The Girl with the Lost Smile

MIRANDA HART

WITH ILLUSTRATIONS BY KATE HINDLEY

Hodder Children's Books

HODDER CHILDREN'S BOOKS

First published in Great Britain in 2017 by Hodder & Stoughton Ltd

1 3 5 7 9 10 8 6 4 2

Written by Miranda Hart
Text copyright © 2017 KingMaker Productions Ltd
Illustrations copyright © 2017 Hodder & Stoughton Ltd

The moral rights of the author and illustrator have been asserted.

ISBN 978 1 444 94137 1

Printed and bound in Great Britain by Clays Ltd, St Ives plc

The paper and board used in this book
are made from wood from responsible sources.

Hodder Children's Books
An imprint of Hachette Children's Group
Part of Hodder and Stoughton
Carmelite House
50 Victoria Embankment
London EC4Y 0DZ

An Hachette UK Company
www.hachette.co.uk

www.hachettechildrens.co.uk

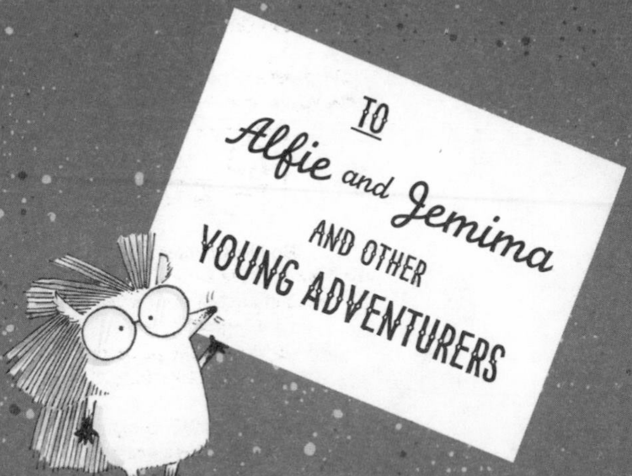
TO
Alfie and Jemima
AND OTHER
YOUNG ADVENTURERS

1

NUMBER 2,
ELMSWATER CRESCENT

Chloe was singing 'Happy Birthday' to herself in bed. *'Happy birthday to me ... Happy birthday to me ...'* Then to amuse herself she stood up on top of her bed and made a speech in a low silly voice. 'Eleven years ago today Chloe Long was born, and what a day that was for the world ...!'

'**PIPE DOWN IN THERE**,' shouted her father as he walked past to use the bathroom. Chloe collapsed back down on to her rather thin mattress.

'Hurry up and get ready for school,' he boomed, then slammed the bathroom door shut muttering to himself, '... can't get any peace in my own home ... I don't know ...'

Chloe whispered a final, rather feeble *'Happy birthday to me ...'* as quietly as she could.

Oh dear, the morning hadn't got off to the start she had hoped for, to say the least. When her alarm had gone off half an hour earlier, she'd lain in bed expecting her parents to burst into her bedroom, laden with presents, and start singing 'Happy Birthday' in funny harmonies, as in previous years. She'd waited and waited but they never came. So … she'd decided to sing to herself instead.

After all, she was cheery Chloe, the girl with the unbeatable SMILE. And when she smiled, people couldn't help but SMILE back at her. It was a gift she believed she'd inherited from Gran Gran, her grandmother and FAVOURITE person in the world. Being happy whatever the circumstances was Chloe's purpose in life and it was one she prided herself on maintaining, come what may.

But sometimes, especially on a day like today, it was hard. She scrambled out of bed to get dressed, and felt less of a spring in her step than usual. Understandably. It was her eleventh birthday and she was beginning to worry that her parents had … well, **FORGOTTEN**. They couldn't have, could they …?

I mean, admittedly Mr and Mrs Long had not

been the cheeriest people of late. And it was true that at Easter a few months ago, they had given her just two eggs. Not chocolate eggs. Not coloured or painted eggs. Not even boiled eggs with toast soldiers, just ... *two eggs*. Which she then had to boil herself for breakfast. But even they wouldn't forget their only daughter's birthday ... would they?

With all this in mind, Chloe quickly reached under her pillow for her emergency joke book. It was a large, thin notebook, now very battered, with a faded map of the world on the cover. Gran Gran had bought it for her years ago and ever since she had been filling it with her favourite jokes so she'd be ready to pull out the perfect one-liner for every situation. Oh yes, Chloe was truly committed to making the world a *happier* place.

The notebook was nearly full now with her joke collection and any one of them was guaranteed to make her laugh, even the very old ones written in large childish writing that probably weren't that good any more.

Like the one her dad used to tell her and loved because he was a bus-driver:

HOW DO **FISH** WITHOUT CARS GET AROUND?
ON THE OCTO-BUS!

She definitely needed a good one today. She flicked to her favourite section – the one she called 'Just Silly'.

WHY DOES THE **SEA** ROAR?
SO WOULD YOU IF YOU HAD CRABS ON YOUR BOTTOM!

That was very silly and funny but, oh dear – she peered in the mirror – there she was, looking just the same as ever: same freckly face, same long dark hair sticking out in all directions (her mother used to help her brush it and keep it under control, but she was too big for that now, apparently), same wide dark brown eyes staring back at her BUT … with only a very faint smile. How strange, Chloe thought. That's not like me.

She took a deep breath, determined to remain cheery about the day despite its strange start. This was her **BIRTHDAY** and her parents were bound to greet her with smiles and a hug and the biggest, best breakfast EVER as soon as she got downstairs.

Before heading down she gave a quick look round her bedroom to make sure she had everything for school. It was not a large room – Mr and Mrs Long had never been rich – but it had everything she needed. A bed, a bedside table with a little lamp, a wardrobe, and a small wooden desk where she did her homework and drawing. Chloe loved to draw animals, especially horses. All over one wall she had tacked up her pictures of galloping horses, and on another there were her drawings of sweet puppies and funny-looking penguins. There weren't so many recent pictures because her favourite hobby of all, these days, was *daydreaming* and she'd been doing more of that than ever recently – sometimes she would sit at her desk, staring out of the window and just IMAGINE ...

Chloe lived at the top of Elmswater Crescent, a semicircular cul-de-sac of detached houses with neat uniform gardens at the front and back of each house.

It was not a large room – Mr and Mrs Long had never been rich – but it had everything she needed.

Her window faced a few of the houses opposite and some of the street, but she could mainly see the park and fields beyond. They were on the edge of a small market town that had built up around a wool factory hundreds of years ago. (Even at the height of summer the older generation would wear their locally produced jolly jumpers and knitted hats, out of loyalty to their town's brand, despite a **lot** of sweating!) It was only a ten-minute walk to school and the shops, but Elmswater Crescent was right next to the greenery where the town ended. One of her favourite **DAYDREAMS** was to imagine herself flying out of her window, over next-door's house, brushing the treetops and flying on and on until she found herself in *Chloe's Magic Land*.

Chloe had created her imaginary land as a brilliant place to escape to if she ever felt sad or lonely, or if her parents were arguing. She called it her *Magic Land* because it was her favourite elements of all four seasons in one day there. Yes, JUST IMAGINE – all the best parts of every season existing together. There was a lake where she could skate with friendly penguins (yes, penguins that skate, well it is called *Magic Land*,

.☼ 7 ☼.

remember), but in her shorts and T-shirt because of the summery weather. And of course because it was *Chloe's Magic Land* the ice never melted.

Once hot from all the skating exercise she could dive into the cool waters of the neighbouring lake and ride on the back of dolphins (who couldn't skate but could dance upright on their flippers – I **KNOW**, dancing dolphins!) to the nearby waterfall, to listen to the rushing water. After that, there were piles of lovely, crisp autumn leaves just waiting for her to crunch and stomp through on the nearby banks. There were Easter eggs to hunt for (and eat!), bonfires where you could cook (and eat!) marshmallows, and all year round there were Christmas presents to unwrap (and eat! Well, only if you could eat them. It would be strange to eat a pair of woolly gloves, for example). It was all her **FAVOURITE** things in one place and she spent hours in this brightly coloured land.

In her mind.

Keeping herself happy.

Escaping when she needed to.

Suddenly, from below her window, in the real world, Chloe realised she could hear voices: Mr and

Mrs Sweet next door, chatting to each other and their flowers. 'Now come on, Mr Sunflower,' Mrs Sweet was saying, 'you gorgeous plant with your lovely yellow face, you can grow taller than that! Here's some delicious water from my best watering can, aahhh, doesn't that feel better?'

Chloe peeked out of her window – Mrs Sweet was a pink-cheeked woman with perfect auburn hair, always styled with a neat little flick at the ends. Chloe often wondered why Mrs Sweet did her hair so perfectly as by the end of a day of gardening there would be leaves and petals stuck all through it, or the back would be so messy it would look like she had gone through a hedge backwards. Because she quite often literally had!

This morning she was still in her nightie but with a pair of bright yellow wellies on underneath.

Mr Sweet, with much plainer hair (black, peppered with grey), and wearing a checked shirt tucked into his rather high-waisted sensible brown trousers, was pruning his magnolia tree by their fence whilst looking over with concern at Chloe's house and overgrown lawn. As Chloe watched, Mrs Sweet joined him. 'Don't you worry, lawn, we'll soon have you shipshape!' she said cheerily.

'But look at all the weeds, Mrs Sweet, tut, tut, it's very upsetting, those flowers used to be cared for properly.' Her husband shook his head, worried.

The Sweets were both very keen gardeners and abhorred mess in a garden. They were forever posting leaflets into everyone's letterboxes with suggestions about how to keep the cul-de-sac gardens tidy and blooming with flowers. If you didn't comply, they might suddenly be at your door with a wheelbarrow, spade and fork and insist they do it for you. (Chloe imagined they had special powers and moved hovering just above the ground so no one could hear them approaching!) They might sound a little bossy, but everyone loved them anyway, especially Chloe. The Sweets were very gentle, and indeed, very sweet.

And their garden was gorgeous – a **RAINBOW** of brightly coloured flowers, almost as bright as *Chloe's Magic Land*. There was a perfect green lawn, a splashy water fountain set in the middle of a small pond and a bush in the shape of a peacock. Mr Sweet had created a bird banqueting suite and Chloe liked to watch the greedy robins, the tiny wrens and the swooping black, white and red woodpecker that came to hammer at the peanuts, twittering more loudly than in any other garden. In fact, their neighbours in the cul-de-sac would hang birdseed up in the hope of attracting some of the birds into their gardens, but still they all flocked to the beauty of the Sweets' garden. Which was good for Chloe because her bedroom was always full of birdsong. And it was part of what made her feel safe there, along with the sound of Mrs Sweet chatting to her plants as if they were her children.

It seemed like Chloe's parents hadn't chatted to her in that kindly, encouraging way for a long time. They had stopped tucking her in to bed or asking about her day at school too. The Sweets didn't have any children, and on some difficult days of late Chloe had guiltily wished they were her parents, and that her bedroom was in their house, with a fat, fluffy, soft duvet, like the one she could see on their bed from her own bedroom window. All Chloe had was a worn sheet and an old blanket.

Actually, a duvet would be the perfect birthday present, Chloe reflected. Especially with horses or puppies on it. But ... maybe there **IS** one, waiting for me as a surprise downstairs, she suddenly thought. It would be too big to bring upstairs without me guessing straight away what it was. Of course ... they must have been planning a birthday surprise all along...

With that happy thought, and her **SMILE** determinedly back in place, Chloe ran downstairs towards the kitchen. But as soon as she reached the bottom of the stairs she could hear her parents arguing. Oh dear ...

She crept into the small kitchen and sat down at

the round table in the middle of the room. The kitchen tops were covered with papers and letters that Mr Long never seemed to get around to dealing with, and piles of her mother's favourite nail kits.

Mrs Long was **obsessed** with her nails. She might leave her long brown hair unwashed and wear an old, stained, fluffy dressing-gown with holes in it where fluff was coming out (there would sometimes be bits of dressing-gown fluff in a trail around the house, showing where she had been), but her nails had to be done to *perfection* at all times. Chloe's dad had used to joke about it, saying, 'All ready to meet the Queen, darling – I'll just fetch the limousine?' But Chloe hadn't heard him say that in a long time.

'What's that smell? You're burning the toast!' Mrs Long screeched suddenly. '**QUICK!**'

Mr Long leapt up, banging his head on the lampshade, he was that tall, and rushed to rescue his toast. 'Well it wouldn't be burning if we still had a toaster and I didn't have to use the blasted grill ...' he shouted, his furrowed brow now furrowing so much there were big dented lines between his eyes.

Chloe smiled slightly at the memory of the day

Mrs Long threw the toaster out of the window, nearly knocking a passing Mr Sweet on the head, because the sudden **POP** of the toast had made her jump and splash glittery nail polish along her finger.

'That's your fault for buying such a loud toaster, you stupid moo!' Mrs Long blew agitatedly on her Russet Red nail varnish.

'Don't call me stupid, who are you calling stupid?'

'You, I am calling you stupid, do you see anyone else here?' quipped Mrs Long.

Mr Long looked around the room, suddenly spotted Chloe at the table and jumped so high in the air he actually hit his head on the ceiling. 'What on … What were you doing creeping in like that?'

'Sorry, I didn't want to disturb you,' said Chloe quietly. 'I just wanted some cereal before going to school, and I thought, er, today, maybe you might—'

'Well, hurry up and eat quietly.' Her father plonked himself back down at the table, straightened his tie – part of his bus-driver uniform – and began gulping his tea down, it has to be said, rather noisily. 'It's bad enough I have to put up with people getting on and off my bus all day, blathering away, opening and closing the doors, letting traffic fumes in, all I want is a moment's peace before starting my day, and now my own daughter is trying to give me a heart attack,' he muttered to himself between gulps.

Mr Long had been fed up with his job since not getting a promotion to work in the bus depot office, but Chloe was sure she remembered a time he used to **LOVE** driving the bus, chatting and laughing with all the passengers. Why did her parents seem so sad?

For the next few minutes, Chloe's family sat in silence. She kept trying to catch her parents' eyes, to give them one of her brightest **SMILES**, to see if she could help them to start their day in a better mood – but neither of them looked up. No matter. SURELY they were about to surprise her and sing 'Happy Birthday' any second …?

'What's that racket?' bellowed Mr Long suddenly.

'The racket is you asking what the racket is. There isn't a racket, there was no racket until you made a racket!' Mrs Long retorted.

Mr Long ignored her. 'It's coming from Chloe's place mat.'

'Sorry. It's my Crispy Crackles ...' Chloe apologised.

'Well next time, choose something that doesn't **CRACKLE** and **POP**. I am trying to read my newspaper.'

Usually this might have made Chloe chuckle inside – even cereal being too loud for her grumpy dad – but not so today. For a moment she had a terrible thought – what if this unhappiness was all *her* fault? If she wasn't around they wouldn't have noisy cereal or frights at the table to deal with, and maybe Mr Long wouldn't have to work such long hours at a job he hated to put cereal on the table. Chloe wasn't sure where the terrible thought had come from, but she didn't like it one bit. She usually saw the **BRIGHT** or **funny** side of anything in life. She jumped up from the table.

'I think I will just go to school.' She plastered her best **SMILE** back on to her face and waited hopefully for a birthday goodbye, but her mother was concentrating on turning the page of her favourite magazine without smudging her nails and her father had stuck in the earplugs he liked to wear to work so he couldn't hear his annoying passengers.

Chloe told herself she wouldn't make her parents feel bad by reminding them it was her birthday. She never wanted to bring anyone down; besides, they were her parents and the Longs were still a team, weren't they?

'The Longs against the world!' her father used to say as he saluted Chloe and her mother before putting on his bus cap and bouncing off to work. Though not bouncing too high lest he banged his head on the door frame. And, thinking about it, he hadn't said that for a while either …

Chloe set off for school as cheerfully as she could. **SURELY** they would have remembered by tonight. Besides, she knew her best friends at school wouldn't have forgotten and maybe Mr Broderick, their headmaster, would crack her up in assembly with one of his embarrassing guitar solos. Chloe had once tried so hard to stop LAUGHING at him she'd snorted orange juice out of her nose. Yes, the day would soon be back on track …

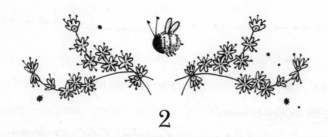

2

THE
MAGICAL OAK TREE

'Morning, Chloe, have a lovely day at school,' Mrs
Sweet called to her as she walked down her path and
past the Sweets' front gate. Chloe gave them both a
SMILE and a wave but didn't stop to chat. She was
busy opening the card she'd found on the doormat as
she'd let herself out of the house. True to form, Gran
Gran had found her a perfect birthday card. This time
it was of a sweet brown bear made out of fur that stuck
out from the card. Chloe stroked it before opening it.

Dearest Darling Chloe,

I can't BEAR the fact that I can't be with you on your BEAR-thday as usual!

My plane back from my cliff-walking holiday in Jersey (where I bought a new jersey) was cancelled due to bad weather so I have had to grin and BEAR it and stay another day or two until the flights are running again.

It has given me PAWS for thought to think of how much I miss you and I can't wait to see you very soon.

BEAR with me!

All love and big BEAR hugs, Gran Gran

P.S. I have just realised it would have been funnier to buy a new jersey from New Jersey!

Chloe **laughed**. Typical Gran Gran, always having wild adventures. Last year she had ONLY JUST made it in time for Chloe's birthday, dashing back from some crazy-sounding holiday in the Alps where, aged sixty-five, she had been on a zipwire down a mountain, amongst other things!

Chloe walked on down the road and as she did so she smiled at the postman as always. He SMILED back, felt renewed energy in his weary legs and found himself delivering the rest of his letters at twice the pace, whistling all the while. She smiled at the angry businessman who had just missed his train. He **SMILED** back and calmly decided he would use the time until the next train to sit happily for a moment in the sun before going in to the office. She smiled at the lollipop lady as she crossed the road. The lollipop lady **SMILED** back, and felt her patience and kindness returning, before skipping over to collect her next gaggle of unruly children.

You see, sometimes the world seemed hard to Chloe, full of adults who were sad and shouty and tired all the time. Which was why she made sure she was always **SMILING** and joking, ready to cheer everyone up. Gran Gran would say it all the time:

'A SMILE COSTS NOTHING, BUT IS ONE OF THE ✦ BEST GIFTS YOU CAN GIVE ANYONE.' ✦

And though it felt a little harder than usual today, Chloe had to agree. For that reason, this morning Chloe smiled at her exhausted-looking headmaster Mr Broderick too, as she crossed the playground. He had big bags under his eyes that seemed out of place with his jolly ginger hair and moustache, and was carrying a litre-size flask of coffee to keep him awake. But even he took a deep breath, SMILED back and felt a little bit better about the day ahead as Chloe marched past.

Once inside the school building, Chloe went straight to assembly and plonked herself down next to her three best friends – Ruby, Hannah and Benjamin.

'Morning,' the three of them said at once to Chloe. 'And Happy Birthday!' Then they *laughed* because they had all said it at exactly the same time and in exactly the same way.

'We are so in tune, we are like some kind of girl band,' said Hannah. Benjamin looked a bit put out, but before he could say anything they were rudely interrupted.

'Urgh, don't think so!' quipped Princess, the leader of the cool girls gang, as they all strode past with their long fair hair, in identical ponytails, swishing violently from side to side. They were the kind of girls who thought they were prettier and cleverer than everyone else, and Chloe and her friends really didn't like their arrogance.

What IS the point of being mean? Chloe thought. Surely it can't make you happy? No one in the school actually knew if Princess was Princess's real name, or just what her mum called her (very loudly) at the school gates. Either way – in Chloe's opinion – it was an abomination. No one so set on making others feel bad about themselves should be allowed to answer to a name as regal as that, quite frankly!

Mr Broderick walked on to the stage of the assembly hall, swinging his arms over-enthusiastically. The truth was, Mr B was actually a little shy and he always found assemblies slightly terrifying. The thought of them even kept him awake at night. But to hide his shyness he would make his infamous assemblies as peppy, energised and over-the-top as possible. He took a big breath and with as much POSITIVE energy as he could muster shouted out a silly-sounding, holiday-camp style,

'Good mooooooooooooorning!'

Ruby snorted back a giggle and Hannah leant forward and whispered to Chloe, 'See you at the oak tree at lunchtime – we've all got PRESENTS for you!'

Chloe's SMILE widened. That was better – her birthday was getting back on track.

And though Mr B didn't get out his guitar as Chloe had hoped, and do a random song like an embarrassing dad trying to be a rock star, he did ask Mrs Bucks the chemistry teacher to say a few words about the new science club … and the most *hilarious* thing happened. As she tried to get up out of her chair, it was plain to see that she was completely wedged in it. Mrs Bucks had arrived late to assembly and by the time she'd got there, the only seat still available was a teeny tiny reception-class chair.

But she stood up proudly, with the chair still attached to her bottom, and continued to tell the whole school about the science club, even though she couldn't really be heard for the sniggering. No one was being mean, except Princess probably, but it was just too funny **not** to *laugh.* And a lovely gift for Chloe. By the time assembly had finished she had virtually forgotten all about her disappointing morning at home.

Chloe couldn't concentrate in the lessons before

lunch break, she was so excited about her birthday lunch. The oak tree was her friends' **FAVOURITE** place to hang out. It was right at the edge of the school grounds, beyond the playing fields, and in the summer term it was where they would go to have their lunch under the shade of the big oak branches.

To Chloe it often felt like a *magical* tree, because they were always so happy and calm there.

The four of them had been firm friends for years, ever since they sat together once in a home economics lesson. They'd got a recipe for a treacle sponge cake so wrong that it started oozing out of its baking tray, and when they quickly whipped it out of the oven, it fully exploded, sending bits of hot treacle flying everywhere so people were ducking for their lives! Especially Princess, who was terrified it might land in her perfect hair. Thankfully, their teacher ended up seeing the funny side of it all and named their concoction the *Volcano Cake* and the four of them the **CHAOS CREW.** They had stuck together ever since. Much like a lump of treacle sponge had stuck to the ceiling of that classroom ever since.

When the lunchtime bell went, Chloe and her

friends made a mad dash for their beloved oak tree and it wasn't long before they were sitting on the grass beneath it, munching on the birthday picnic lunch that Hannah had organised for them all. Hannah was tall, had ruler-straight dark hair and could be very bossy but in a well-meaning way, so Chloe knew it was definitely her that had planned and laid out the picnic. Especially since the food was arranged alphabetically on each plate.

Ruby immediately started weeping with joy at the whole occasion. She was physically the opposite of Hannah, small with wavy strawberry-blonde hair, and would get emotional at the smallest thing. She had been known to burst out crying even at an ant getting squashed, so her friends were quite used to it. But she started getting even more teary than usual when Hannah brought out some flapjacks for their pudding. She was virtually wailing.

'What on earth could be sad about flapjacks, Ruby?' asked Ben, or rather Benjamin, since he preferred to be called by his full name at all times. Benjamin was the super-sensible one in their group, always very neat and organised. He had deep, dark green eyes that looked slightly oversized, which Chloe thought was appropriate really because nothing ever seemed to get past him. 'I mean really, they are just **FLAPJACKS**!'

'But ... you see ...' spluttered Ruby. 'Well, this is my birthday present for you, Chloe.' She handed Chloe a sticky parcel and when Chloe unwrapped it she found a huge slab of home-made flapjack inside. 'I actually cooked something and it didn't go wrong and I thought it was perfect for you ... but Hannah got there *firrrrst!*'

'But who can have too many flapjacks? Not me!' said Chloe, giving Ruby a hug. 'In fact, I am placing an order for **TWENTY** Ruby-baked flapjacks, and in time for breakfast tomorrow please!'

Ruby sniffed, then smiled. Good old Chloe, always cheering everyone up.

'I thought we were going to do presents after pudding, but OK ... here's mine,' said Hannah.

Chloe unwrapped Hannah's present – it was three pairs of rainbow-striped socklets, to be worn under trainers in the summer. Chloe loved them, even when Hannah added, 'After all, you spent the whole of last summer wearing long purple socks with pink trainers, Chloe – it was NOT a good look!'

'True, although I'll rather miss it …' Ruby said, her lower lip trembling.

'Why are you welling up now?' asked Hannah impatiently.

'I was just thinking of our lovely summer holidays last year, that's all, these are happy tears.'

'Perfect timing then for my present,' announced Benjamin, who handed Chloe two gifts, both of course perfectly neatly wrapped. Chloe opened the long thin one first and found a shiny new ruler inside.

'A ruler?!' said Hannah, her eyebrows raised questioningly.

'Just wait … it goes with the other one …' said Benjamin defensively. Chloe opened the other parcel he'd given her to find a lovely hardback notepad with a *seaside* scene on the front. 'I thought you could use it to write down all the things we want to do over the *summer* holidays. And then you can draw all the things we do in it too. The ruler is obviously to make all your lists as neat as possible.'

'Obviously,' laughed Hannah and Chloe

together. 'Thanks, Benjamin,' Chloe added. 'It's a **perfect** present.'

'Oh that is too much, a summer notebook, how **BEAUTIFUL** ...' Ruby started crying AGAIN. This time they all knew it was with *happiness*.

But despite the lovely moment under her favourite oak tree, Chloe was surprised to feel a sudden twinge of *sadness*. The hugs and presents from her friends had reminded her that she'd got neither of these things from her parents that morning. Chloe needed to cheer herself up quickly, keep the day on track ...

'Let's play a round of School-amentary.' This was their current **FAVOURITE** game, invented by Chloe. It involved giving a running commentary on everything they saw around them in a nature documentary style.

'You start, Chloe,' Ruby begged. 'You're the best at it!' The others nodded smilingly.

'OK.' Chloe looked around at the playing field and beyond to the school, and began. *'And here we see a strange beast prowling the school grounds ... Mr Broderick, sometimes known as Mr B, seems to walk on two legs but with his head hanging so low it's like he's about to fall over at any moment ... oooh and he*

'A ruler?!' said Hannah, her eyebrows raised questioningly.

bangs *into a bench he didn't see coming ... he's a clumsy species and looks a bit like a baboon* **farting** *and rather embarrassed about it ...'*

They all burst out laughing, although Chloe noticed her *laugh* didn't make her feel as free and light as usual. In fact, if anything, there was a tight knot in her stomach. Her favourite game felt like an effort, and it wasn't making her smile like it should. She looked desperately about her but couldn't see anything that seemed remotely funny. 'Actually, lunch break is nearly over, we should probably head in. We don't want to be, er, late ...' She bowed her head and started stuffing her presents into her bag – whatever was wrong with her?

Benjamin looked at Hannah, a bit confused. Chloe was usually the last person to want to leave their oak tree at breaktime; it was Benjamin who kept his eye on the time.

As they headed back across the fields for afternoon lessons, Hannah asked, 'By the way, what did your mum and dad get you?'

'Oh, er, we usually do presents at teatime,' Chloe said quickly, telling herself that had to be her parents' plan anyway, so it wasn't strictly a lie.

'Remember when your dad borrowed one of his company buses and turned it into a **PARTY BUS**,' Ruby chimed in a little hysterically. 'That was my **FAVOURITE** birthday party ever – that Snakes and Ladders game your mum brought, and the balloon animals, and the ice-cream machine on the back seat! And then he drove us all the way to the beach …'

'… and bought us all fish and chips,' Benjamin added.

'… then the seagulls swooped down and stole your mum's portion,' Hannah finished off. 'That was *hilarious*!'

Oddly, Chloe found it hard to remember any of this. It seemed like much longer than a couple of years ago. Dad hated the buses so much now – she couldn't imagine him getting on one for **FUN**.

'Shall we come for a Chaos Crew birthday sleepover?' Hannah suggested. 'Or are they planning another trip …?'

'Er …' Chloe mumbled.

'Put something in the **SUMMER BOOK**, somewhere your dad can take us …' suggested Benjamin.

'Can we just stop talking about my dad?' Chloe snapped. They all stared at her – wow, that was not like Chloe.

She quickly changed the subject back to the game. *'And there's Mrs Bucks, a turtle-related species with a very unusual shell – yes, they sometimes grow chairs out of their bottoms.'* Her friends couldn't help but laugh and Chloe breathed a sigh of relief as her momentary grumpiness and potential birthday day out was forgotten.

The rest of the afternoon passed quickly, although not especially happily for Chloe. She couldn't focus in her classes, worrying about home. But she had to think POSITIVELY and when school was finally over she waved goodbye to her friends at the corner gates, before heading home for the birthday tea she had decided would be waiting for her.

As Chloe approached her front door, she paused hopefully. Maybe they're waiting to surprise me as soon as I step inside, she told herself. She opened the door ... and ... nothing. The house was no different from any other day. Her dad wasn't home yet and her mum was sitting in her favourite leather reclining chair in the sitting room where she did her nails all day. There were usually piles of nail clippings and discarded nail varnish bottles dotted around the chair.

Once her nails were groomed, she'd obsessively read her way through several glossy magazines. There was a pile as high as the ceiling next to her chair, and when she finished reading one magazine she would remove the next from the pile, being very careful not to topple it over in the process. It was like magazine Jenga. Sometimes it took Mrs Long a whole hour just to extract one magazine from the pile!

Chloe reckoned the reason her mother loved to read about the glossy world of other people's lives was because she was convinced that hers wasn't as *glamorous* or **EXCITING** as everyone else's. Chloe didn't believe her mum had always felt like this, but recently she never saw her without a magazine by her side.

Chloe poked her head around the sitting-room door.

'Oh you're back, tea is on the kitchen table, then it's bedtime, isn't it?' Mrs Long said automatically, so engrossed was she in the glamorous world of her magazines. 'Good to get an early night on school nights, I always think.'

'Right, thanks, Mum,' Chloe said as cheerily as she could.

Chloe went into the kitchen; there was a sign saying:

Make your own dinner

with an arrow on it pointing to a box of cereal. It was only half past four but nowadays Chloe often went to bed that early. She thought her parents liked to get her out of the way so they could argue in peace – but Chloe didn't really mind. Early evening and bedtime had become her **FAVOURITE** part of the day. She felt safe closing her bedroom door behind her; drawing and *daydreaming*; watching over the activities of her little cul-de-sac.

She took her bowl of cereal upstairs and ate it on her bed watching the Sweets gardening outside. The Sweets would make such brilliant parents, she thought to herself again. Though Chloe knew deep down she just wanted her own parents ... but as the parents they used to be.

Although it was ridiculously early and very light she got ready for bed and slipped under her old thin sheet, feeling her scratchy blanket through it. Now she felt stupid to have hoped that Mr and Mrs Long might have got her a duvet for her eleventh birthday: not only was there no duvet, but the worst had happened – they hadn't even remembered her special day **AT ALL**.

Oh dear. She clearly needed a trip to *Chloe's Magic Land*. Her secret, perfect place. Of course, she knew it wasn't a real place, it was all in her imagination; but it was somewhere that no one else knew about, that nothing could spoil, somewhere that made her *happy*.

Surely it would make her feel cheery again …

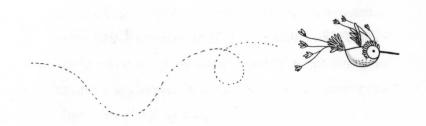

3

CHLOE'S MAGIC LAND

Chloe stared at the sky outside then slowly closed her eyes. She imagined herself flying out of her bedroom window, over the houses, over the fields, up and up and on and **on**, the wind cooling her cheeks, until finally she landed in her very own, special, *Chloe's Magic Land*. She went straight to the banks of the summery dolphin lake and ran through the bright red and orange autumn leaves. In fact some of the leaf piles were *so* high that she could climb the surrounding trees and fall backwards from the branches into the leafy heaps – it was like landing on a soft crunchy mattress.

And these weren't just any trees, they were apple trees, and these weren't just any apple trees, they were **TOFFEE APPLE** trees. Oh yes, DELICIOUS toffee apples hung from their branches ready to be picked and eaten. Chloe sat on a pile of leaves and munched one. It might have been *imaginary*, but it was still the best-tasting apple she had ever eaten.

At that moment she noticed a bush smouldering nearby. You might think this was scary, but not in *Chloe's Magic Land* for these were sausage bushes. Yes, **SAUSAGE** bushes! And when the sausages were fully grown, they would start to heat up and a bundle of cooked sausages would land perfectly on the ground beneath them. **IMAGINE!**

Chloe reached over and plucked one from beneath the bush – yum, freshly BBQ'd sausage, her **FAVOURITE** (of course). She took a bite and was about to wolf down the rest of it when she saw all the dolphins in the lake had gathered and were waving at her with their flippers. She waved back. Immediately they lined up on their tummies in a row across the lake and Chloe hopped across their dolphin bridge to the other side.

By now she was on the bank between the summer dolphin lake and the winter ice-skating lake. As she pulled on her skates the penguins waddled excitedly across the ice towards her; and as she swooped on to its slick, white, sparkling surface, they fell into line behind her. Before she knew it, they were doing their own little *dance* routine together – Chloe and the penguins sliding in a zigzag across the surface, the black and white birds with their long yellow beaks pointed forwards, their stubby black flippers extended elegantly behind them.

Chloe whizzed off on a full circuit of the lake, feeling the icy breeze in her hair. She wasn't cold though, because of course with four seasons in one day the weather was summery, so there was a lovely warm sun on her face. PERFECT. Wasn't it? Of course it was. So why don't I feel properly happy yet? Chloe fretted.

Chloe started mimicking the penguins' waddling walk and flapping her arms like wings. They **LOVED** her doing this. It was exactly the sort of thing that usually made Chloe feel on top of the world; the perky penguins never failed to make her *giggle* – especially when they fell over and slid sideways on their tummies. Percy, the King Penguin, once slid off so fast he continued over the bank of the lake and plopped into the dolphin waters next door. By then he was LAUGHING so hard one of the dolphins had to flip him back on to land before he glugged too much water and drowned.

Oh yes, in *Chloe's Magic Land* penguins could laugh. Sweet little giggling penguins. **IMAGINE!** The problem was, CHLOE wasn't giggling, not at all – the most she had managed so far was a half-hearted smile. She looked about – what could she do to **REALLY** cheer herself up …?

Just then, one of *Magic Land's* bunny rabbits hopped past, so Chloe jumped on to its soft back. Yes, in *Chloe's Magic Land* you rode rabbits, not ponies, because then you could hop instead of trot which was much more fun. A massive hopping bunny you could ride. And hunt for chocolate eggs together. **IMAGINE!**

But never mind chocolate eggs. Now the rabbit was hopping past her favourite water slide which looped along the dolphin lake shores before dipping down into the lovely warm waters. Surely that would return her *cheeriness* in full? Percy the King Penguin was waiting for her at the top and gave her a friendly wink and a helpful shove so she flew down at speed.

SPLASH! Chloe snapped her eyes shut as she hit the bright blue water, then blew big bubbles as she swam underwater back towards the shore.

Another amazing thing about *Chloe's Magic*

Land was that when you got out of the water you immediately dried off, so you never needed to change your clothes to swim, you never felt cold and wet and you never needed a towel. **IMAGINE!**

Yes, this was the life ... wasn't it? At the water's edge she pulled herself up and out of the lake ...

And found herself back in the reality of her bedroom, with her itchy blanket, the horrible memory of her difficult day and, worst of all, the realisation that her trip to *Magic Land* hadn't made her **SMILE** like it normally did. What if ... what if turning eleven meant that she was growing out of *Magic Land*? That she was meant to be more of an adult somehow and things wouldn't be so fun any more?

She looked at her new rainbow socks and notebook, finished the final bit of Ruby's birthday flapjack, and held Gran Gran's card close, almost hugging it. *'Happy birthday to me ... Happy birth ...'* she sang to herself. But there were tears in her eyes, spilling down on to her pillow as she slowly started to fall asleep.

4

CAN YOU REALLY
LOSE A SMILE?

When Chloe woke the next morning her stomach was churning and her face felt funny. Sort of frozen, as if she'd lain awkwardly on it all night. Or as if she'd been to the dentist and had part of her mouth made numb. While she was getting dressed she glanced in the mirror – she looked like her normal self, but something was definitely *odd*. She felt tired, that was for sure, but beyond that she couldn't work out what specifically was *odd*. How *odd* not to be able to work out what was *odd*. Everything was *odd, odd, odd*. It was time for the emergency joke book. She grabbed it from under her pillow.

WHY DID THE BANANA GO TO THE HOSPITAL?
BECAUSE HE WASN'T PEELING WELL!

She left her bedroom and started walking down the stairs, but stopped suddenly halfway down. Hang on, she hadn't *laughed* at all, and there was even less of a SMILE than yesterday. She ran back upstairs and read *another* joke.

KNOCK, KNOCK.
Who's there?
THE INTERRUPTING COW ...
The interrupting
... MOO!!!!

Only a tiny SMILE, well, more of a teeny turn-up at the corners of her mouth. She walked downstairs heavy-hearted. What was happening to her? Was she ill?

In the kitchen she found her parents both silently reading. She was about to grab herself a banana and leave when Mr Long, who had got up to make himself a tea, let out a low screech because the door of the kitchen cupboard he was opening had come away in his hand.

As she crept out of the room her parents were already bickering again.

'I have been telling you that door was *wonky* for months.'

'No, Mrs Long, I have been telling **YOU** for months … you need to fix it.'

'Me fix it? Why should I fix it?! It would ruin my nails thank you very much, **MR LONG**.'

'Well I don't know if you have noticed, **MRS LONG**, but I have to drive buses all day and don't have time to be fixing cupboards …'

'Bye, Mum, bye, Dad!' Chloe called as she exited, but doubted they'd even heard her.

'Hello, Chloe,' Mrs Sweet trilled. 'Have you seen, we've got some lovely *butterflies* making their home on our buddleia …?'

Chloe tried to SMILE and wave back, as she normally would, but all she could think of was a sad thing. That they had a lovely duvet, and she didn't. Mr and Mrs Sweet looked at each other with concern as Chloe disappeared around the corner. Chloe hadn't SMILED at them on her way to school. And that was a very worrying first.

As Chloe slouched along the road she saw a policeman. She tried to muster a **SMILE** for him. It must be a very difficult job and they are so brave, she thought. If anyone needs a **SMILE** it's a policeman. She looked at him, but found herself only able to stare. And the policeman didn't look best pleased. She didn't even look at the lollipop lady – who snapped at a small boy dawdling as he crossed the road and made him cry.

And there was a dishevelled Mr Broderick, pedalling across the playground ahead of her, already late for the start of his day because that morning his car had broken down before he'd even backed out of his drive; and the seat of the bike he'd jumped on had fallen off, so he'd come to work on his daughter's tiny pink bicycle shaped like a *unicorn*! It was exactly the kind of sight guaranteed to make any child *laugh* – not least one as humorously inclined as Chloe – but …

NOTHING. Today, the world stayed grey. There was no doubt about it, Chloe had lost her smile. And she hadn't a clue how, or where. Or indeed what **ON EARTH** was going to happen to a girl with a **LOST SMILE**.

By the time Chloe slid into her seat next to Hannah, that morning's assembly was already underway.

'And I know you can all feel the summer holidays looming,' Mr B was saying, sweat dripping down his face from all his frantic pedalling, 'but there is still work to do. Not to mention the house athletics competition.'

There was a group groan in the hall.

'I believe I heard a cheer then, didn't I?' said Mr B, thinking he was being rather funny. No one *laughed.* 'Didn't I?' he said, desperately looking around the hall, until some of the kinder children including Hannah, Ruby and Benjamin took pity on him and there was a raggedy '**HURRAAAAYYYY ...**'

'That's better, especially as this year we have, of course, included our new teachers versus seniors three-legged race.' He laughed at what he thought was another funny idea of his, and turned around to the teachers sitting behind him, who all gave him fake encouraging nods. Mrs Bucks' fake *laugh* was so over-the-top it sounded like a crow being strangled.

'Do you want to partner with me, Mrs Bucks?' Mr B asked. 'Come on, let's show them how to do it!'

'He is so *cringe!*' whispered Hannah. Ruby and Benjamin laughed. 'Oh no, look!'

Mrs Bucks looked outraged as Mr B hoisted her up out of her seat to link arms with him (thankfully the chair remained off her bottom this time) and demonstrated how they would run tied together. Mrs Bucks' enormous bosom was heaving up and down as she half-ran-half-hopped across the stage whilst Mr Broderick's tie kept whacking her in the eye. By now, most pupils were *laughing* hysterically – Mr Broderick thought WITH them, but it was most definitely AT them, I am afraid.

And when I say MOST pupils, I mean all but one – Chloe. It was Hannah who noticed first. 'What's wrong with Chloe?' She nudged Benjamin. 'Why isn't she *laughing*?'

'I don't know. And something about her looks really ... *different*,' he replied, looking quizzically at Chloe.

'Right,' said Mr Broderick, still high on how well his three-legged race demonstration had gone down, 'I think before we go to class, there's time for a little song on our theme.'

He grabbed his guitar from the stand beside him and began a mash-up of songs about running including 'Run Rabbit Run', and 'Don't Stop Me Now' by Queen.

Before long, Benjamin, Hannah and Ruby – along with much of the rest of the school – were cracking up, and clapping along. But Chloe was feeling odd again. Clapping was meant to be a *jolly* thing, so doing it without *smiling* made her feel even *odder*. What an *odd, odd, odd* day. She leant forward slightly, hoping her hair would swing down to hide her face … But it was no good.

'Chloe,' said Benjamin softly. 'I don't mean to be rude, but you look, umm, well … really *weird*.'

'Yes. What's wrong?' Ruby added as she studied Chloe's face.

'I don't know … nothing,' said Chloe grumpily, quickly looking away. She could barely admit to herself, let alone her friends, that she had lost her smile. She was the fun one of the group, she loved making them *laugh.* And who would want to be friends with someone who couldn't SMILE? As Gran Gran would say:

'YOU NEVER KNOW WHAT GOODNESS
A SIMPLE SMILE CAN BRING.'

Chloe was starting to feel a bit panicky, but luckily her lessons that morning were maths and French, which the gang never really enjoyed anyway – so no one would be expecting her to be SMILEY. But typically today was the day Miss White, the French teacher, on bending down to pick up a piece of chalk, did the loudest and longest fart you have **EVER HEARD!** The class was *hysterical* and Chloe had to pretend to have a coughing fit to cover up the fact she was not smiling or laughing, while Miss WHITE went bright RED and said a horrified 'excusez-moi'.

At breaktime, Hannah wanted them to start thinking of fun things to do in the holidays, so they could write them down in Chloe's SUMMER BOOK. Chloe could feel the panic rising in her chest. What was she going to do? She couldn't join in – she felt numb, not fun. And they'd be expecting her to have loads of creative ideas. What would she say when they noticed her SMILE had gone? What if her weird, non-smiley-ness dragged them down too – she couldn't bear to let **ANYONE** down, but especially not her best friends.

Hannah started the ideas list. 'Obviously at least ten picnics … Your go, Ben …'

'… jamin,' corrected Benjamin, before adding, 'Pedalos in the park!'

Thinking fast, Chloe tapped Hannah on the shoulder. 'I haven't finished my homework from yesterday,' she lied, 'so I'm just heading to the library to finish it now. Go ahead without me.'

'Do it later!' said Hannah bossily. 'It's not due until tomorrow anyway.'

'But I, er, really want to get it done,' Chloe stammered.

'What, instead of making our best-summer-ever plans together?' Ruby's lips started quivering. 'Why would you choose homework over this … oh my goodness …'

'I just **REALLY** want to get it done!' Chloe couldn't think what else to say, so with that she ran off, leaving her friends looking very confused. And a bit cross.

At lunchtime it was even worse. As usual, the friends had planned to gather at their oak tree. Never one to give up, Chloe told herself that it might just help if she went. Maybe, she thought, just maybe the oak tree was *magical* in some way and she would find her SMILE underneath it, by spending time with her best friends that she loved so dearly.

Once they had gathered she tried to kick off the school commentary game. *'And there's Princess, so thin and wispy that if someone sneezed she might fall over ...'* but because SHE wasn't finding it funny, her friends began to just stare at her and not find it funny either. She was beginning to feel really guilty. She was clearly making everyone miserable. And suddenly there was that worrying thought again – what if it was her fault too that her parents had been so angry and miserable?

As usual, it was sensible Benjamin who said the thing that everyone else was thinking. 'Umm ... I don't think we should play any more. There's no point playing if not everyone wants to.' He looked pointedly at Chloe.

'I **DO** want to play,' said Chloe. 'You know I **love**

playing and making you *laugh!*'

'Well … oh my goodness … you clearly **don't** any more,' said Ruby. 'This is too awful, I wish you'd tell us what we've done to *upset* you.' Her voice wobbled with emotion.

'You haven't done anything!' Chloe tried, but without an accompanying SMILE to reassure them, her friends were not convinced.

'I think we should all just go back to the playground,' reasoned Benjamin. 'It's OK, maybe you're just not in a jokey mood or something today, Chloe?'

'I'm not sure it is OK actually! She's being very weird and she won't tell us why!' snapped Hannah, before storming off in a huff. Ruby went after her and Benjamin looked at Chloe questioningly, before following the other girls back across the field.

But Chloe just couldn't explain. Or rather, she thought it best not to try. What if it only confused and upset them … what if it meant they didn't like her any more? Now that she no longer seemed to be *funny* Chloe, the girl with the biggest, brightest SMILE in the school? She leant back against the oak tree and

watched as her friends disappeared into the distance.
She found herself looking up into the tree branches in
case there was a SMILE hanging in there. But what does
a SMILE without a face look like? You can't just pick
a smile up off the ground. It's a feeling too, isn't it?
And that feeling had gone.

5

THE LONG
AND SWEET OF IT

The rest of the day was no better. Chloe hid in the toilets at afternoon break and tried practising her SMILE in front of the mirror – but there wasn't even a lip twitch. Not even when she did her famous impression of a giraffe who had just been stung by a bee, her limbs and tongue LOLLOPING all over the place.

As Chloe walked home after school, having dodged her friends at the school gates, she could already hear the shouting coming from her house as she arrived at the bottom of Elmswater Crescent. She usually got home before her dad was back from work, and she liked it that way. Then she could have something to eat, do her homework and get on with some drawing whilst the house was still quiet – but today he was home and her mum and dad were arguing already.

'I told you **NOT** to come back to check on me!' Mrs Long shouted from the other side of the front door as Chloe walked up her garden path. The door was slightly ajar and Chloe peeked round it cautiously.

'I wasn't going to leave you alone with a builder, was I?!'

'Why not? **YOU** wanted that cupboard fixed … Hang on, are you **JEALOUS**?!' screeched Mrs Long.

The builder stood between them, both mortified and slightly flattered that he might be considered someone to be jealous over. He was going on sixty and was carrying a bit of extra weight, so much so that his tummy flopped over the belt of his jeans.

'I am not jealous. I just know what you're like! You're a … a **flibbertigibbet**!'

Chloe's mum couldn't believe her ears. 'What did you just call me?'

'A flibbertigibbet, you heard me – with your *fancy*

nails and your lounging about.'

Mrs Long raised herself up to her full height, which was also very tall (well over six foot), rolled up one of her magazines and **BIFFED** Mr Long on the head. 'I am **NOT** a flibbertigibbet! How dare you. I am a lady of sophistication and elegance.' Some of her dressing-gown fluff fell to the floor and she quickly picked it up and tried to stuff it into her pocket. 'And I am trapped here all day long doing your washing and ironing and keeping the house tidy ... if only I had **TIME** to be a flibbertigibbet!'

'**TIDY**?! There's dust an inch thick on this mantelpiece. Gather it together you'd make a dustman.'

'Very funny,' Mrs Long said sarcastically.

'I thought that **WAS** quite funny,' the builder spoke up suddenly. Mr and Mrs Long stared at him. 'Sorry, carry on ...'

So Mr and Mrs Long did. And all this time, Chloe remained outside on the doorstep. She was feeling anxious. Anxious about opening her own front door. Yesterday her father had told her off for creeping up on him in the kitchen, so now she stood outside wondering whether to push the door open and sneak in or whether to ring the doorbell and make herself known. After all, she didn't want to give Mr Long another fright. And what if ... what if the fact that she always seemed to get in the way was one of the reasons her parents were so stressed all the time? If she couldn't find a way to make them *happy* even when she **WAS** able to SMILE, what would her face do to them now?

She decided to ring the doorbell. As she pressed it, out came the familiar and rather silly circus-themed doorbell chime that Mrs Long had insisted on installing many years ago. When Chloe was little she and her parents used to do a little hip *wiggle* whenever it went off. Now everyone just put their fingers in their ears instead.

'Who the heck is that now?' shouted Mr Long. 'Well, aren't you going to get it?'

'Why should I get it? **You** get it,' her mother replied.

There was a long, furious pause.

'Do you want *me* to get it?' said the builder eventually.

'What?! **NO!**' shouted Mr Long. 'You might be in

cahoots with MY wife but you won't get your hands on **MY** front door too!'

'I am not *in cahoots* with—'

'SHUSH!' Mr Long swung open the door. He looked straight ahead and couldn't see anyone. At six foot six, he often forgot to look down at what wasn't in his line of vision. 'No one here.'

'It's me,' said Chloe, looking up at her father. And as she did so she realised all she wanted was one of his **GINORMOUS** hugs – when he wrapped his long arms right around her and held her tight and safe. She couldn't remember the last time he had hugged her like that, maybe if she …

'For goodness sake, girl, you frightened the life out of me. Again. Is this some sort of *joke*? Pick on your dad and give him a heart attack week? Well, come in then …' Chloe stepped past him into the hall. It definitely wasn't going to be a *cuddly* moment.

The builder was on his way out. 'Hello,' he said, and **SMILED** at Chloe.

'Hello,' said Chloe, realising at the same time that she wasn't even able to **SMILE** when someone was actually smiling at her first.

'Not you and all, Chloe, stop taking sides with the builder, I think it's best you get upstairs!'

'I haven't had any tea,' exclaimed Chloe.

'Don't worry, I'll throw you up some pop-tarts,' shouted Mrs Long from the sitting room.

'Right, er, thank you,' said Chloe as she ran upstairs trying not to cry. She flopped on to her bed, didn't even turn to her joke book or her drawing pad, and the tears started to fall as she heard a box of pop-tarts land in the hallway outside her bedroom.

'Do you know what I am going to bring in at the garden centre this summer season – **GNOMES**! They'll sell like hot cakes, I'm sure of it!' Mr and Mrs Sweet were talking about Mr Sweet's job, just outside Chloe's window.

'**GNOMES**! You are silly!' Mrs Sweet chuckled.

Chloe peeked out of her window and saw Mrs Sweet hugging her husband lovingly.

Chloe stared up at the ceiling and couldn't help remembering her last birthday. Gran Gran had been there, of course, and she'd given her some new drawing pencils. She always made her feel *loved* and encouraged, because she remembered all the little things Chloe told her. That was why Gran Gran had bought her the pencils, because she'd remembered Chloe telling her all about the horses she loved drawing. She was so grateful to her grandmother for taking the time to come and see her, especially on her birthdays.

And Chloe had gone to bed that night, a year and a day ago exactly, her SMILE intact, and had the most *marvellous* party. Albeit in her head. But it was a fabulous evening DREAM, flying over the treetops to a party in *Magic Land.* She'd eaten a delicious summer ice-cream pudding, served on the back of a majestic polar bear that she could hug and stroke. The squirrels who lived in the toffee apple trees performed a dance routine including a section where they juggled conkers SPECTACULARLY. And the party finished with the penguins conducting a multicoloured firework display which spelt out CHLOE in the sky.

Tonight, there was nothing inside her to drum up even a short imaginary trip to *Chloe's Magic Land.* She missed Gran Gran – though thank goodness she wasn't here, Chloe told herself. She was now a girl without a SMILE – would her grandmother even recognise her? Who will love me like this? And how on earth do you go about getting a lost **SMILE** back?

It wasn't vaguely dark, it was still a summer's afternoon, but with these anxious thoughts in her head, all Chloe could think of doing was getting ready for bed. She put on her favourite spotty pyjamas with shorts for bottoms, listened to the soothing sounds of the birds tweeting in the Sweets' garden, then fell into a fitful sleep. Until something **EXTRAORDINARY** woke her up …

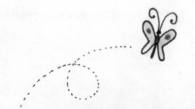

6

GODFREY AND HOPPY

RuMble, GRuMble, RuMble!

Chloe woke up with a jump. What was that massive rumbling, grumbling sound? She'd fallen asleep with her window and curtains open, it had been such a warm summer's afternoon. Now she looked out of her window into the night, convinced there must be a large animal or even a **MONSTER** out there, such was the strange noise. But there was nothing. Just moonlight and stars – a beautiful bright night.

She saw everyone's cars parked neatly on their driveways, the local plumber's van parked on the road and the postman's trolley bag in his garage. A couple of children's bicycles lay discarded on the pavement after some post-school cycling around the cul-de-sac. And she could see Mr and Mrs Sweet in their sitting room spraying their indoor plants with water – Mrs Sweet would sometimes even polish them with a duster – before switching the lights off and going up to bed under their lovely fluffy duvet. Everything seemed as normal.

Then suddenly – another **HUGE** grumble. She whipped her head around, searching for the source of the sound. Was it a fox? There were sometimes foxes sniffing in the bins outside at this time of night. But no – besides, it sounded louder than a fox. She considered the monster option again before telling herself to stop being silly. 'After all, monsters don't exist, Chloe!' After the third rumble, she twigged where it was coming from. It was her. It was her stomach growling with hunger. She'd hardly eaten all day and was completely ravenous now.

Chloe crept out into the hallway to see if the pop-tarts were still there. No sign. Her parents' bedroom door was open; she tiptoed very carefully towards it and peered inside. Her mum and dad were fast asleep, their feet hanging off the end of the bed. Mr Long was snoring and he had the pop-tarts tucked under his arm. He had obviously been eating them in bed. Chloe thought this was rather mean, considering he knew they were meant for her. But on the other hand, it was probably her own fault for leaving them there. As her dad often said, he worked long, hard hours to provide food for his family – so he was probably hungry after a tiring day.

If she'd still had the strength her SMILE gave her she might have tried to tiptoe up to her snoring father and sneak the final pop-tart out from his grasp. In fact, she thought she remembered a time when she might have bounced on to her parents' bed and made them *giggle*. When she used to wake them up by tickling the bottoms of their feet that always stuck out of the bed sheets. Or was that a *dream* she'd had? Whatever it was, right now, she didn't want to risk waking her dad since he had become so long-faced and short-fused.

Chloe crept back into bed, trying not to think about food. But it was hard to fall asleep feeling so hungry. She noticed her scratchy blanket more than ever tonight, all prickly against her skin. She turned over in bed, away from the window, to try and sleep that way.

But as she turned, she thought she saw something or someone walk past her window. She stopped, half sitting up, still facing away. What on earth was that? No one could walk past her window – she was upstairs on the first floor, which would make the person about twenty foot high. But by now she was convinced she felt a presence there, behind her. She slowly turned around and … Nothing. It was obviously just her hunger playing tricks on her. Then **SUDDENLY** …

… an **ENORMOUS** face appeared right in front of her, almost the size of the whole window. She was so startled she couldn't even scream. She just stared, open-mouthed and wide-eyed, wondering what on **EARTH** she was looking at.

In fact, the face before her at the window was mostly hidden by a very large-brimmed hat with a colourful ribbon around it, but from what she could see the person attached to the face had yellow straw-like hair that stuck out from the hat like the *sun's rays*, looked neither young or old, and had a **big,** beaming GRIN. And if a person hadn't lost their SMILE, they would have been sure to SMILE directly back, it was such a friendly grin.

But as it was, Chloe just remained mouth open. Eyes wide. Aghast. She couldn't believe what she

*What on earth was that? No one could walk past her window –
she was upstairs on the first floor, which would make the
person about twenty foot high.*

was seeing. She closed her eyes and slowly opened them again, assuming the face would disappear as she did so, because it **MUST** be her IMAGINATION. But instead, well, she couldn't believe this ... the big face was still there and there was now **ANOTHER** face at the window, much smaller, as small as a bird, peering over the brim of the big face's hat. Chloe gulped with astonishment but weirdly, she realised, she was *not* scared. Even though you would have thought it would be scary, a twenty-foot person appearing at your window all of a sudden, with a miniature creature perched on their head.

'Hello,' said the beaming face, in a booming yet calm sort of a way. Chloe continued to stare, motionless.

'Hello,' said the smaller face in a squeakier tone. As she did so, she swung down from the hat brim to reveal that she was a small, shiny, SPARKLING girl in what looked to be a white, floaty dress and tiny shoes with fun pom-poms on the end. She had petite, pointed features, dark, penetrating eyes and hair piled up on her head like a messy nest. Chloe thought she looked a bit like a miniature *ballerina* who'd been dragged through several hedges both forwards and backwards.

They both SMILED at her again. Chloe was **STILL** open-mouthed, wide-eyed and motionless.

'This is normally when you say hello back,' bellowed the big-faced one eventually.

'Hello,' Chloe croaked at last.

'There you go.'

'Who are you?' Chloe managed to add.

'My name is Godfrey,' said the tall, big-faced figure. At least Chloe assumed he was tall, given his head was at her window level.

'And I'm Hoppy,' said the sparkly girl. 'Well, my real name is Holly but everyone calls me Hoppy …'

'… because she is always hopping happy. *Happy* hopping Hoppy,' Godfrey finished.

'That's me,' said Hoppy, and she dropped to the windowsill where she boinged up and down for a moment, leaping so high she disappeared from view momentarily, before she settled back on the sill. It was like she had springs in her feet. 'So that's us. Hello.'

'Hello. Again,' said Chloe, still blinking her eyes to see if the faces might go away. 'I'm …'

'You're Chloe, you are eleven years old, just, you didn't get the duvet you wanted for your birthday and you have lost your SMILE, your friends are cross with you and your parents are grumpy ...' said Godfrey.

Chloe was back to being open-mouthed and **WIDE-EYED** again.

'You might want to shut your mouth. What happens if a fly flies in?' Hoppy *giggled*.

Chloe forced her mouth shut with her hand. 'It's just, how did you know ... who are you ... **WHAT** are you?'

'Never mind that. **WE** know **YOU**, my dear Chloe; we always know when a child loses their SMILE. We're here to help you get it back.'

'Oh thank goodness,' Chloe gasped. The relief she felt coursing through her was immense – so her SMILE was somewhere safe, she would find it and be back to her normal self before anyone noticed a thing, and these strange people ... **CREATURES** ... whatever they were, were here to take her to it. She still couldn't believe she didn't feel scared by them. Perhaps it was because she was so used to imagining weird and *wonderful* things that this didn't seem so very strange to her. Or maybe it was because their faces looked so safe, friendly and ready to help.

'By the way, are you really that tall or are you standing on something?' Chloe asked.

'I'm really this tall,' Godfrey answered.

'Wow, you're even taller than my dad.'

'Mr Long is six foot six and a half, I believe, so yes, I am way taller than your father,' agreed Godfrey.

'You know about my father too?'

'We know everything,' said Hoppy. 'May I try your bed out?'

'OK.'

Hoppy leapt from the windowsill to land on the bed beside Chloe. 'Oh deary me, it's even harder than I thought ...'

Behind her, Godfrey pulled himself up so he was sitting on the windowsill, his upper body in Chloe's room and his legs and feet dangling down to the flower bed outside. But even though Chloe felt sure he should fill her room, given just how immense he was, somehow he suddenly sort of shrank and didn't seem much bigger than her dad after all. He sat down in her bedroom chair.

'**WOW!** How do you do that?!' she exclaimed.

'Oh yes, sometimes he's tall, sometimes he's smaller, sometimes he's something else altogether. He can be anything he needs to be. It's so much **FUN**.'

'Shush now, Hoppy,' said Godfrey. 'Let's get back to the business at hand. Which is a question for you, Chloe ... What would you like?' He paused. Up close Chloe could see more of his face – he had a wide nose to match his wide **SMILE**, and *warm* brown eyes. And even though his face was in the shadow of his big hat it seemed to have a kind of **INTENSITY** about it that made it hard to look at him closely for too long.

'Apart from this sandwich,' Hoppy added, as she reached into one of Godfrey's enormous brightly coloured pockets in his long, dark velvet coat, and pulled out a cheese and tomato sandwich.

'Cheese and tomato ... my **FAVOURITE**,' Chloe said dazedly. She took a bite – it was the most amazing cheese and tomato sandwich she had ever tasted. 'I was just thinking about sandwiches ...' Chloe mumbled with her mouth still full, so desperate was she to eat.

'I knew it. I could tell how hungry you were. I can always tell exactly what people are thinking and feeling,' said Hoppy. 'And it's horrible feeling hungry.' As she spoke she sprang back up off the bed, but a little too strongly, and flew head first into Chloe's lampshade. 'Ow!'

'Some calm now, please, Hoppy,' said Godfrey. He was obviously the leader of this strange duo, Chloe thought. 'We have something important to discuss with Chloe, after all.'

'What do you mean?' Chloe asked.

'Well, the thing you want most right now, over everything else, is to have your **SMILE** back. Is that right?'

Chloe paused. She thought about her mum and dad and wished she could make them feel better. She wished adults' frowns generally would be turned upside down into **SMILES.** She thought about her friends and wished they weren't cross with her. Then she wondered whether the thing she most wanted was to look into the future to check she would have a duvet of her own when she was older. But when it came down to it, she was meant to be *cheery* Chloe, a granddaughter that Gran Gran could be proud of, and who was *cheery* Chloe without her **SMILE**?

'Yes. I want to be able to **SMILE** again!'

'In that case, I think we should start our adventure to get your smile back **RIGHT NOW**!' boomed Godfrey.

'Ooooh yes yes yes!' squeaked Hoppy joyfully, bouncing up and down so fast all over Chloe's bedroom you could hardly see her, just the pom-poms on her shoes wobbling madly. 'Come on, let's not waste another minute.' She leapt on to the windowsill and Godfrey jumped down, becoming twenty foot tall again in the blink of an eye.

And suddenly, despite their obvious **EXCITEMENT**, Chloe felt hesitant. 'I feel a bit shaky, I don't know what sort of adventure you mean, how will it get me my **SMILE** back because nothing normal seems to work, like jokes and, well, I don't really know who you are.'

'But you are so courageous, Chloe, we know YOU,' said Godfrey gently, looking back through the window, directly into her eyes. 'Come on, what do you have to lose?'

'OK, you're right.' Already Chloe couldn't imagine how she had been able to keep going without Godfrey and Hoppy, and she had only known them for two minutes. 'I don't have anything to lose right now.'

'That's my girl! Come on then.' He turned around carefully, so as not to completely trample Chloe's garden under his immense feet, and offered her his shoulders for a piggyback.

'But I'm still in my pyjamas,' Chloe said.

'And very pretty they are too,' Hoppy chirped, as Godfrey waited expectantly.

Chloe took a deep breath, grabbed her trainers, and clambered through her window and on to the back of her new **GIANT** friend.

And it suddenly hit her. What on **EARTH** was happening? Or more to the point, was this **REALLY** happening at all?!

Then Godfrey asked Chloe, 'So, how do you want to travel?'

7

THE SURPRISING WAVES

'How do I want to travel? Ummm ... I'm not sure,' answered Chloe, still amazed about what was happening, and all the more amazed that she was even contemplating going on this sudden **ADVENTURE**.

Then, just as Chloe was about to say, 'Umm ... I'd love to fly, if you **CAN** fly, that is ...?' Hoppy leapt into the air and zipped through the sky above Mr and Mrs Sweet's house. And for the first time, Chloe noticed the tiny bird's wings sprouting from Hoppy's back – they shimmered blue, a bit like kingfisher wings. 'Ooooh!' Chloe gasped. 'It was like she knew what I was going to say!'

'Oh, she always knows what all of us are going to say. You can rely on Hoppy, however silly she may seem,' said Godfrey reassuringly. 'Ready?'

'Nothing to lose!' said Chloe.

'Brave girl!' called Godfrey over his shoulder at her. He launched into the night sky and Chloe found herself sitting snugly between his shoulders as he flew over houses, then trees, then way into the countryside beyond her little town. It was similar to the flights Chloe often imagined for herself. But it was **ACTUALLY** happening. She was actually in the night sky, looking down on everything below, able to reach out and touch the tops of the trees. Ahead, Hoppy flew figures of eight and loop-the-loops like an aeroplane at an air show, *giggling* the whole time, but Godfrey maintained his sedate, steady pace to make his new passenger feel as safe as possible. All Chloe had to do was sit back and enjoy the starry skies, crisp chill in the air and this EXTRAORDINARY journey.

Just as Chloe was beginning to feel like she wanted to land, to see where they had flown to and where and how she was going to go about retrieving her missing SMILE, ahead of her Hoppy started to descend. It's like she's reading my mind again, Chloe thought.

They landed on what Chloe guessed was a riverbank – it was hard to see at first because it was still dark, but she could hear the splash of rushing water and feel the occasional droplet pinging her skin. Godfrey set Chloe gently down.

Is my **SMILE** somewhere here? Chloe wondered, but before she could ask the question, Godfrey and Hoppy began walking along the bank. The sun started to come up and she could feel it warming her face. Then, as she looked about, she realised something **COMPLETELY AMAZING** – they were walking along a riverbank she had seen before, one she knew very well. In fact, they were walking along the riverbank that led into Chloe's very own *Magic Land!*

'No way!' Chloe shouted in shock. 'How … how could you know about my *Magic Land*?! I made it up, it's all in my head, how can it really be here?'

But there it was. The two lakes, one iced and one summery, with a waterfall for swimming under. And there were her funny penguins, already slipping and sliding across the ice to say hello. And it was all as bright as ever – the red and orange autumn leaves, the vibrant spring flowers and the bluest clear skies.

'We know everything about you, remember?' Hoppy's whisper was suddenly in Chloe's ear and she felt the brush of bird wings on her hair. 'We love *Magic Land* too, all the seasons in one day – such a clever idea of yours.'

'I can't believe you have made *Magic Land* come true.'

But Godfrey was already out of earshot on the icy lake, gliding across its surface wearing enormous skates instead of his enormous dusty espadrilles (what size his shoes must be, Chloe could barely imagine …), his coat flapping about him so wildly that some of the *Magic Land* exotic birds would get caught up in it, if they didn't duck and dive quickly enough. Chloe assumed he was enjoying himself but he was **SO** enormous at this moment that she couldn't really see his face, all she could see was the bottom half of his legs. And he could only do about three slides of his skates before he had to turn around and go back in the other direction.

Chloe pulled on the skates that were always resting on the shoreline waiting for her, then she paused. She knew she should be **HAPPIER** than she'd ever been before – after all, *Magic Land* was **REAL** and she was here, actually *here*, about to go skating

*In fact, she felt so far from being able to smile that
she thought her face might turn to stone any minute.*

with her unusual new friends and experience who knew what escapades – but she couldn't help noticing that despite how incredible this precise moment was, she still wasn't *smiling.* In fact, she felt so far from being able to SMILE that she thought her face might turn to stone any minute.

Ahead of her, Godfrey spun on the spot, creating a small whirlwind as he did, sending some of the smaller penguins flying off the ice, through the air, only to plop gently head first into the soft mounds of snow piled along the banks on one side. Chloe's favourite, Percy the King Penguin, even whirled so high into the sky that when he fell down he got wedged in the top branches of a toffee apple tree and had to be carried down by the strongest squirrels.

But when Godfrey saw that Chloe wasn't joining him on the ice, he skated back to her, his feet spraying her lightly with ice as he skidded to a stop at her side, then crouched down to her level.

'What's wrong, Chloe?'

'I am worried I will never get my SMILE back. Not even the thought of skating in *Magic Land*, one of my favourite things in the world, is making me feel even remotely **SMILEY**!'

'I understand,' Godfrey began, 'but—'

Chloe felt panicky, and she couldn't hold it in any more. 'And you **PROMISED** you'd help me find it. So where is it? How do I get it back? NOW!'

'Shhhh, ssshhh.' Hoppy flitted in front of Chloe's face, cooling her hot cheeks with her whirring wings. 'We know how sad you feel right now, and we are going to help. We want your **SMILE** back as desperately as you do. But one step at a time. Trust us, all will be well. I promise.' She alighted on Chloe's wrist. Chloe realised she did feel calmer, thanks to their understanding. 'Now, come on, let's skate ... In fact, let's make up a routine ... *Yippeeeee* ...' And with surprising strength for a girl the size of a bird, she pulled Chloe up by her hand and propelled her on to the ice.

As Hoppy and Chloe skated, a routine began to take shape between them quite naturally and easily. So much so that the penguins she normally skated with couldn't keep up, and one by one they fell back to watch, beaks agape, giggling and clapping, as Hoppy whizzed about the ice like a spinning top and Chloe swept in big, graceful *arcs* around her.

Chloe was so busy concentrating she didn't notice Godfrey pointing and waving at something or someone in the trees. But she couldn't miss it when a band of woodland animals appeared on the banks of the frozen lake, each with an instrument, and started playing a TUNE that fitted their moves perfectly. There was a badger with a flat cap and a violin, a squirrel with a fluttery pink scarf and a flute, an otter in a stripy waistcoat with a trumpet, and a bespectacled deer with a double bass. A woodland band! Wow! That hadn't happened in *Chloe's Magic Land* before – she wondered where they had been hiding all this time. It wasn't long before the penguins were joining in with the music-making too, beating bongos with their flippers and tapping triangles with their beaks. Godfrey towered over them all, conducting with great gusto.

Chloe felt very *special*, like a professional skater – she even found the courage to copy one of Hoppy's little spins in the air. It all felt so good, especially when Godfrey and Hoppy clapped and roared. (You can imagine the noise of Godfrey's clapping – if his feet were large, then imagine the hands, as big as bin lids!) Chloe put her fingers to her face – surely there would be a **SMILE** there now? No …? But before she could dwell on this, Hoppy dropped an ice cream cone the size of a beach ball into her raised hand and chivvied her off the ice – and into the summer lake.

PLIP!

Hoppy dived neatly into the lake behind her, with barely a splash. Godfrey on the other hand took such a long run-up that he started from two fields away and when he dive-bombed into the water he caused a wave big enough to wash up and over the lake's banks and across the neighbouring icy lake, giving the penguins quite a shock! 'Top splash marks!' yelled Hoppy. 'Ten out of ten!'

Amazingly, Chloe's ice-cream cone was still intact and she lay on her back in the warm water, her hair floating about her head like a **MERMAID'S**, licking away at it, until a cheeky dolphin swam quickly to the surface and grabbed it, thinking it was a beach ball. Hoppy giggled, hovering overhead, and as Chloe's beloved dolphins leapt in *arcs* over her, spinning in the air and then splashing back into the water, she found her spirits leapt with them – so could her SMILE be returning …? She could almost sense it touching her lips …

But at that moment, Chloe felt something VERY different in *Magic Land*. At first it was just a wind, blowing across the lake. Not the usual warm summer breeze that Chloe liked to conjure up, but something colder, harsher. It seemed to come from the autumnal trees along the banks of the lake.

In seconds it was more like a full-blown gale, chilling Chloe to the core. Because even more SPOOKILY each tree now seemed to have a strange shadowy face hidden within its leaves and branches, all blowing as hard as they could to cause the storm.

Waves started appearing on the lake surface, getting larger and larger. It was becoming harder to swim. As one, the dolphins disappeared, presumably to the very bottom of the lake to hide. Chloe spun in the water, looking desperately for Godfrey or Hoppy.

'Hello? Where is everybody, help!' But the waves were too high – she couldn't see them. Water broke over her head, pushing her under for a moment, and she swallowed a mouthful before bobbing back up, coughing. 'Godfrey, **COUGH**, Hoppy, **COUGH** – where are you?' She started to feel really frightened. Where were they, what was happening, and why? *Magic Land* in her imagination never had any problems in it; now in its reality something awful was happening, and she was all alone.

Still, she didn't have time to tread water and complain, she needed to get out of the water **NOW** before it was too late. But which way is the shore? Chloe wondered.

Just then she caught sight of Hoppy briefly, as one wave dropped and before the next rose. '**HELP!**' she shouted at the top of her voice, and the next thing she knew the bird-girl was right there, hovering in the air next to her, bedraggled but determined.

'Don't worry,' Hoppy shouted, 'Godfrey is coming – he'll get you somewhere safe!'

'Isn't he big enough to just pick me up out of the water, can't he do it **RIGHT NOW**?' Chloe gasped.

'Knowing Godfrey he's got an even better plan than that … he won't let you down.'

'Seems like his plan is to let me **DROWN**. I don't think I can tread water for much longer,' Chloe coughed.

'Stay strong, Chloe, I know you can, I'm right here!' But the waves were getting higher and higher, crashing over Chloe's head and even pushing them both under from time to time, so that Chloe had to swim hard up to the surface to get her breath back, and Hoppy's wings began to droop with the weight of the water.

'Hop … py … Hop …' Chloe could feel herself weakening as she struggled in the waves, she couldn't even call out to Hoppy any more. Where *was* Godfrey?

SMASH! Another wave came down on her head and she found herself underwater again, being whirled around like an old sock in a washing machine. She couldn't fight the water any more, she was so *tired* … she stopped struggling and felt herself begin to float down, down, down. This was it, she was drowning, now she'd never find her SMILE …

WHOOSH! Suddenly a hand the size of a small

boat appeared in the water and scooped her up and out into the fresh air above. Godfrey had arrived. At last. She gulped in breaths gratefully as Godfrey plopped her into a beautifully carved wooden canoe, a smaller version of the one he was sitting in himself, and started paddling his way through the waves at pace, pulling Chloe's boat along behind his own.

'Jump in with Chloe, Hoppy!' he shouted over the howling gale. 'I'll get us out of here.'

'But … but the storm, there's nowhere to go to get away …' Chloe just managed to pant as she grabbed her own paddle and tried to help them along.

'Don't worry, Godfrey knows somewhere to go,' Hoppy gasped before flopping gratefully on to her canoe.

'The gale is coming from the trees,' Godfrey stated with calm authority, like he was a sea captain in a crisis. 'I am going to *use* it, let it push us towards the waterfall. Once we are under there it will be calm. Hold on.'

All Chloe could do as she was sprayed from every direction by the fierce waves was hold on and hope they got to the waterfall before she capsized. Her heart was beating so fast. She looked back at the trees and saw that the shadowy faces amongst their branches now seemed to have bodies too. And they were shaking the branches, blowing the leaves themselves, almost as if they were encouraging the wind, and *laughing* an evil-sounding laugh as they did so. Where they blew, colour seemed to leach from the leaves, and blossoms shrivelled and dropped. Who were these horrible shadows and what did they want?

She heard the roar of the waterfall from above.

'Duck!' shouted Godfrey. Chloe bent forward protectively over Hoppy. For a brief moment she felt the hard flow of the waterfall against her back, then they were through and in the calm, still waters behind it.

'There were things in the trees ... I saw horrible scary-looking **CREATURES** ... it was like they were *making* the wind,' Chloe panted, still trying to get her breath back.

'I know,' said Godfrey sadly.

'But why?' Chloe exclaimed. 'Why are they there? This is **MY** *Magic Land*, and it was all perfect in my head, but now you've actually brought me here it's ruined with evil shadowy people trying to make me drown ...'

'But we didn't drown,' said Hoppy, buzzing beside her in the air once more, drying off her wings as she fluttered. 'And more to the point, how brave were you, Chloe?! WHAT an **ADVENTURE** that was!'

'Are you mad?' shouted Chloe above the noise of the waterfall. 'An **ADVENTURE**?! That was *terrifying!*' She suddenly felt really angry. 'I don't want to have to be brave ... that's not why I'm here. PLEASE tell me, what's going on?'

Godfrey nodded. 'It's true, Chloe – there is something afoot in *Magic Land,* though even I did not realise how strong THEY had become ...'

'I thought you brought me here to find my SMiLE,' Chloe said. 'Not to tell me that *Magic Land* was under attack from, from whatever ... This is all too much ... And ... and ... there's nowhere to go, we're trapped here now and—'

'We're not trapped, are we, Godfrey?' said Hoppy soothingly.

'Not at all. Let me surprise you, Chloe, because as you may have noticed, I like doing that.' Godfrey tapped his canoe paddle against the rock wall behind them and it started to move, opening away from them like an enormous rock door. Chloe was back to her wide-eyed and open-mouthed expression because as the rock extended fully she found herself looking out on to the most magical landscape she had ever seen. They paddled through and the rock wall closed behind them.

'There's so much more to you and your **IMAGINATION** than even you know, Chloe – and now it's time to explore! Welcome to the rest of *Magic Land*!'

8
DOWN THE RAVINE

They continued down the river in their canoes and into the **MIND-BOGGLING** world beyond. The banks were lined with lush trees full of beautiful, colourful birds, some so small they would fit on the side of Chloe's canoe, some so huge they were the size of Mrs Long's armchair – and some particularly friendly parrots that flew down to perch on large boulders in the river and greet them with squawky 'hello's. Butterflies fluttered lazily past, leaving trails of colourful dust in the sky that settled in *rainbows* on Chloe's eyelashes.

There were plump, pink berries the size of fists that fell into their canoes without prompting – they smelt like sweets and tasted like peaches and strawberries rolled into one (Chloe's two **FAVOURITE** fruits, of course). The juice dripped from Chloe's chin as she bit into her second one, while Hoppy zipped through the air in zigzags lest one dropped and knocked her flat!

Bright orange monkeys jumped from tree to tree and rainbow-coloured gazelles leapt along the rocky banks. Behind the trees on both sides of the riverbanks were huge reddish rock faces and Chloe realised they were in a deep ravine. The world above them, on either side of the ravine, seemed miles away.

It was **SO AMAZING.** The water was calm and the trees were still, and Chloe did almost feel grateful that she had been through the wind-wave storm if it meant she could get to this.

Godfrey must have brought them here because it was safe from the shadow creatures, whatever they were.

She wanted to ask Godfrey that right now, but his canoe was too far ahead. And at the thought of the leering faces in the trees she shivered, and that made her think of something else – the thing she loved to do at home whenever she needed to relax ... have a **BUBBLE BATH**.

'How nice would a bath be right now?' Hoppy's voice said in her ear suddenly. 'It would really top this off perfectly, wouldn't it?'

'I was just thinking about baths, that's SO WEIRD!'

'Not really,' Hoppy chuckled. She hopped up and down, pleased with herself.

'But how can we have a bath when we're already in a river, Chloe?' Godfrey called back to them, his voice echoing off the ravine walls.

Chloe could feel her mind racing ahead – how great would it be if you could have a canoe or a little boat that was *also* a bath? So you could be lying in a hot bubbly bath as you made your way down the river. You'd be in a **BOAT BATH**! And then once you had got warm and relaxed enough in your boat bath you could let the water out with a plug, into the river, then plug it back up, and the bath becomes a boat again.

'Utterly brilliant!' exclaimed Hoppy, without Chloe even saying a word. 'Now close your eyes and open them again.' Chloe did as she was told and she couldn't believe what her eyes were showing her. They were floating down the river in the boat baths she had **IMAGINED**. Chloe's had rubber ducks floating in it and was full of bubbles. Hoppy was already swooping over

Chloe's boat bath, popping bubbles with her pom-pom shoes as she passed.

Godfrey's boat bath was white marble with huge golden taps, the most ornate bath you have ever seen. And although it was incredibly long, his feet still dangled over the edge. But Chloe could see he was very *happy*. As she watched he SMILED, reached into one of his patched pockets – and pulled out a shimmering gold shower cap and swapped it for his old black hat. 'Oh yes, fit for a king.' He let out a hearty *laugh*.

Chloe took a deep, calming breath and lay back looking up at the birds flying all around them. A bath in pyjamas and trainers – who knew it would feel so **RIGHT**?! She was all right, she had fought her way through those waves … so was this it, was her SMILE just around the bend in the river waiting for her, or would it find its way back to her face all by itself at last—

WHOOOSH!

Chloe sat upright in her boat bath. What was that noise? Why did the air suddenly feel cool around her again?

'The Shadow Bandits are back!' shouted Godfrey.

It was true: on both sides of the river trooped an army of shadows like those Chloe had seen by the lake, part person-shaped, part formless. Colour seemed to soak out of the world and disappear from every place they touched. Suddenly the parrots looked almost grey, not green and red and yellow, and the monkeys were a dull dark brown.

'I didn't think they would have the strength to follow us here!'

'Shadow Bandits?!' asked Chloe. 'What **ARE** they? What do they want?'

'No time for that now, but I am afraid us having fun has angered them,' Godfrey growled.

Chloe noticed the birds and butterflies were all flying upwards away from the bandits; the gazelles and monkeys had already disappeared from sight. There was an eerie quiet in the ravine. An expectant feeling. But not in a good way. What was going to happen?

Ahead, Chloe spotted a bridge across the river. She saw with horror that it was lined with Shadow Bandits. They were still hard to make out properly, but somehow Chloe could tell that they were blowing again. This time straight downwards on to the river. And on their side of the bridge, it was creating rapids. Dark, **WHIRLING** waters with white-topped angry waves crashing into each other. Rapids that their boat baths were heading straight towards. And on the other side of the bridge Chloe could see it was even worse. A waterfall, dropping away to NOTHINGNESS.

There wasn't enough time for Godfrey to shout to Chloe before he hurtled into the rapids. Moments later, Chloe blasted into them too. The boat baths made such a noise as the rapids pummelled their sides: **THUMP-BUMP, THUMP-BUMP, THUMP-BUMP**. She could feel Hoppy's wings humming against her cheek as the bird-girl shouted something in her ear, but she couldn't hear what it was over the roar of the water. It was all so turbulent and fast that it was impossible to steer.

Chloe knew she had to start thinking clearly, and quickly, because otherwise she was going to capsize and she couldn't risk going over the waterfall, she would be bashed to bits below. Even in her boat bath

Chloe looked at the bandits lined up above her.
Her heart was thumping.

that was a very strong possibility. Horrifyingly, she couldn't see Godfrey anywhere.

Chloe suddenly had an idea. Hopefully that meant Hoppy had the same idea, she thought. She was about to go under the bridge: her plan was to stand up and try to jump up and cling on to it. She knew this was risky, because the bandits might attack her by kicking her hands off the bridge, but she also thought it might be her only hope.

She stood up, her boat bath rocking wildly from side to side as she did so, and reached up high, ready to seize the bridge. And as her boat sailed underneath she grabbed its edge and held on with all her might. Her little craft sailed on without her, crashing over the waterfall and out of sight.

Out of the corner of her eye she saw Hoppy hovering anxiously in the air at her side, her wings zipping frantically back and forth like a hummingbird's. Chloe looked at the bandits lined up above her. Her heart was thumping. Were they about to stamp on her hands and kick her back into the tempestuous river below?

But dark as they were, the Shadow Bandits

weren't very solid. They were a bit like thick clouds. If she had a sword, she thought, and the hands spare to use one, she could pierce them through and they would dissipate like a puff of smoke, or like a popped BUBBLE. It didn't seem likely they could stamp on her hands and hurt her in that way at all.

But she was still struggling to hold on, and then seeing one of them blowing on the river, she had another idea. Could it ... would it work? Well, it was worth a try. She took a deep breath ... and started blowing back at them as hard as she could. Two of the bandits dissolved immediately. She carried on blowing and another floated away to nothing, then another, then another.

One by one they screeched as they were forced up and away, eventually evaporating from the bridge altogether. Having cleared several of the shadows from around her she was able to drag herself on to the bridge. Hoppy joined her and together they blew and blew with all the strength they could muster, Hoppy also flapping her wings furiously to beat them back. And as the last bandit dispersed, the river rapids stopped swirling and calm water gradually returned.

Godfrey's face appeared over the top of the waterfall. He seemed to stretch momentarily until he was big enough to step **UP** the waterfall as if it was a tiny shelf, then to shrink back down again to his usual twenty-foot-sized self. With just a few strong strokes he swam back upriver.

'Everyone all right?' he asked as he clambered out of the water and joined them.

Chloe was slumped on the bridge getting her breath back. By now, Hoppy was doing a **CELEBRATORY** dance in the air. 'Well done, Chloe, well done. Godfrey, she was amazing! So brave and resourceful, she saved us all.'

'I do not feel remotely amazing,' said Chloe crossly, looking up. 'I was just feeling a bit better in my lovely boat bath and then that happened, just like it did before at the lake. We nearly **DIED**, that was so so so scary.' She felt a few tears trickle down her cheeks as what had just happened sank in. '**WHY**, whenever I think everything is going to be all right, does something nasty happen? And why have you brought me here – none of this can possibly give me my **SMILE** back.'

As she began to cry, Godfrey morphed into a normal-sized person for her to cry on his shoulder. Finally, the hug she had been craving. It felt so safe. Safer than being under the covers in her own bed.

'The time has come to tell you something important, Chloe. **THIS** is why we brought you to *Magic Land* in the first place. It's not just about your **SMILE**. We need your help. We need to stop the Shadow Bandits before they suck the colour and light from this beautiful world and reduce it to nothing. *Magic Land* needs you. We can't do it without you.'

It was true that where the bandits had been there were little patches of grey, wilted plants that the returning animals skirted around fearfully.

'What can I do?' Chloe said. 'I'm no good for anything without my **SMILE** ...'

'That's not true,' said Godfrey. 'Look at the courage you showed just now – it was **YOU** who blew those bandits away. We know you can do this. You *have* to. The shadows are here and they're spreading their darkness and feeding on the sadness that it brings, getting stronger all the while. We can help you, but only you can stop them once and for all – it's YOUR *Magic Land*.'

'It's not fair!' said Chloe furiously. 'How am I ever going to get my **SMILE** back, when bad things keep happening?'

'Maybe you can do *both*,' said Hoppy's small voice in her ear. 'Save *Magic Land* and your **SMILE** ...' Then she darted enigmatically away, into the sky.

'What does she mean?' demanded Chloe, but as she did so she yawned. She couldn't help it – it had been the longest, busiest night of her eleven-year life ...

'Come on,' said Godfrey, picking Chloe up. 'I'll tell you on the way home. You've done enough for tonight.' He straightened and swung Chloe on to his back, so she was snuggled safely again between his shoulders.

He took off, rising straight up from the river to the top of the ravine and then swooping onwards over what looked like a beach, as the *Magic Land* sun began to go down and the sky turned to night again.

'What will it be when I get home?' mumbled Chloe tiredly. 'Day or night, I'm so confused.'

'Don't worry, when we take you on an **ADVENTURE,** time stands still. It's stayed night in your town the whole time you've been here. So when we take you back, you still have a good night's sleep ahead of you.'

'Ummm ... Now please tell me what Hoppy meant about the *Magic Land* and the **SMILE** thing ...'

'You see, my girl, it will take courage to save *Magic Land,* and it takes courage to be cheerful too. Life isn't always easy and it sometimes takes strength to see the happy side ...'

Chloe thought she was beginning to understand. But she was feeling so sleepy after her adventures ... That, plus the soothing nature of Godfrey's voice, and she found herself slowly starting to close her eyes. No, this was important. 'Go on,' she whispered.

'Your **SMILE** is something special. And we'll be back tomorrow night to explain it more. So ...'

But Chloe was fast asleep.

As they flew over the Sweets' house back to Number 2 Elmswater Crescent, Godfrey grew smaller and smaller so he could fly straight into Chloe's window and put her safely to bed. Hoppy, who had travelled the rest of the way in Godfrey's chest pocket, *kissed* Chloe's forehead.

'Good night, sweet child,' whispered Godfrey as he stepped out of the window, returning to his twenty-foot height as he did so, and walked off into the night with Hoppy alongside, proud as punch of his dear Chloe.

And Chloe slept through it all.

9

AN **UNANNOUNCED VISITOR**

Chloe woke up the next morning to banging and crashing and shouting and nothing short of a commotion going on downstairs. She heard the front door slam, and peering out of her window Chloe saw her mum shrieking across the front garden and out into the street, fully dressed and with an apron on too. Chloe hadn't seen her mother out of her dressing-gown for months. What was going on?

'Mrs Sweet, Mrs Sweet, *Mrs Sweeeeettttttt!*' screeched Mrs Long. 'I need your help, bring your garden cutting instruments and your mower … *Mrs Sweeeeeeeeettttttttt.*' She disappeared into the Sweets' house.

Then Chloe heard the hoover on downstairs. Who could that be? Mr Long had never hoovered in his life. Chloe sat on her bed wondering what was going on. She swung her feet to the floor to get up and go and see, and she felt a surge of **ENERGY** rise from her toes, all the way through her, into the rest of her body. And then **WHAM**, it hit her: the memory of last night, meeting Godfrey and Hoppy, visiting *Magic Land* for real, the woodland band, the waves, the boat baths and the Shadow Bandits. Did it all **ACTUALLY** happen?

She noticed something on her bedside table. It was a small china penguin ornament with skates that you could take on and off. She slipped one of the skates off and it was tiny in her palm. Its white leather gleamed brightly and the blade glinted in the morning sunlight. Next to it was a frosted cupcake with rainbow-coloured icing – almost too pretty to eat – and what looked like a tiny ballerina with marzipan wings on top. Hoppy! It **HAD BEEN** real. **WOW!**

And even though her **SMILE** was still missing – Chloe had already checked in the mirror – and even though the thought of having to encounter those bandits again terrified her, she somehow felt more able to face the day.

'Mr Long!' Chloe was startled by her mum coming back towards the house, with Mr and Mrs Sweet and a variety of gardening and cleaning equipment in tow. 'Mr Looooong!' she screeched again, causing many net curtains in the cul-de-sac to twitch.

Chloe pulled her school uniform on and rushed downstairs. Goodness, it **WAS** her dad hoovering. He was in the sitting room with a small apron on and a dust buster sucking up all of his wife's toenail clippings and the dust off the mantelpiece.

'Mr Looooong!' Chloe's mum marched past her into the room. 'The Sweets have got a toilet brush, now get upstairs and get it down the loo and scrub like you have never scrubbed before.'

'I literally *have* never scrubbed before,' replied her dad, bumping into Chloe on his way out of the sitting room. 'Move along, Chloe, man on a mission, no time to waste.' They both stepped the same way in an attempt to get out of each other's way, and then the same way again, and again, until Mr Long irritably lifted Chloe up, sidestepped her, then put her down again behind him before rushing off muttering something about '*being in the way*'.

Chloe's heart sank. That was probably it, probably why they were so unhappy, she was always in her parents' way.

'What's going on?' Chloe dared to ask nonetheless, as Mr Long hurried up the stairs.

'Oh, nothing much, just that …' and he suddenly shouted, 'MY **DRATTED** MOTHER HAS JUST RUNG UP TO SAY SHE IS ON HER WAY FOR A TWO-NIGHT SURPRISE **VISIT**! Argh!' and he disappeared upstairs with the loo brush.

'Gran Gran is coming?!'

'Yes, and unannounced. I usually get some notice, but not this time, so I've lots to do. She will be here in an hour, so stop mucking about and no causing a mess. You know how particular Granny Evelyn is!' said Mrs Long.

'I am just standing here, I am **not** causing a mess,' Chloe found herself retorting. Mrs Long gawped at her, not used to such a tone from Chloe. But the girl was only rightly and politely sticking up for herself. Remembering the waves and the Shadow Bandits from last night, she'd had a surge of courage and spirit, and it had just blurted out of her mouth. Frankly, she was ' a bit shocked herself, but it felt right and good.

'You … you shouldn't answer back, young lady,' Mrs Long shouted up the stairs. 'Mr Long, Chloe has just been incredibly **RUDE** to me. I think.'

'I can't deal with that *and* have my hand down a toilet, now, can I?' he shouted back.

If anyone was rude it was them, muttered Chloe to herself in another unusual act of defiance. Gran Gran always visited on or around her birthday, so had they remembered her birthday it wouldn't be a surprise visit at all and they wouldn't be in this **PANIC**. Grabbing a banana off the kitchen table, she picked up her school rucksack and went outside. She leant against the front door, relieved to be out of the house. Despite her night-time **ADVENTURES** with Godfrey and Hoppy, things felt even less right than ever. And normally the announcement of a visit from Gran Gran would most definitely give Chloe a *spring* in her step.

Ironically for someone called Mrs Long with a son who was over six foot six, Gran Gran herself was absolutely tiny. Only just five foot and so petite she barely took up any space. In fact, they usually made a spare room for her by putting a camp-bed in the garden shed. She fitted perfectly in there and was **very** happy with it. She always brought a travel kettle and mug, a little rug, and her *own* pillow and blanket, and made it a very tidy HOME from HOME.

You see, Gran Gran, however lovely a lady, was **very** particular. She might like **ADVENTURE** and excitement in her life, but she *didn't* like arguing or mess in the home, she liked neat and ordered lifestyles and households. Hence Chloe's mum and dad cleaning like maniacs this morning.

Chloe loved her grandmother being so small because she felt like she had even more of an ally in someone of her own height. Someone who literally and metaphorically didn't look down on her.

Chloe and Gran Gran had always seen eye to eye. They got on 'LIKE A HOUSE ON FIRE' as she used to say. In fact once, when Gran Gran was babysitting for Chloe, they'd been making pancakes, but left the oil on the heat for a bit too long and it caught fire in the pan. They nearly really did set the house on fire. But they always *laughed*, even then. Another one of Gran Gran's sayings was:

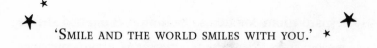

And Chloe admired her so much for this, because it wasn't as if her grandmother hadn't encountered sadness. Gran Gran had lost her husband very soon after Mr Long was born, and she had been on her own ever since.

But she never complained, never moaned about feeling lonely, even though she once told Chloe that not a day went by she didn't miss having someone to *love* as she had Chloe's grandfather. She just kept on **SMILING**. Something Chloe knew she was now singularly failing to do.

'Good morning, dear,' said Mrs Sweet, who was pruning the bushes in the Longs' front garden as ordered by Mrs Long. 'Say good morning to Chloe, sweetie pie,' she said to her husband.

'Sorry, can't lose my concentration, I am in the middle of sculpting the beak on what will be a chicken *topiary* made from this fine yew hedge. Never will the Longs' front garden have looked so neat,' replied Mr Sweet cheerfully. 'I might even find a place for a **GNOME!**'

'We have wanted to have a go at your garden for such a long time, this is giving us SO much pleasure,' Mrs Sweet added.

'Well, er, thank you,' said Chloe as she swung her rucksack on to her shoulders and set off to school.

'Are you all right, dear?'

'Yes, thank you, absolutely fine, really wonderful, great. Bye!' said Chloe unconvincingly as she dashed off down the street with a grey sinking feeling back inside.

'Sweetie pie, have you noticed that Chloe hasn't been herself recently, I haven't seen her SMILE for days. I am sure there is something wrong,' said Mrs Sweet.

Chloe heard this. Indeed her SMILE already seemed a distant memory. She felt even lower – and feeling low was a good way to describe it. She just wanted to fall down and crawl along the ground. Without her SMILE she had noticed her face and shoulders were pulled down towards the pavement, her legs felt heavy like they just wanted to collapse on to the road and sit there and not move. She tried to look up, to find some energy and *light* in the world like she normally would by SMILING at others, but all she saw was a dullness.

She saw the postman tired and grumpy, flinging letters over hedges rather than bothering to put them in people's letterboxes. She saw stressed-out parents rushing back and forth between their houses and cars, forgetting children, packed lunches, purses, hats, coats, before finally realising they had everything (even if the purses were in the lunch boxes and the hats were strapped into the car seats and the children were sticking out of their handbags) and could reverse out of their drive and be on their way, at too fast a pace that wasn't good for anyone. She saw early-morning joggers on their way back home, sweating and exhausted, nearly crashing into lampposts. Everyone looked *tired* and *grey* and *busy*. Without **SMILES**. Just like her.

Chloe came to a sudden stop in the road. Which was lucky because she was about to go crashing into a bin she hadn't noticed. But she had also suddenly realised something ... Yes, good, she would be seeing Gran Gran later, but no, no, no, bad, very bad – she couldn't BEAR for Gran Gran to know that she had lost her **SMILE**. Surely she'd be desperately sad and disappointed with her.

Right, she MUST get her SMILE back **TODAY**. She couldn't wait until tonight to ask Godfrey and Hoppy again, she needed it **NOW**, even if she had to bash a billion bandits to get it. GULP. So where were they when she needed them? Hadn't they said they knew where she was and what she was thinking at all times?

'Umm ... hello, are you there?' said Chloe tentatively.

'Are you talking to me, kiddo?' A binman had suddenly appeared to move the bin Chloe had stopped by. 'Because yes, love, I am here.'

'Sorry, no, I was ... Don't worry ...' She walked on, embarrassed. 'Godfrey, Hoppy, where are you?' she tried again. 'Oh, this is so unfair!'

'Not you as well. I know it's unfair, but it's my job, for heaven's sake!'

She looked up and a traffic warden was writing a parking ticket for someone pulled up on a yellow line. 'Oh sorry, no, I wasn't talking to ...'

But the traffic warden wasn't listening, he was moaning to himself. 'And it's an important job actually, without traffic wardens there would be **CARNAGE** in the streets, cars everywhere, parked all over the place, on pavements, in playgrounds, under swimming pools … I mean, I am just doing my job …'

Chloe moved along quickly, hoping that Hoppy might know by now that she needed the two of them urgently. She **HAD** to get her smile back today and **QUICKLY.** Not just for Gran Gran either. Maybe if she had **SMILED** at the traffic warden he wouldn't be having such a moaning morning. Argh – where were they? Surely they could go on an adventure now, to get her back to normal? Then she could have **FUN** with her friends at school too.

She had another worrying thought – what if she'd already failed Godfrey and Hoppy by not doing enough last night, what if they were never coming back, what would she do then?

Chloe's anger and worry gave her so much fresh *energy* that she ended up walking super-fast and arriving early at school. When there was still no sign of Hoppy or Godfrey as she reached the near-empty playground she gave up and headed glumly into school, feeling lonelier than ever.

Once inside the school hall she deliberately

sat herself down on a different bench to the one she normally chose alongside Hannah, Ruby and Benjamin. She'd decided this was the right thing to do. So that she didn't upset the rest of the Chaos Crew, she would stay away until her SMILE came back.

But she was so distracted by everything going on that she didn't realise she'd plonked herself down on the cool girls' bench. Not until Princess arrived and stared down at Chloe wordlessly, with an indignant look on her face. Eventually she breathed loudly through her nose and said very sarcastically, 'Er, hello ...?!'

'Yes, er, hello,' chorused her band of followers sneeringly. Chloe stared back up and didn't move. Once again she found herself thinking of battling the waves and the bandits last night, nothing's as scary as that. She took a deep breath and said, 'I am not going to move, I'd like to sit here today, thank you, there's room for all of us.'

Princess and her friends were so shocked by having someone stand up to them that they simply sat down in silence. But before Chloe could feel even a little bit pleased or proud of herself, she saw Hannah,

Ruby and Benjamin looking over at her. Their expressions were a mixture of hurt and incredulity. Chloe suddenly realised how it must appear. Her friends thought she was dissing them and wanting to hang out with the cool girls. Quickly, Chloe waved at them and made a move in their direction, determined to explain, but they just spun away huffily and sat down on their usual bench without another glance in her direction.

At that moment, Mr Broderick bumbled on to the stage, without his usual guitar case and looking very grumpy indeed. In fact, he was still carrying his morning litre of coffee and sipping it desperately.

'Right, good morning ... **SHUT UP!**' he shouted. The whole room went quiet – it was so unlike Mr B to let a small bit of chatter make him angry, he was usually so over-the-top *positive* in the mornings. Mrs Bucks and the other teachers on stage jumped in unison out of their chairs and fell back down again in a jumble.

'Just a few notices this morning and then you can get to class quietly and on time, please,' said Mr Broderick soberly. Chloe immediately began to worry that because she hadn't **SMILED** at him either today, she was the reason he was in a bad mood.

Of course, it wasn't her fault. Cheering as the headmaster usually found Chloe, he was in fact having a small crisis of confidence, having overheard some of the children talking about him in the changing rooms the day before. He had spilt some coffee in an unfortunate place on his trousers so it looked like he might have, well … wet himself … and he rushed into the changing rooms to quickly wash it off with water. Then, realising the water looked just as bad, he stood underneath one of the hand driers. But the drier was so powerful that the fan behind it sucked up his trousers into it, with him attached.

Mr B always had a lot of bad luck this way. It was partly why he looked so tired. As he desperately tried to pull the trousers out of the drier, they ripped in the most **UNFORTUNATE** of places (yes, you guessed it!) and he quickly ran into a toilet cubicle to work out his next move. And that was when some pupils came in to change for PE and he overheard them saying how tragic his guitar playing was – more embarrassing even than any of their parents attempting to dance as if they were all young and cool at a disco.

But how could Chloe know all that? Well, she couldn't. Still, what pressure she put on herself to keep everyone *jolly*.

As everyone filed out after the most boring assembly for a long time, Hannah strode past Chloe and blurted out, 'I can't believe you want to be friends with **THEM** over us. Is that what this has all been about? Well, you're welcome to them.'

'But …'

'I knew something was wrong,' said Benjamin sadly, following close behind Hannah. 'But I didn't think it would be about being a cool girl …'

'It's not …' Chloe tried again.

'**SOB!**' was all Ruby could say, then the three of them turned their backs and headed off down the corridor without her.

Chloe stood frozen in the school corridor, everyone around her bustling to their lessons, until the corridor was quiet and she was the only one left.

Her life was falling apart. She had lost her **SMILE** and now she was losing her friends, just like she was losing her parents.

Just then, she heard buzzing, and realised there were two bees hovering beside her head. She thought she heard a whisper in her ear, '*Things will change*', before the bees flew off down the corridor and back outside. She couldn't be sure, but she wondered – well, she hoped – that the message had been something to do with Godfrey and Hoppy and those were their wise words. She took a deep breath and said to herself over and over as she walked down the corridor to her classroom, '*Things will change, things will change, things will change.*'

But if things did change over the course of the rest of the day, it most certainly was **NOT** for the better. She seemed to have caught Mr Broderick's clumsy bad-luck gene: she walked past the school gardener at breaktime just as he switched on his leaf-blowing machine and it blew her skirt up, revealing her spotty PANTS to everyone in the playground; then she tripped up in art class and fell head-first into a tin of bright green paint and got nicknamed '**FROG FACE**' for the rest of the lesson; and at afternoon break she tried to hide out by the long-jump sandpit, making sandcastles on her own to try and cheer herself up, but she had forgotten it was seniors athletics that afternoon and everyone saw and *laughed* at her, so she kicked all her castles down and ran off.

Chloe didn't think she'd ever had such a *spotty* **sandy** PAINTY **bad** day.

10

CAKE IN THE
MICROWAVE

As the last school bell rang for the end of lessons, Chloe started feeling nervous about going home all over again. Could she cover up her lost **SMILE** to Gran Gran somehow – maybe wear a neckerchief and tell her that cowboy-style fashion was all the rage right now? And things had changed dramatically at home since Gran Gran had last visited. How would she be about that?

Before heading home, she waited for her friends by the school gate to try to explain one last time. As they strode past, she heard Benjamin telling a joke:

WHAT **VEGETABLES** DO **LIBRARIANS** LIKE? **QUIET PEAS!**

Hannah and Ruby laughed.

'Good one!' said Chloe.

'Well you should tell your face,' said Hannah. 'It clearly didn't think so.'

'Too cool for us now, that's why,' sighed Benjamin. And they went off down the road without her.

Chloe put her key in her front door, and took a deep breath. She remembered blowing the bandits off the bridge last night. 'You are brave, things will change,' she muttered to herself.

As she closed the door behind her and put her school rucksack on the hook in the hallway, her mother came out to greet her. 'Here she is, our precious little daughter,' said Mrs Long with a strained GRIN. She had done her hair up, had a huge amount of make-up on, and was wearing a skirt and pretty top, with her apron over it.

She escorted Chloe into the sitting room where Mr Long was back early from work and wearing smart trousers (ones that came only halfway down his calf, as he could never find clothes long enough) and a shirt and tie (the tie not even reaching his tummy button).

Chloe's grandmother was perched on the sofa in the newly arranged spotless sitting room with a neat tea set in front of her.

'Hello, sweetie,' said Mr Long, kissing Chloe quickly. 'Good day at school? Say hello to your Gran Gran.'

Chloe ran to her grandmother and gave her the tightest **SQUEEZE**.

'Hello, my *sunshine*,' (Gran Gran always called her this, because she said Chloe was her personal little ray of *sunshine*) 'how's my lovely Chloe?'

'Good, great, yes really great,' said Chloe, burying her face in Gran Gran's shoulder. It was so **WONDERFUL** to see her – she looked the same as ever. Her long dark hair was perfectly set as usual, with a bright red scarf tied over it into a neat bow that sat on the top of her head. Her bright blue top was tucked neatly into her handmade polka-dot skirt, with perfectly polished practical shoes below. And of course atop all this sat her forever *twinkly* eyes and warm **SMILE**. She smelt of lemony fresh linen, as always, and Chloe could have stayed with her face hidden in that comfort for ever.

But what were her parents doing? What was this charade they were putting on for Gran Gran? It only made Chloe feel even worse that she no longer got this kind of welcome home for **REAL**.

'Happy belated birthday, my *sunshine* girl,' said Gran Gran. 'I only wish my flight had got me here sooner. Now let me fetch your present for you.' Chloe pulled away, careful to keep looking downwards so Gran Gran couldn't see her mouth. Her grandmother tried to push herself out of the sofa. 'Oh,' she *giggled* breathlessly after a moment, 'I've got stuck in the sofa, how FUNNY.'

She did indeed look rather wedged in – she was so small that she'd sunk deep into the gap between the sofa cushions, so much so that Chloe couldn't see any sign of her bottom. 'Be a dear and get it yourself, Chloe, it's over there on the table.'

Chloe collected a parcel wrapped in purple paper with pink horses on it and sat down on the sofa next to her grandmother to unwrap it, while her mum and dad looked on with confused expressions.

'Did you have a nice day?' Gran Gran went on.

'Ummm ...' said Chloe. She tried to make

it sound like an excited *ummm* but she wasn't sure she'd succeeded.

'What's wrong with her? Are you bored of us grown-ups now you are so old …' Gran Gran looked over at Mr and Mrs Long and *laughed*; they did a fake *laugh* with her.

'Yes, I mean now you are the ripe old age of …' Mrs Long paused. She looked at Mr Long for help.

'Eight …?' said Mr Long at the same time as Mrs Long said, 'Ten?'

'Oh, aren't your parents FUNNY.' Gran Gran *laughed* and Mr and Mrs Long joined in fakely again. 'Teasing you like that, Chloe, as if they'd forget your age!'

'Ummm …' said Chloe again. Luckily she had the present to open and keep her face looking downwards.

'Can you believe she's eleven now? How fast it goes, eh?' said Gran Gran.

'Eleven, just the other day, really?' said Mr Long. 'Yes, eleven, I mean, I know, eleven …'

'Ah thanks, Gran Gran,' said Chloe as she revealed her present at last. 'It's GORGEOUS.' And it was. It was a *beautiful* dark wooden box with 'CHLOE'S

TREASURES' engraved ornately in the lid.

'Well I know, like me, you like to go on **ADVENTURES**, especially with those lovely school friends of yours, so I thought you might want somewhere to keep any *memorabilia* you find. With the summer holidays coming up there must be adventures galore afoot?'

'You have a nice chat with your Gran Gran, my precious little eleven-year-old daughter,' said Mrs Long, standing up and patting Chloe's head awkwardly. 'Mr Long, my dearest, can you come and help me get my cake out of the oven?'

Chloe's parents moved through to the kitchen. Chloe refused to believe that her mother could possibly have been baking. And if she hadn't, these lies to Gran Gran were shocking.

From her vantage point at the end of the sofa, Chloe quickly learnt she was right to doubt. From there she could just see down the hall and into the kitchen, where Mrs Long had started removing a ready-made cake from its box.

'Cough, will you, so your mother doesn't hear me opening this cardboard?' Mr Long had a fake coughing fit as Chloe's mum unwrapped the cake and put it into her own baking tin.

'If you'd just baked it, it would be warm,' pointed out Mr Long.

'Well, let's shove it in the microwave then, clever clogs.'

'There's no need to take that tone with me, I am just trying to help!' Mr Long whispered angrily.

'Well if you want to help,' seethed Mrs Long through gritted teeth, 'then for goodness sake throw the packet away, so she doesn't see it. I will not have her looking down on me for not being a good enough wife and mum.'

Just then, out of the blue, Chloe's dad leapt forward and *tickled* his wife at the waist. She shrieked loudly.

'Argh! What on earth did you do that for?'

'To cover the microwave ping, come on … let's get this over with.' Mr Long came back into the sitting room. 'My little lovebird has made a delicious cake.'

'Oh well, it's nothing, just a Victoria sponge; you know, Chloe, how I am always knocking them up for you for when you come home from school.'

Chloe's mum gave her a pleading look but Chloe was too shocked to say anything. 'And like I did for your birthday the other day of course. And ...' She trailed off. 'Evelyn, what are you doing?'

Chloe turned round. Behind her, her grandmother had finally levered herself out of the sofa and was pushing the coffee table back against the wall. Now she whipped a CD from her handbag and brandished it cheerfully. 'What every birthday celebration needs – MUSIC! Put it on for us, son, would you?'

As the bouncy-sounding MUSIC filled the room, Gran Gran beckoned Chloe over. 'I've been taking cha-cha lessons,' she explained above the bop of the drums. 'Let me show you some steps!' Usually Gran Gran's enthusiasm would sweep Chloe along, but dancing without SMILING felt even weirder to Chloe than clapping without SMILING had the day before. She stared down at her feet, pretending to be concentrating on the steps.

'So much FUN, eh, Chloe?' said Gran Gran. 'Come on, you two!' she encouraged Mr and Mrs Long. Reluctantly they got to their feet and started dancing together in a very awkward way. Mr Long's

Gran Gran trod on Chloe's foot. 'Oops, oh dear, sorry.' She started laughing. 'Look at your mother and father, don't they look ridiculous!'

head kept banging the lightshade above as he swayed from side to side.

Gran Gran trod on Chloe's foot. 'Oops, oh dear, sorry.' She started *laughing*. 'Look at your mother and father, don't they look RIDICULOUS!' Chloe looked over at them lumbering about attempting the cha-cha with complete lack of skill. 'Oh dear, excuse me, I must go to the toilet, that *laughing* has brought on a little wee, hee hee.' Gran Gran pottered neatly off humming 'You Are My Sunshine' as she went.

When she left the room, Chloe's mum and dad collapsed on the sofa with a groan. For a moment they almost seemed united, even if it was in pain, but then, 'Get off me, Mr Long!' her mum snapped. 'Move up – you're crowding me!'

'I can't help having a long body,' her dad retorted.

'I wouldn't mind as much if you were as shiny and gorgeous and SOPHISTICATED as a film star in a magazine. I bet they don't go around shouting all the time and have breath that smells of a badger's bottom and an ill-fitting tie that smells of bus fumes!'

'We can't all be like the people in those magazines of yours ... There used to be a time that you liked my tie … no one's here – how about a little peck for your poor old husband, my fluffy bunny?'

Urrrh, yuck! thought Chloe.

She realised they hadn't even noticed she was still in the room. A surge of courage rose in her again. 'That's very upsetting to me actually, as I am your child and I am right here.' Her mum and dad sprang apart, shocked and slightly embarrassed. Chloe was expecting a shouting match in return, but she had silenced them.

Chloe dashed from the room, passing Gran Gran on her way back from the bathroom.

'Well isn't this lovely?' said Gran Gran, beaming at Chloe. 'Oh, are you all right, dear? Where's your usual lovely *cheery* face gone?' She cupped her hands warmly around Chloe's cheeks.

'Actually I'm, er, going to bed, Gran Gran,' replied Chloe.

'Now?'

Her parents quickly poked their heads around the sitting-room door. 'Yes, now?! … It's very early to go to bed, SWEETIE … We never send her to bed this early … Absolutely not …'

'Well of course not,' said Gran Gran.

'I'm just not, er, feeling very well … sorry!'

'Is she all right?' Chloe heard her grandmother ask as she ran up the stairs.

11

A SPARKLE IN THE SKY

Chloe ran into her room and slammed the door behind her. Her parents just didn't know anything about her any more. They forgot her birthday. She was nothing but in their way. Even her SMILES and jokes – her winning features – hadn't been enough to lift their spirits in recent months … maybe that was why her SMILE had gone; she didn't deserve to have a SMILE if she wasn't making good use of it. And nothing she tried seemed to make things better. Even saving *Magic Land* from the terrifying Shadow Bandits suddenly seemed like it might be easier than her real life right now …

Desperately, she jumped on to her bed, leaned out of the window and whispered, 'You've got to come now, please, come quick, Gran Gran is here and I …'

'Are you talking to me, dear?' Mrs Sweet shouted up from her garden where she was setting up the sprinkler for their perfect lawn. Unfortunately Mr

Sweet was also using it – to cool himself down from a hard day's gardening – and at just this moment he took a mighty run-up and jumped right through the jet of water ... in just his pants!

'Mr Sweet!' exclaimed Mrs Sweet admonishingly.

'Oh no, sorry, Mr and Mrs Sweet.' Chloe ducked down on to the floor below the window, embarrassed that she had been heard talking to herself and slightly regretting having seen Mr Sweet in his pants!

She couldn't believe that Godfrey and Hoppy hadn't reappeared by now. For a moment she considered grabbing her joke book for a distraction, but remembering that Benjamin's joke earlier hadn't caused even a SMILE tremor, she knew it was pointless. She felt so angry and unloved and hopeless. 'Things **DON'T** change!' she said to herself.

She looked over at her homework – but she couldn't face it. She looked over at her drawing book and pencils. She couldn't face them either. She could start her *summer book.* But she couldn't face that even more than all the other things put together. So she just sat there.

She sat there and sat there and got crosser and

crosser – why weren't Hoppy and Godfrey here? It started to get dark. She was **STILL** just sitting there. **STILL** cross. **STILL** worried.

Gran Gran came to the door and whispered goodnight, but still Chloe didn't move. The moon came out. An owl hooted. Still no sign of them. Finally Chloe realised that her legs and arms had been crossed all this time and she was getting sore muscles. Then, just as she started to unfold her body and think about giving up and going to bed, no one was coming, there was nothing more to be done … in flew several *glow-worms* through her open window. They landed on her bed, RADIATING brightly.

'Is that you?' asked Chloe, but the glow-worms didn't answer. She stood up stiffly, looked out of the window and gasped. Stretching out into the night sky was a trail of glow-worms and fireflies, pulsating gently in unison. As Chloe watched, a large, dark shape travelled along the line of glowing insects, drawing closer and closer to her window; alongside it zipped a flicker of something else, like a star that keeps blinking in and out of being. Chloe knew what it was immediately – Godfrey and Hoppy were on their way!

At last, Godfrey made a running landing in her front garden, careful not to disturb the newly tended shrubs. He paused in front of her window to sweep his hat from his head and bow grandly. 'Hello once again, my lovely Chloe!' Hoppy alighted on Chloe's shoulder with an excited squeak and stroked a strand of her hair **LOVINGLY** in greeting.

'Get off me,' said Chloe a little crossly.

'What's wrong, my sweet girl?' asked Godfrey calmly.

'What's wrong?' snapped Chloe as Hoppy shot into the air in alarm. 'What's wrong?! I have been calling out for you all day, things never changed, and you never appeared, and my grandmother is here and she is going to see that my **SMILE** is gone and I had to wait here all this time on my own and ... and ... and ...'

'If only you had trusted we would come, like we said we would, and waited patiently, or got on with your homework and not sat crossly on your bed, then you wouldn't feel so angry and sore.' Godfrey beamed warmly as he put the remaining fireflies and glow-worms back into his pocket.

'But you don't get it ...'

'Oh, we do. We know you tried to get your smile back with your wonderful sandcastles at school, before you crushed them. We know you. But you lost sight of your HOPE, didn't you, Chloe?'

'I hoped I would get a duvet for my birthday but it never came,' Chloe retorted. But while Godfrey's responses didn't necessarily make full sense to her (yet), his calm confidence was already affecting her mood for the better.

'Oh yes, there is always HOPE,' said Hoppy, hopping back on to Chloe's bed. 'Thank goodness for HOPE. I love the word "HOPE" because it's only one letter away from "hop".' And off she went, bouncing joyfully up and down as usual.

'But PLEASE, PLEASE, **PLEASE** can you help me get my smile back TONIGHT ... I really don't think I can go on without it.'

Godfrey leant in through the window emphatically. 'Patience. First, *Magic Land* needs your help – you know it does.'

'But—'

'Besides, there's so much more of *Magic Land* for you to meet and explore!' interrupted Hoppy.

'Are you with us?' asked Godfrey.

Chloe gulped. She reflected on her newfound courage, despite her dreadful day – and that was because of *Magic Land*. Besides, what other choice did she have? No one else was offering to help her find her **SMILE**.

'All right, yes. Nothing to lose!'

'Come on then. All aboard!' said Godfrey, facing the window in a preparatory way.

'Ooh, are you going to be the *bird plane*, Godfrey?' asked Hoppy.

'I thought I might.'

'*Yipppeeee!*' said Hoppy. 'Come on, Chloe, this is **BREATHTAKING**.'

Hoppy beckoned Chloe on to her windowsill and from there she did a small jump to land on Godfrey's back, as if he was offering her another piggyback ride. He began to run – first he jumped over their garden hedge, then over the cars parked in the street, and then his feet were **SLAP SLAP SLAP SLAPPING** the road as he ran faster and faster towards town, but just as Chloe was beginning to worry that surely someone would see him, or he would smash into a building, he seemed to lift into the air and suddenly Godfrey was *flying* again. But hang on, no, it wasn't Godfrey flying, it was … an enormous EAGLE, bigger than Chloe had ever seen in her life. Its wingspan must have been the size of a house at least. Chloe sat up in shock – but how had that happened, where was Godfrey?

'Just look,' said Hoppy's tinkling voice in her ear. So she did look, and she noticed that, very oddly, the giant eagle was wearing a black hat and its large hooked beak seemed to be … SMILING?

'The eagle is Godfrey!' she said breathlessly. **BREATHTAKING** indeed!

Hoppy alighted on eagle-Godfrey's back with a rapturous sigh. 'Feel how soft his feathers are!' It was true, beneath Chloe's hands the long, golden feathers of the bird's giant back were smooth and soft and comforting. Hoppy nestled deeper into the shorter, fluffy feathers around eagle-Godfrey's neck, while Chloe settled between his shoulders, and they both watched the world disappear beneath them, the glow-worms and fireflies lighting their way, as they soared off on their next **ADVENTURE.**

12

SAND LAND

Godfrey the majestic eagle swooped, regal and strong, over the trees beyond Chloe's town, and *ooh look* there was her school in the distance, fading to a tiny little dot. Wow, they were truly high in the sky. Scary! On the plus side she was pleased the school was disappearing because it only reminded her of falling out with her friends, and she felt even luckier that Godfrey and Hoppy had found her ... but on the down side – oh my goodness, how HIGH WERE THEY?!

But Chloe was not going to miss this experience, so, trying not to look down, she gathered all her bravery and, first crouching and then standing tall on Godfrey's back, she spread her arms wide like wings, the sky sliding through her fingers as if she was flying herself. It was more *magical* than she'd ever expected anything to be. And such a **BIG** moment her own worries briefly seemed small and insignificant.

The sun was beginning to come up as they finally dipped downwards and Chloe saw they were over the plains that surrounded the ravine of the night before. She looked behind her and saw the more familiar parts of her *Magic Land* – could she just make out the dolphins flipping over the water and her penguins waving at her? She certainly couldn't see anything shadowy, which was a relief.

She nearly asked to get off there, wanting to visit her familiar lakes and precious penguins, but knew that Godfrey had other places to show her. Besides, hadn't she glimpsed a beach as they headed home the night before? Chloe **ADORED** the beach, and she hadn't been to one in so long – a *Magic Land* beach was something worth waiting for, surely? There she'd be able to make sandcastles galore without anyone laughing at her.

'Look!' squeaked Hoppy, pointing towards the end of one of Godfrey's beautiful eagle wings. A family of yellow parrots was catching a ride on his wing tips, all squawking happy 'hello's and 'good morning's! In fact, one of the baby parrots was flapping so excitedly, it fell off Godfrey's wing and its mother had to swoop down and catch it, much to the amusement of its brothers and sisters.

Godfrey continued to soar elegantly over the river ravine. The plains either side of it were covered with a red soil that made the early sunlight even rosier. Occasionally he dived down into the ravine and Chloe screamed in a mixture of delight and fear, her stomach flipping as if she were on a rollercoaster.

But Chloe knew she was safe. Nestling into his soft feathers was like snuggling up in the most perfect feather duvet.

Hoppy was now flying ahead of Godfrey, warbling joyfully. As Chloe watched, Hoppy spun round to fly backwards and get a singsong going. Godfrey seemed to have taken on a kind of *bird-bus* role: various BEAUTIFUL birds of all shapes and sizes, from robins and kingfishers to geese and puffins, were hitching rides on his huge wings. It was like a bird commute! And now as the birds sat there, they started to trill and tweet along with each other, following Hoppy's tune: 'We love you Godfrey, we do, we love you Godfrey, we do ...' Chloe hopped up again to stand on his wings and began humming along.

In that *happy* moment, Chloe really thought her SMILE might come back again – it was **SO JOYFUL**. She wished humans, especially grown-ups, would sing and celebrate more, for no reason – like the beaming, trilling birds all around her right now. A birdsong singsong – brilliant! But she forced herself not to feel cross that people didn't celebrate enough, and that her SMILE still showed no sign of reappearing.

She noticed the river below her was widening to meet the sea and she lay down on eagle-Godfrey's back and leant out over his wing to see a stunning beach coming into view. All around her the hitchhiking birds headed off on their separate ways, flapping goodbyes as they did so, but Chloe only stared down.

Yet again, her mouth was wide open with awe. This time because she was witnessing the wide sandy beach and crystal-clear waters of her dreams.

She'd only ever been to pebbly beaches on the coast near Elmswater Crescent, with just occasional tiny patches of sand. And whenever she asked her mum and dad if they could go to a *golden* beach like the ones she had seen in holiday brochures they would say things like, 'Who wants sand in their sandwiches or shoes, or anywhere else for that matter?' 'Yes, last time I got itchy grainy sand right up in my pants, thank you very much.'

But this beach looked so heavenly Chloe thought her parents couldn't mean it when they said that. They had to have lost their smiles too, a long time ago, if the idea of a beach as glorious as this brought no pleasure. She couldn't remember the last time she'd seen Mr and Mrs Long properly **SMILE** … their faces had just been getting longer and longer and more and more creased and furrowed.

In the memory she had of them all **SMILING** and tickling each other on their bed, she was sure she could remember them having the widest and warmest eyes of anyone in the world when they smiled. But she was so confused about what was real any more. And if they had lost their smiles too … how much of that was her fault?

As if she knew what Chloe was thinking – and she probably did, after all – Hoppy swooped in to nestle comfortingly on Chloe's shoulder. It was as if she was saying, 'No worrying, Chloe, no, no. I don't want any child's face to become long and furrowed, no, no, no, not on my watch.' And Chloe felt herself relax again – but not for long …

They started descending towards the beach when suddenly eagle-Godfrey jerked up, then down, then up again. Chloe's stomach churned. 'Hold on,' called Godfrey, in a voice that sounded half-shout-half-squawk.

'Bit of crosswind at the beach, grab a feather,' he added calmly. But for the first time since climbing aboard, Chloe didn't feel safe. They were buffeted left and right as Godfrey tried to land smoothly on the beach. He was finally about to set down, his talons almost stroking the sand, when another larger gust whistled around them and he overshot the beach altogether. They found themselves heading straight for the SEA.

'Help!' said Chloe. 'We're going to crash-land in the water. Can eagles swim?'

'Abort eagle!' she heard Godfrey squawk. Abort eagle – what did that mean?

Chloe's mind raced – did he mean jump **OFF** the eagle? To where? From up here into the sea? But what other option did she have – she didn't have wings like Hoppy and Godfrey.

In a panic Chloe leapt up, took a deep breath and stepped out on to Godfrey's wing. The air whistled past her ears. The sea was coming towards them at such a rate – the crash would come ANY MOMENT. She lifted her right leg, leant forward and ...

'**STOP**!' Hoppy's tiny hand grabbed her ankle and pulled her down. Once again her strength, given her miniature size, surprised Chloe. But this was no time to ponder the physics of tiny magical bird-girls ...

'We're going to crash in the sea and drown!' screeched Chloe.

'Trust him,' said Hoppy, in what looked to Chloe very much like a brace position, which didn't give her much confidence.

Then, as they were a few metres from the water's surface and Chloe was also braced for impact, she felt the feathers beneath her hands begin to *shiver* and shift. They were toughening and merging and changing colour from golden to blue-grey until they were much more like rubber, or skin, or ... whale skin. **SPLASH!** A beautiful, big, beaming blue whale hit the water and glided gracefully into it.

Godfrey had morphed into a ... well, a **WHALE** ... and Chloe and Hoppy were sailing the sea safely on his back, whooping and cheering with relief and for Godfrey's magnificent skill.

Chloe patted Godfrey's back experimentally – yup, definitely a whale ... *amazing*. He even seemed to have acquired a huge pair of goggles! What Chloe didn't realise was that she was patting right over his whale spout and Godfrey chose that moment to blow water out of it – suddenly Chloe found herself being blasted into the air on top of a whale water fountain!

She bubbled there for a moment, enjoying the view, with Hoppy giggling in the air beside her, before he dropped her down to his back again. Cheeky Godfrey!

As they neared the shoreline, whale-Godfrey caught the biggest waves and surfed them in to the beach. Chloe took her shoes off, slid off his back and on to the softest golden sand she had ever encountered. It felt like she was walking on rabbit fur mixed with velvet. Or like baby duckling feathers mixed with cotton wool. It was **SO** soft, even Hoppy was choosing to walk rather than fly. She was darting about at Chloe's feet, throwing sand in the air like confetti.

It was also the biggest beach Chloe had ever seen, even imagined. And so much sand. Everywhere. Even above – at the back of the beach there were dunes as high as houses. Beyond them lush green hills bumped up and down towards craggy mountains.

'Welcome to *Sand Land*,' boomed Godfrey in almost his usual voice, though it sounded a bit gargly too, as he morphed back into his natural giant self, with his bright round friendly face and long limbs wrapped in his velvet coat, putting his enormous whale goggles back into one of his pockets.

'Wow!' said Chloe. 'I can't wait to play … I'm going to make a **SANDCASTLE** and then—'

'Hold on, we need to get permission from the Royal *Sand Land* Family first,' said Hoppy.

'Is that one of your silly jokes?' asked Chloe affectionately.

'Actually no,' Hoppy chirped. 'There IS a Royal *Sand Land* Family.'

'Seriously?!' said Chloe. 'No!'

'Yes!'

'Really?!'

'Yes, yes, yes!'

'No, no, no, you're joking …'

'**Stop!**' said Godfrey, before Chloe and Hoppy went on like that for days. 'It IS true, Chloe. And they love people playing on their beach, but by polite permission only. They protect their lands very fiercely.'

'Plus,' added Hoppy excitedly, 'they live in a Sand Castle. An **ACTUAL** Sand Castle!'

'Now you ARE being silly, Hoppy,' said Chloe.

'I'm not – it's true.'

'An ACTUAL Sand Castle … no?!'

'Yes!'

'No?!'

'STOP IT!' Godfrey got between the two of them again. 'It IS true, Chloe, we would never lie to you or tease you. About anything.'

WOW! A real Sand Castle. That sounded PERFECT. Because Chloe hadn't mentioned her real reason for suggesting a sandcastle. She felt sure that if she did one of her favourite things, and wasn't *laughed* at for doing so, like in the school long-jump pit, then SURELY her **SMILE** would turn up. She didn't say it out loud, though, because she knew Godfrey and Hoppy had other plans for her first. But however much they told her she was destined to help them, Chloe still found it very hard to believe. Because without her **SMILE** she felt blank, like a nobody.

'Right. Onwards we go, to the Royal *Sand Land* Family. Best behaviour please,' Godfrey said, rather grand and king-like himself.

'Do the Royal *Sand Land* Family ever say no to playing on their beach?' Chloe was suddenly worried.

'Very rarely.'

'They'd definitely say no to a Shadow Bandit, though, wouldn't they, Godfrey!' squeaked Hoppy, her bird's-nest hair quivering indignantly at the thought.

'Oh no, not the bandits again? Here?' trembled Chloe.

Godfrey gave Hoppy a stern look. 'Let's not worry her with that right this moment, Hoppy! However,' he turned back to Chloe, 'as I said, I will never lie to you. And one of the reasons I am here is to ask the Sand King whether he has noticed any unusual shadow activity on his beach, and to scout the area myself if I get the chance.' He put a reassuring arm around Chloe.

'But there are no bandits here now, are there? Just look!' He waved a hand around airily, indicating the blue skies and gently drifting clouds.

It really was extraordinary. The sea was that kind of clear turquoise that meant you could see fish of every colour of the RAINBOW darting about in the waters, and the seabed was just the same sand as on the beach. There would be no fear of putting your foot down painfully on a sharp pebble like at the beaches

Chloe had been to before.

'Enjoy this moment.'

Chloe gave herself a firm shake, knowing Godfrey was right. She gazed about again. There were palm trees at the bottom of the sand dunes behind them and as Chloe looked over she realised they were filled with fluffy monkeys collecting coconuts from the top of the trees, smacking them open at one end, then popping a straw in so you could drink the coconut water. **IMAGINE!**

Ooh, and fun: the palm trees had ropes to swing on between them.

There were pineapple bushes, and Chloe saw turtles waiting underneath for a pineapple to fall so they could collect it, peel it with their claws and present it to you on a shell plate. **IMAGINE!**

There were rock pools to fish in and craggy rock cliffs to climb. It was wild and adventurous and as magical as *Chloe's Magic Land* had ever been.

'Is this all still my *Magic Land*?'

'Yes,' explained Godfrey. 'You just haven't needed it until now. Our imaginations are one of the greatest forces in the world. And those of us who know best how to use them can come to places like this whenever we need to …

'Now, let's focus on the task in hand. Getting permission from the Royal *Sand Land* Family to explore this wonderful creation of yours …'

'Yes, come on, come on, **COME ON!** I can't wait for Chloe to see the Royal Sand Castle …' hopped Hoppy.

Hoppy's excitement was always catching. Chloe felt her courage and sense of **ADVENTURE** return and she buried any worries about the Shadow Bandits and strode onwards.

Ahead of them, at the end of the crescent-shaped beach they were on, there was a small cliff jutting out into the sea, with just enough space at its foot for them to climb around to the next section of beach.

'This way, we're nearly there!' said Godfrey.

They clambered over the wet rocks, friendly crabs scuttling ahead of them and obligingly wiping dry any very slippery sections with seaweed dusters, then clapping them on with their claws. **IMAGINE!** Eventually they emerged into the next sandy bay.

Chloe gasped so loudly, she nearly sucked up and swallowed a passing sandfly. Because nestled into the dunes before them was the biggest, most **GLAMOROUS, ACTUAL** Sand Castle she could have dreamed of. As ever ... just **IMAGINE!**

13

WALRUSES AND TRUMPETS

It was a Sand *Palace* really. With turrets, a moat and a bridge made from twisty driftwood. The windows, which were just rectangular holes in the sand walls, were surrounded by pretty shells and bits of worn-down coloured glass to mark them out. And the walls around the castle's large doorway were decorated with spangled dried seaweed. It reminded Chloe of the ivy that she'd sometimes seen growing up the sides of large old buildings.

The sand itself had little bits of shiny dust in it and in the sunlight the whole castle *sparkled.* As they approached the driftwood bridge, Godfrey rang a GLEAMING golden bell that was hanging from an old ship's mast just outside the castle.

Immediately a loud trumpet fanfare began.

The bridge started to wobble as a marching band consisting of dozens of large trumpet-playing walruses – the instruments wedged between their massive tusks – exited from the Sand Castle's entrance and began to cross it at pace. The flappy waddling of their flippers in perfect time with each other was loud enough to drown out any speech, so everyone was forced to watch and listen. Which was fine by Chloe. It was quite the sight.

Massive trumpet-playing WALRUSES! **AMAZING!** I certainly wouldn't have got this on any beach back home, thought Chloe. As they reached Chloe's side of the bridge they began to fan out into lines along the castle moat before giving a final, perfectly timed blast on their trumpets and falling silent. As one they swivelled their heads back towards the castle.

Out stepped two figures.

They were normal-sized and relatively human-looking, in an old-fashioned sort of way. King Sandy (Hoppy chirruped his name into her ear before Chloe could even ask, of course) wore an outfit not unlike Chloe had seen in pictures of Henry the Eighth – he was the same sort of shape as him as well, almost as broad as he was tall. But as he drew closer Chloe realised the tasselling on both his shoulders wasn't that at all, it was two miniature seagulls, stitched out of gold cloth, so that the king had the air of a slightly bonkers **PIRATE**.

On top of this, the king's buttons were seashells, and on his head was an extravagant *crown* made entirely of coral, complete with the occasional sea snail still living in it. Despite what Chloe thought must be very uncomfortable headwear, the king had a friendly face with a bristly blond moustache that stuck out beyond his ears.

Beside him walked Queen Sandra. ('Sandy and Sandra of **SAND** Land, so *funny*,' giggled Hoppy.) Queen Sandra wore a long, elegant gown that shimmered from pink to pale blue and silver as she moved. Chloe thought it might be because she had fish scales stitched into the skirt; oh, and her belt was held in place by a bright pink starfish.

Both the king and queen had blond, sun-kissed hair with strands of seaweed woven into it, but what really made Chloe stare was their footwear. Despite the kingliness and queenliness of their outfits, the

'That's Prince Barnacle,' Hoppy whispered, her wings brushing
Chloe's ear. 'Though everyone calls him Barnie.'

royal couple were wearing bright yellow **FLIP-FLOPS** with fish patterns on the straps. On a different sort of day, this would definitely have made Chloe *laugh* out loud. For now she had to settle for a sort of startled snort.

Moments later, Chloe realised there was a third figure crossing the bridge behind King Sandy and Queen Sandra. 'That's Prince Barnacle,' Hoppy whispered, her wings brushing Chloe's ear. 'Though everyone calls him Barnie.' The prince was dressed in a similar sort of outfit to the king on his top half, but along with his own neon **FLIP-FLOPS** he wore a pair of long blue shorts with shark fins all over. Chloe guessed he was about her age.

As the royal family stepped off the bridge and on to the sand, Godfrey lowered himself to one knee, removed his hat and bowed respectfully. Chloe quickly followed suit. She felt Hoppy do a little curtsey on her shoulder too.

'Your Majesty,' said Godfrey, head still bent. 'This is Chloe.' He paused significantly and Chloe thought she heard a kind of muffled gasp and a shiver of flapping flippers travel through the walrus trumpeters, but she didn't dare look up until she was given permission.

'We come to enjoy *Sand Land* May we stay and play?'

'Rise!' commanded King Sandy in a gravelly voice. Godfrey raised his head, though he stayed down on one knee, and Chloe stood up straight beside him with Hoppy still on her shoulder. His Majesty approached Chloe and as he did so his eyes narrowed and his moustache twitched. Chloe tensed – what would he make of her? They were such a warm-looking family, it seemed unlikely they'd be impressed by the current gloomy state of her face – and if they weren't, what then? Did kings and queens of sand-based kingdoms have the power to order executions? Chloe hoped that the answer was a most definite NO!

After a few wordless moments of sniffing, prodding and peering, the king swivelled on his feet and marched back across the bridge to the entrance of his castle, nodding to Prince Barnacle as he passed.

In the grand doorway he turned and said with a smile, 'Please do stay for as long as you like and enjoy our sumptuously sandy *Sand Land*, presided over by me, King Sandy of said *Sand Land*!' The walrus trumpeters sounded a short triumphant note then dived one by one into the castle moat for a celebratory dip.

'And we're so pleased you came,' added Prince Barnacle. At this remark, the king looked a bit surprised. Clearly the prince didn't usually speak at these formal occasions, so what had prompted him today? Just then the prince took a step closer to Chloe and seemed to give her … a **WINK**?

Chloe's jaw dropped and she blushed – did an actual **PRINCE** just … **WINK** at HER? In return, the prince suddenly looked a lot less sure of himself – he'd probably been hoping for a more enthusiastic response than the aghast expression he was receiving. Suddenly he rubbed his eyes rapidly and tried for all the world to look as if he'd got sand in his face and had not, under any circumstances, been **WINKING** at anyone, ever.

'You make quite a delightful band of adventurers,' said Queen Sandra, oblivious to all this, as she followed her husband back across the bridge.

'What? You as well?! It is usually just I, the KING, that does the talking …' said the king, a little put out. 'So. Enjoy our *Sand Land*, presided over by me—!'

'You already said that bit,' said Queen Sandra.

'All right, yes, thank you ...' muttered King Sandy as he flustered his way back inside the Sand Castle, the walruses now out of the moat and following behind.

Chloe couldn't believe it – she had just met a whole family of royals and had possibly, maybe, been **WINKED** at by a prince. I bet not even Princess at school can say that, Chloe thought.

'So I can explore now?' she asked Godfrey. He nodded, before stepping over the nearest Sand Castle wall to shrink down and join the king at a table inside.

Chloe dug her toes into the soft sand, took a deep breath and ran towards the sea, splashing back and forth in the shallows. She watched as Hoppy zipped over the waves, waving to the rainbow-coloured fish below.

Under the warm sun Chloe did *cartwheels* across the beach, almost colliding with Godfrey as he came out of the castle.

'Can you bury me in the sand? Please!' she panted. She had always wanted to do that, to feel what it was like to have the weight of spadefuls of soft sand on your body.

It only took Godfrey a matter of seconds to cover her completely, what with his big hands and the giant spade he pulled from another of his patchwork pockets. And it was a strangely comforting feeling.

But she didn't have time to rest. She burst back out of her sand bed and ran towards the sea to wash it all off. Now she had a **SHELL** necklace to make …

Chloe was so busy she didn't spot the figure at one of the Sand Castle windows – it was Prince Barnacle, watching her with *fascination*. Despite her friends playing with her and how entranced she was with the beach, to him, Chloe made a rather sad and lonely figure in the distance.

'Come on, Chloe,' said Hoppy suddenly in her ear as Chloe was just threading the last of her shells on to her shoelace and hanging it round her neck. 'We haven't even begun to show you the best of what *Sand Land* can do yet, and it's all thanks to you …'

14

SAND ANIMALS

'Thanks to me?' Chloe said in surprise.

'Yes, yes.' Hoppy grabbed Chloe's hand and pulled her towards the flat wet sand left behind by the tide.

'The best thing about *Sand Land* ...' Hoppy began again. 'But what am I saying ... you know what the best thing is, this is **YOUR** *Magic Land*.'

'I'm still not sure I do,' said Chloe, bemused.

'But you remember how much you love drawing animals ...' nudged Hoppy.

'Well, I guess I can draw animals in the sand,' said Chloe.

'To start with, yes, yes, yes!' said Hoppy excitedly.

Chloe picked up a large, fan-shaped shell and used the sharp edge to draw the long neck of a giraffe in the harder, wetter sand. She added a head, body and legs and stood back to admire her work. It was fun, of course, but not quite the wonder

Hoppy was making it out to be.

Not wanting to seem spoilt, Chloe started to draw another animal. This time an elephant. They were always slightly trickier, but she managed to do one that she thought bore a strong resemblance to an actual elephant, then using a tiny mussel she added more detail, like its big eyes and long eyelashes.

She stood back and looked at Hoppy.

Hoppy *giggled* at her perplexed expression. 'It's not just drawing them, you know. Now remember the boats in the ravine, remember what happened to them when you **IMAGINED** your perfect bath?'

Chloe nodded. And as she did so, she suddenly realised what Hoppy might be trying to say. The most AMAZING thing about *Sand Land*, of course ...

'Oh my goodness, any picture I draw in the sand, can I ... can I imagine it into a real-life sand animal?'

'Yes, yes, yes!' squeaked Hoppy, turning somersaults in the air.

'NO WAY!' said Chloe. '**NO WAY!**'

'Yes, yes, yes.' Hoppy hopped and boinged.

'NO!'

'YES!'

'So can I make a lion, I've always wanted a pet lion?' asked Chloe, finally believing Hoppy.

'Yes! And I am going to make a …'

'Kangaroo!' Hoppy and Chloe said at the same time. Obviously Hoppy would choose a kangaroo!

They started drawing their animals. As Chloe really focused on it this time, everything else around her seemed to fade away: the beach, the whole world, even her worries. She enjoyed the sensation of the sand peeling away beneath the sharp edge of her shell. She drew the long, sweeping line of her lion's back and tail; she carved out its curved legs and claws. She moved to the shaggy mane, then finally its face – large, warm eyes, long whiskers and a *smiling* mouth. It was the biggest, friendliest-looking lion.

Beside her, Hoppy squeaked, 'Finished!' The bird-girl's kangaroo was only the size of Chloe's sand lion's foot, but its tail and hind legs looked more powerful than a ten-tonne truck. 'Ready?'

They both stepped into the middle of their drawings and closed their eyes. Chloe IMAGINED hard: her lion standing there, blinking its eyes open for real. She told herself to believe it was possible.

There was a long pause – Chloe felt herself slump; it wasn't going to work, she couldn't do it, probably because— but hang on … **OH MY GOODNESS** … All around her, the sand was beginning to *shift*. Chloe fell to the ground and watched as the beach seemed to ripple and rise in front of her – and in no time at all, there was a large, *three-dimensional* lion and a smaller kangaroo, made entirely of sand, standing tamely on the beach before them.

Chloe stood up, reached out tentatively and stroked her new pet lion. It felt as grainy as sand should, but somehow warm and furry too. The creature prowled majestically around, making big paw prints in the sand. Then he came and leant against her, kind of nudging her to climb up on his back.

Chloe scrabbled up on top of her sand lion and there she was, riding him. As he bounded playfully up and down the beach, Hoppy's kangaroo followed, springing higher than any kangaroo has sprung, with Hoppy sitting in the pouch!

For a moment Chloe closed her eyes, threw wide her arms and let the sand and sea splatter her – could this really be happening? Had she really **MADE** this happen? But yes, it was, and yes, she had. Well, in that case … She slid from her lion's back as he slowed to a trot, and ran over to the elephant she had drawn earlier. She stood in the middle of it and closed her eyes. Once again the sand rumbled, rippled, and a beautiful sand elephant emerged.

WOW, WOW, **WOW**! 'Look, Godfrey, **LOOK**!' Chloe shouted to him. He was some way up the dunes, peering up at the mountains above, presumably scouting for Shadow Bandits, but it didn't take him many leaps to get all the way back down to the beach.

He clapped so hard that the beach shuddered. 'Carry on like this and you could have quite the sand ZOO before long,' he shouted back. She was just thinking which animal to do next when she heard a very loud clucking, quacking noise coming from the Royal Sand Castle. Godfrey and Hoppy were already *laughing* as they turned to see what was happening.

Approaching were what must have been over a HUNDRED sand ducklings and chicks, rushing about in a complete frenzy, with a frazzled Prince Barnacle running behind, desperately trying to get them under control.

'Gosh, I am frightfully sorry ...' said Barnie, trying to stop them surrounding Chloe and tripping her up. Unfortunately, Prince Barnacle wasn't very good at drawing and some of the birds were enormous (a rather scary duckling the size of a cow!), some were so tiny they kept nearly being trodden on, and some had only one leg and kept going around in circles. It was duck and chick chaos!

'So sorry, so sorry ...' was all Barnie kept saying. 'I was trying to create one chick and one duckling for you, something sweet to cheer you up, I mean, well ... but anyway, by mistake, all the ones I had been drawing for practice became real too!' He chuckled. But then he looked up and realised Chloe wasn't *laughing*, she wasn't even SMILING, and his laughter trailed off worriedly.

The chicks were pecking at Chloe's bare feet.

'Oh dear, so sorry ... sorry, no really, so sorry ...' Barnie tried to shoo them away.

By now Chloe was feeling bad for the embarrassed prince and she desperately wanted to SMILE at him to let him know her toes were fine. 'I really don't mind,' she tried instead, but knew it didn't sound at all convincing when her mouth was as straight as a ruler.

Still, the prince didn't seem to have been scared off altogether. 'Your lion and elephant are, well, **INCREDIBLE,**' he said. 'Well done ... Oh gosh ... now your elephant is being attacked by my chicks ... shoo, shoo ... there's nothing for it ... BACK TO SAND!' The chicks and ducklings dispersed into the sand as one, whilst Barnie fled back to the Sand Castle looking more than a little mortified.

'I think someone is trying to be your friend, Chloe,' said Godfrey knowingly, as Barnie disappeared.

'I am not sure I should have any friends at the moment.' Chloe's good mood was gone again. 'Back to sand,' she muttered, and her lovely lion and elephant fell back into the beach as if they had never existed.

'Until having you and Hoppy to really talk to, I didn't realise how ... how lonely I have been.' Chloe plonked herself down on the sand and burst out crying. 'Who in the real world wants to hang out with someone who has lost their **SMILE?** Oh, I want it back so badly.'

Hoppy immediately flitted to her face and began dabbing at Chloe's tears with the corner of her dress.

Chloe appreciated the effort, even if it was a little ineffective given that the corner of Hoppy's dress was so small it was soaked through after one teardrop.

Godfrey lowered himself to the sand beside Chloe. 'What exactly happened with your friends?' he asked gently.

'I just didn't want to bring them down too,' wailed Chloe.

'Sounds to me like you didn't give them the chance to make that choice for themselves.'

'I …' Chloe trailed off. Was that true? She hadn't really thought about it like that.

'Trust us, Chloe.' Godfrey pulled a tissue from one of his pockets as he spoke and handed it to her. But it was so big it covered her completely like a *blanket*. 'Oh sorry, that's one of mine. Here you go.' And he handed her a human-sized tissue from another pocket. 'Things will get better, all in the good and right time …'

'There's always Hoppy's hope,' Hoppy added. 'Excuse me whilst I HOP for HOPE.' She went on another one of her mad **BOUNCING** sprees.

But Chloe's mood wasn't lifting.

'Do the *clouds*,' whispered Hoppy in Godfrey's

ear. 'That will cheer her up.'

Chloe lay back on the sand next to Godfrey. 'Do you mean the *cloud-shape* game? Gran Gran and I sometimes play that, looking for shapes in the clouds.'

'Oh, we can do better than that,' said Godfrey. 'We're in *Magic Land*, after all. Watch this.'

He lay back on the sand, his hands behind his head. Chloe found herself curled safely next to him, staring up at the sky.

He took her finger and pointed it upwards. He drew a circle in the air with it. As he did so, a perfect circular cloud appeared in the clear sky overhead.

'**Wow!**'

'I make clouds all the time,' said Godfrey. 'Weather is one of my favourite things to play with. I am going to make this one a bit rainy as I feel like cooling down. And the plants on the sand dunes could do with a nice watering.' He created a puffy cloud with a few swoops of his hands, then with a subtle movement of his fingers, as if he was playing the PIANO in the air, he made it begin to rain gently. *Pitter-patter, pitter-patter* went the tiny drops as they bounced off the leaves behind them.

All Chloe could say again was, '**Wow**.'

She put her finger up towards the sky and drew a *heart* shape. And sure enough a cloud in the shape of a heart appeared in the sky.

'I feel a bit bouncier now, thank you, Hoppy,' Chloe had to admit.

'You're welcome! Enjoy the moment!' Hoppy paused for a second and drew a tiny, perfect cloud in the shape of a smiley face, then whizzed away.

Godfrey looked down at Chloe, who had her tongue stuck out in concentration as she drew a huge *cloud bus* in the sky.

'Chloe, if you can trust us, we will help you get stronger. But you mustn't forget that there are challenges to overcome and fights to win, even in *Magic Land*.'

'Umm ... I know. Right now is perfect, though,' said Chloe.

Godfrey nodded slowly. He looked as if he was going to say more, but at that moment there was a cry of excitement above their heads. A flashing blue shape swooped towards them from high in the sky. It was Hoppy, of course.

'It's Trevor!' she cried. 'I can see Trevor! I went to the taverna again and he's there! He's come back!'

'Who's Trevor?' asked Chloe.

'A lovely old friend,' Hoppy chirped.

'Hoppy.' Godfrey suddenly seemed rather stern as he pulled her out of the air and placed her carefully on his hand. 'Do remember, though, if Trevor is here, it means something has happened. Quick, we must get there before he goes.' As he said this, Godfrey scooped Chloe and Hoppy up and slid them into one of his giant pockets – yes, some of Godfrey's pockets were big enough for an eleven-year-old girl to fit into. And they were perfect for travelling in because they were specially padded, a bit like being in a **BOUNCY CASTLE** box. And Chloe quickly discovered this was necessary: the minute Godfrey set off running, she found herself flying through the air, very grateful she could land safely in his spongy pocket.

Godfrey ran. Faster and faster.

Chloe and Hoppy **BOINGED**. Higher and higher. Despite it being an urgent situation, Chloe was rather enjoying being inside Godfrey's enormous pocket. **BOING, BOING, BOING!**

15
TREVOR'S STORY

After more bouncing than even the most enthusiastic bouncy castle fan might enjoy, Chloe found herself wedged head-first in the deepest corner of Godfrey's pocket as he screeched to a halt. He gently pulled her out by her feet and set her back on the ground. Hoppy zipped out behind her, looking even more dishevelled than usual – her hair was like a bird's nest that had been in a torpedo, so big it was almost the same size as her. Hoppy gave it a little brush with a small fan shell, before the weight of it caused her to topple over!

Chloe looked around. They had arrived at a small cluster of trees at the base of the dunes. And the taverna was simply a lovely kind of CAFÉ surrounded by colourful pot plants.

The three walls of the taverna were built from driftwood, the same as the Sand Castle bridge. It only had three walls because the front was fully open to the beach, giving it the most perfect view. Perfect for sipping from a coconut given to you by a friendly monkey on arrival.

The taverna had an appealing ramshackle feel. Nothing matched. Some tables were made from large steering wheels taken off ships that had been wrecked on the shores in the past. Others were ornate eight-legged tables made from, well, **OCTOPUSES**, of course, actual ones. Others were giant *turtles*. You had to be careful if you sat at the octopus or turtle tables, because they might suddenly get bored and move off, albeit slowly and not very far in the case of the turtles. The chairs for the turtle tables were strong, kindly seals who would shuffle you along if the turtle table moved.

There was certainly never a dull moment at this taverna. The most normal chair was made from fan shells with a starfish for legs.

'There he is!' yapped Hoppy. As Chloe followed Hoppy into the taverna she spotted a gentleman sitting at one of the wooden wheel tables. He had a cloud of white hair, bushy white eyebrows and wore a shabby linen jacket that looked like it had never seen an iron. Chloe understood – she didn't see the point of ironing. Clothes only get crumpled when you wear them, so just wear them crumpled in the first place – that was her theory!

The old man was gazing out to sea as he plucked a melancholy tune on his **UKULELE**. He looked sad, but Chloe also thought he had a warm, cosy feeling about him. She had never known either of her grandfathers, but she imagined Trevor was just like a perfect, wise, kind grandfather might be. Although it was quite a shock to her, seeing someone so ordinary in her *Magic Land*.

Hoppy flitted up to him and landed on his table, folding her bird wings neatly behind her as she leant on his glass and tapped gently on it to announce her arrival.

'Trevor, we're here!'

Godfrey joined them, slowly shrinking so he fitted perfectly into the chair beside Trevor. He gave Trevor a warm hello hug. No one's too old for a hug, thought Chloe. Hugs are **SO GOOD**.

Trevor's eyes widened at the sight of Godfrey and Hoppy, the sadness on his face instantly wiped away and replaced by a **SMILE** so big that it made Chloe jealous.

'We've missed you so so **so** much,' said Hoppy, with tears in her eyes.

'Soppy Hoppy,' teased Godfrey. 'But it is wonderful to see you again, Trevor, whatever the reason.'

'I didn't think you'd want to …' said Trevor, his gloom settling back over him as he spoke. 'See me again, I mean – after all these years …'

'We always want to see you, if you want to see us,' said Godfrey. He sounded almost fatherly, even though Trevor was an old man himself.

Trevor looked up and saw Chloe. He jumped in his shell seat, looking as surprised to see her in *Magic Land* as she had felt to see him.

'Hi, I'm Chloe,' she said shyly, as a seal chair scuttled up so she could sit down next to Trevor. 'Did you … did you lose your SMILE too?'

It was the first time she had spoken this aloud to anyone other than Hoppy and Godfrey, and it felt like the hardest thing she had ever said to anyone.

Trevor sighed heavily and reached across the table to pat the back of Chloe's hand. 'Oh, I see …' he said with understanding. 'Not exactly … but I have come very close.'

'Everyone's troubles are different,' said Godfrey gently, looking at Chloe as he spoke. 'We all need a *Magic Land* of some sort, at some time in our lives, for different reasons …'

'I can tell you the story of what's been happening to me since I last visited many, many years ago now … Shall I, Godfrey?'

'Please do.'

'A story, a story!' Hoppy sprang up and down on the back of a giant turtle table, who got fed up and moved out of the taverna even as she bounced. 'I **LOVE** a story!'

Trevor began. 'Right. Well, last year I went on a summer holiday abroad – to the **MOUNTAINS**. It was an arts holiday where we learnt drawing, dance and music. You could pick which lessons you wanted to do every day. Oh, it was just wonderful. And I learnt to play the **UKULELE**. Though I am still only just getting the hang of it. Anyway, there I met this wonderful woman …'

'Evie,' said Hoppy.

Trevor smiled slightly. 'Of course, you'd already know …'

'Let him tell his story in peace, Hoppy.' Godfrey wagged a finger at her.

'Yes, so … Evie …' continued Trevor. 'She was the most beautiful, charming and **ADVENTUROUS** woman I had ever met. We were both on holiday on our own and ended up chatting on the first day. We got on so well that by day three we thought we might as well have our dinners together at the same table rather than sitting alone.

'So every night for two weeks, we ate together. And my goodness how easy it was to chat. We shared so many interests and boy did we *laugh*, always about the silliest things. Once I tripped over a pot plant on my way out of the restaurant and brought Evie down with me. We were in a crumpled heap *laughing* so much we couldn't get up. The waiters just left us there until we pulled ourselves together! I felt like I had come truly alive for the first time, well, ever. Quite the thing, when I am sixty-five this year. Then it came to our last day and I asked her if she wanted to dine a bit earlier because the hotel was doing a dance after dinner and I would love to dance with her. I'd seen her dance the first day we were both there, before we'd even spoken, and she did so with such joyful *sparkle* in her eyes that I wanted to share that with her, see it up close.

'I also told her I had something important to ask her. You see, I was going to ask her to marry me. I know some people might think that was too soon, we'd only known each other for two weeks, but I just knew … I thought we both just knew. Finally I had found *love*, I was sure of it. But …'

His voice wobbled and Godfrey stepped in quickly.

'Trevor has spent his whole life writing, Chloe – he is an author who has written more than fifty wonderful books. Your parents may have read a few of them, he is very well known. But all that time he was writing, he was alone, never finding anyone to fall in *love* with.'

'I could never understand it,' Trevor chimed back in with a tinge of frustration in his voice. 'It seemed I could write about *love*, and I could make other people feel *loved* when I wrote, but I couldn't find it for myself. So I just kept writing. And of course coming to the taverna on and off for many years to talk with Godfrey and Hoppy when I felt lonely.

'Then last year I wrote my final book, decided it was time to retire, and went on that much-needed holiday. And there she was. Evie. **MY LOVE.** The woman I had been waiting for.'

'So what happened?' asked Chloe impatiently. 'Did you ask her? It sounds **SO ROMANTIC.** Did she say yes … what happened …? Please carry on!' By now she was completely gripped.

Trevor was about to continue when there was a tremendous **CRASH** outside the taverna. Everyone spun around.

'Oh gosh, sorry, sorry, so very sorry … sorry to interrupt …' It was bumbling Prince Barnacle again. This time he was causing a *commotion* by colliding with two young storks carrying teetering piles of crockery for the taverna.

'I saw you were all here and thought I would make you some of my special thirst-quencher drinks; they come with coloured straws and umbrellas and everything … I was just going to *creep* in, no fuss … sorry, sorry …'

'Please, stop apologising, Prince Barnie,' said Godfrey with a **SMILE.**

'Golly … yes … ummm … Sorry … Oops, apologising again … sorry … Oops, there I go again!'

Godfrey, Hoppy and Trevor couldn't help but *laugh*. And even Barnie ended up joining in. He looked at Chloe (who of course wasn't *laughing*) and she could see him thinking she must be very unimpressed by him. Oh dear.

'So … would you all like a Prince Barnacle *Classic Beach Quencher*?' he asked tentatively.

'YES!' everyone said at once. Barnie flushed with pleasure and immediately busied himself at the back of the taverna, pulling down glasses, gathering ice and making sure the young storks he had brought over from the Sand Castle to help didn't smash into him again. They were the clumsiest of their royal waiters.

'And please can we have the end of the story?'

Barnie and Chloe had said that at **EXACTLY** the same time. Barnie looked over his shoulder at Chloe and SMILED his slightly crooked, but very charming SMILE at her. But she could only stare back – there was of course no smile to steal across her face, however much she was growing to like this slightly strange prince.

She turned away quickly. He probably hated her by now, she seemed so unfriendly, or boring, or sad, without her **SMILE**.

'The story, Trevor ... Please, I am desperate to know ...' said Chloe, keen to deflect the Sand Prince's attention away from her.

'Yes, story, story!' hopped Hoppy.

'Right. Where was I ...?' Trevor continued. 'Yes, so on the last night of our holiday ...'

'Here you go ... oh sorry, Trevor ... Sorry ...' said Barnie. 'I didn't realise you had started again ...' Barnie had bustled over with his special drinks. 'Passion fruit, mint, sea cucumber and honey, with a dash of shrimp syrup. It may sound unusual but it's ... ummm, very **DELICIOUS**, if I may be so bold.' He handed Chloe hers first, waggling his eyebrows happily as he did so. Chloe took the drink, surprised that he was still talking to her.

'Right ... now, shall I carry on ...?' asked Trevor as Barnie handed round the remaining glasses.

'**YES!**' everyone said together.

'So, I dressed in my black tie for our dinner and dance, I hid the plastic ring I had bought in the souvenir shop in my pocket, and I went to our table and waited. And waited. But, well, she never came. Evie never arrived. After two hours of counting the seconds, I saw a waiter approaching me with a note.'

Everyone silently took a sip of their Prince Barnacle *Classic Beach Quenchers*, wondering what might happen next in Trevor's story. Chloe swallowed back her tears. 'What did it say?' she whispered.

'It said, *Sorry, Trevor. I can explain. One day. In fact, if you are willing to trust me, I can tell you exactly a year and a week from now. Meet me on that day, at noon, at the Horse Fountain we both love. Evie.*' Trevor took a deep breath. 'So there it was. I had hoped for love, all my life, and it had happened, but just like that I had lost her. I have waited this whole year in anticipation of the day … but now it's **TOMORROW**, and suddenly I am so afraid.'

'Why?' they all said in unison, taking another sip of their delicious drinks.

'After all this time, I just cannot believe she will be there. If she loved me the way I love her, why would she have left like that, without a word? And why would she love an old fuddy-duddy like me, full stop?

And I'm so angry that I found someone, only for it to be taken away – it's even more cruel than never falling in love at all. I just don't have the courage to deal with the disappointment if she doesn't turn up.'

'You're scared to hope.' Godfrey nodded sadly to himself.

The group had another silent moment, not knowing what to say to poor Trevor. Chloe so wanted to do what she would usually do after hearing somebody's sad story – crack a *joke*, pull out a SMILE, and see a SMILE come back to the face in front of her. She was desperate to cheer him up.

Then she saw something that gave her an idea.

'Do you like *board games*, Trevor?' she said.

Trevor looked a bit surprised at the random question but he answered, 'Umm … yes, yes I do.'

'Well … look …' Chloe had noticed that at the back of the taverna there were several games set up on tables, all ready to play. There was chess and Cluedo. There was also draughts, ludo, backgammon, Monopoly and a football game. And on the table nearest to them, it was Snakes and Ladders.

Another wave of sadness came over Chloe. It

reminded her of the times she would play at home at weekends, and sometimes weeknights if Mr Long had had a difficult day at work, to cheer him up. Chloe would sit sandwiched warmly between her parents and there would be teasing *laughter* when Mr Long rolled the dice and landed on the longest snake, taking him all the way back to the beginning when he was just about to win.

Chloe was about to get really sad reflecting on how those times didn't happen any more, when she noticed something on the Snakes and Ladders board that made her leap off her seal chair. You wouldn't believe it, but it seemed like one of the snakes twisted its head in her direction.

Chloe told herself her IMAGINATION had gone into overdrive, until she realised Trevor had also leapt up and was standing next to her.

'Did you see that?' asked Chloe.

'Well, dear, I don't know what **YOU** saw, but I think I saw … it sounds rather odd to say it … but …'

'A snake move?'

'Yes! It did, didn't it? How **EXTRAORDINARY**!'

Bravely, they moved closer to the table, and

suddenly the whole board was moving. All the different varieties of snakes, in their different sizes, were sliding up and down the ladders.

Chloe and Trevor gasped and jumped backwards again.

'That board game is **ALIVE**!' shouted Chloe.

'Indeed,' agreed Godfrey.

She didn't know whether to feel excited or scared by what they were seeing, but having Trevor there definitely made it feel easier.

'Look!' Chloe shouted. She pointed at the chessboard table, where a little white wooden pawn had sprouted legs and was running over to the other side of the board to swap places with a black pawn. And there was a cross-headed bishop sliding diagonally with a sophisticated **WHOOSH**. On the Cluedo board there was a miniature Mrs Peacock and Professor Plum having an argument as to who had stolen the candlestick!

'Seems like they all want to play with you,' Godfrey said as he slipped out of the taverna, indicating that Hoppy should do the same. It wasn't a coincidence that Trevor was in *Sand Land* at the same time as

Chloe. Godfrey had wanted them to meet.

'How do we play?' Chloe asked, turning back to look at the board. She wanted a game of Snakes and Ladders with Trevor very much. It could be fun.

'There aren't any dice and if the pieces keep moving, then I don't know how we'd play properly.'

'Oh well … ummm … if I may …' Barnie stepped in. 'In *Sand Land*, board games are played for real.'

'Imagine that …' whispered Hoppy in Chloe's ear happily, flying out to join Godfrey.

And as Hoppy said it, Chloe understood exactly what she meant, as if it was her idea, and even as she thought it, something REALLY **BIG** began to happen.

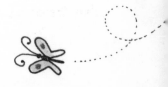

16

SNAKES AND LADDERS

One by one the snakes and ladders began to fly off the table and up into the sky, the now-empty board hurtling along behind them growing bigger and bigger as it flew. Once in the air, hovering over the sea, they re-formed as the biggest Snakes and Ladders game Trevor and Chloe, indeed the world, had ever seen. They could see the whole board: the lower numbers at the bottom, with the snakes and ladders reaching high up to the winning square at the top, as high as a house. At least.

Of everything Chloe had experienced in her *Magic Land* so far this was the most FANTASTICAL. She quickly realised that in order to play, she and Trevor were going to have to climb the ladders themselves, and the surprisingly friendly snakes – multicoloured, with no teeth, cheeky winking eyes and playful smiles – were like water flumes; if you landed on one of those you would slide down and plop into the sea below.

What fun! thought Chloe. Beside her, Trevor was looking a little wide-eyed, as if doubting whether he was sprightly enough to take on the challenge. But Chloe's excitement was hard to resist, so as Godfrey sat himself down to spectate, with Hoppy on his shoulder, Chloe and Trevor walked down the sand towards the sea, Barnie following just behind, where they found a dice about the size of an armchair bouncing up and down excitedly, waiting for the game to start.

'Just shout "**ROLL**" to the dice whenever it's your go,' explained Barnie.

Chloe and Trevor waded out to the bottom of the board. The sun was sparkling on the sea and the warm water lapped at Chloe's legs comfortingly, yet she knew this was quite her strangest experience so far.

Once below the first square of the board she shouted '**ROLL!**', and the dice rolled itself along the sand with glee, landing on a six and whooping *joyfully*!

Chloe pulled herself up on to the bottom of the

board – there was a small ridge she could walk along. When she reached the sixth square she found she'd landed on a ladder. Wow, she was going to actually climb a ladder. It felt surprisingly sturdy and safe as she put her foot on the first rung. It was one of the smaller ladders on the board, and she reached the top of it pretty quickly.

She stepped into her new square, and realised she was next to a green and purple striped snake. She reached out and patted its skin experimentally. It was smooth, soft and spongy, and although she knew the aim of the game was **NOT** to land on a snake, she almost wanted to, to see what would happen if you did. It didn't take her long to find out.

Trevor threw a three and pulled himself up on to the first level of the board.

Then it was Chloe's turn, and the dice rolled a one and made a mischievous *tee hee hee* noise almost like it had done it on purpose. Chloe stepped on to the snake's head, and **WHEEEEEEEEEEEEE!** she slid down the snake at speed and *splash-landed* safely in the water below. It was even better than the water slide at her favourite *Magic Land* lake.

'Don't worry if you land on a snake, Trevor, it was actually fun,' she shouted up to him.

'Phew!' said Trevor. 'Look, I just got a four and it's taken me up this big ladder, I must be halfway up.' Chloe looked up and wondered what it would be like right at the top of the board. What a **VIEW** there would be.

They carried on playing, regularly sliding down snakes and plopping into the water below. As Trevor took his next turn, Chloe looked back at the beach from her perch on top of one of the ladders and saw Prince Barnie waving at her *enthusiastically* from the taverna.

Chloe waved back and as she did so he pointed at the two tables nearest him.

Suddenly there appeared twenty-two life-size football players in yellow and red shirts, with real goals and a pitch marked out on the sand, and a set of chess pieces, all human-size too now, laying themselves out on an enormous checked board, probably as big as a football pitch too. Barnie gave Chloe a huge thumbs-up and shouted, 'Play against me next?' She nodded gratefully.

'Your turn,' shouted Trevor from five squares behind her.

'**ROLL!**' she yelled down. The dice rolled a four. She walked forwards four steps and found herself at the foot of another ladder. She started to climb, wondering how high this ladder would take her, when it wobbled a little. Trevor had started laughing so hard it was making the ladders around him shake. In fact, he nearly toppled off his own wobbling ladder. Toppling and wobbling did not make this game easy.

'Trevor, I'm trying to climb – stop *laughing*!'

'But look at Barnie!' he shouted up to Chloe.

Prince Barnie was trying to organise the chess pieces into their correct starting squares for a game, but they were shuffling about and chatting, not paying ANY attention to him **AT ALL**!

The black bishop was still showing off that he had the smoothest moves of them all, gliding in long diagonals back and forth. The white knight shouted crossly, 'Stop showing off, when you know full well I can only move three paces forward and one pace to the right or left, like a weird jumping *cricket*.'

The black castle shouted back over the heads of the pawns in front of him, 'I could glide up and down just as well as him, if I could get out of this *blasted* corner.'

Barnie was desperately trying to get control. 'Bishop, please stop sliding and get back to your place? Ummm … can the pawns stop bouncing and chatting and form neat orderly lines … ummm … is **ANYONE** listening? I am a **PRINCE**, you know …' shouted Barnie.

At that moment a football flew and sent the white queen shooting through the air, only to land head-first in the sand with an indignant, muffled scream. The footballers had started a game on their own, but instead of working as teams, each player was simply trying to get the ball for himself. As Chloe watched, twenty-two players threw themselves after the ball, landing in a messy clump, still clambering over each other to try and get a foot on it. Even the half-drawn sand chicks and ducklings were less chaotic than this!

Trevor was still *giggling*. Chloe couldn't *laugh* like everyone else, but she was certainly feeling lighter since playing this giant game. She decided she would go and help Prince Barnacle, who was retreating to the taverna to hide from the arguing game pieces. After all, he had been so kind to her.

She was about to climb back down a ladder, when she thought she felt the board shudder. This wasn't a jolly wobble from Trevor laughing. This was something else. It was a serious shudder that went right through her. She looked for Godfrey on the beach. He was no longer reclining on the sand. He was standing up, *alert* and scanning the horizon. Hoppy was on his shoulder whispering furiously in his ear.

Chloe knew instantly what that meant – the Shadow Bandits were back. But where? The trees were still, and everything was just as colourful and picturesque as it had been minutes ago.

'**The footballers!**' roared Godfrey suddenly.

As he spoke, a small group of sneaky Shadow Bandits made a break for it. They wafted out from amongst the pile of footballers and began half-running, half-drifting across the beach towards the Snakes and Ladders board.

They were insubstantial enough not to leave

footprints in the sand, but Chloe thought they seemed darker than before, and where they passed, colour sucked from the sand and sky and shells, leaving a dull greyish trail in their wake.

The lead shadow appeared to be carrying something – it looked like the black, smoking root of a plant.

Chloe's ladder shook as Trevor pulled himself up beside her, panting heavily. 'What's going on?' he exclaimed. But there was no time to explain. The leading Shadow Bandit, protected by a circle of the others, was already planting the root into the sea below their board, twining the other end of it around one of the lowest ladder rungs. Immediately the root began to **GROW** into evil-looking twisted branches, thickening and spreading.

The Shadow Bandits vanished upwards in a dark cloud with an eerie parting **s c r e e c h.**

'Come on!' Chloe grabbed Trevor's hand and started pulling him higher up the board, as far away from the black vine as possible.

'Good idea!' Hoppy said suddenly in her ear.

'Thank goodness you're here!' Chloe gasped.

'What do we do?'

'Don't worry – look at Godfrey,' Hoppy replied. 'He'll soon stop it!'

Godfrey was running down the beach towards them so fast he was creating a small sand whirlwind in his wake. In just five of his long strides he'd got to the sea's edge, where he leapt into the air, his hat flipping from his head as he did so, and *dived* neatly into the sea, emerging seconds later as a majestic, oversized **POLAR BEAR**. His thick white fur glistened, but his eyes were dark and menacing as he powered through the water towards the thickening vine. Blackness puffed outwards from it, darkening the water and making it bubble angrily. Bear-Godfrey leapt up then dived down into the black sea, disappearing from sight.

'What's he doing?' Chloe asked worriedly.

'Stopping it taking root in the seabed,' Hoppy explained, 'before it can do too much damage.'

They all stared expectantly at the seething water.

'He's been under a very long time,' said Trevor after a minute. 'Are you sure he can hold his breath that long?'

Hoppy didn't answer. Even she was starting to look worried.

'We have to help him!' Chloe said desperately after another minute had gone. But none of them knew what to try.

Suddenly a huge white mass exploded from the sea. The polar bear gasped in a massive intake of breath, *golden wings* sprang from its back, and it had already morphed into full eagle by the time it passed the top of the board.

'Oh no!' whispered Hoppy, in a shocked voice unlike anything Chloe had heard from her before.

'What?!'

'He hasn't been able to stop it … the vine has taken root!'

They all glanced down to see its dark *tendrils* growing fast, entangling themselves in the snakes' tails and ladder rungs.

The ladders at the bottom of the board began to creak and snap and the snakes writhed, the colour sapping from them. All the time the vine was creeping higher and higher.

Hoppy whipped a bow out from under her wings

and started firing arrows at the black strands, but the pace was too fast, and the stabs of her tiny arrows made little difference.

Chloe racked her brain desperately – what could she do? Godfrey and Hoppy had insisted she was the one destined to save her precious *Magic Land*, but she was now feeling completely useless. Think, Chloe, think, think think, she said to herself. *Magic Land* was under threat. **THEY** were under threat. Something HAD to be done.

CRACK!

Hoppy buzzed in Chloe's ear, 'Don't look down!' but she didn't say it soon enough. Chloe had indeed looked down. She screamed. Vine tendrils were just inches away, twisting and *snapping* ladders everywhere she looked.

'Move this way!' Trevor yelled. They shuffled backwards into square 100 but there was nowhere left to go. They'd reached the top edge of the board. They were trapped.

The sky began to **DARKEN**. Chloe looked up: a huge grey storm cloud was swelling above them. Eagle-Godfrey was circling the cloud, beating his wings wildly, but to little avail. He grabbed the cloud with his beak and tried to pull it away from the board, but it only got stronger and darker. The sea raged, heavy rain began to fall and there was a loud rumble of thunder. The vines seemed to dance in the grey light of the *storm*.

Chloe was plunged into despair as yet again something wonderful was turned to bad. Even Hoppy seemed to be losing power as her wings were battered by the storm's heavy rain.

Trevor's white hair was flattened and stuck to his face, and he looked scared and defeated. Chloe felt a surge of angry **ENERGY**. She was not going to give up. No, she decided, absolutely not.

She looked about frantically for an undamaged snake that they might slide down – at least the beach would be safer.

But the worst had happened. The snakes had … *turned*. They were emerging from the constricting vines one by one, their smiling faces filled with **teeth**, their colourful stripes replaced with an oily blackness, and they hissed **MENACINGLY**. They began to slide up the board. There was nowhere for Chloe and Trevor to go. The biggest snake pulled ahead of the rest, opening its jaws wide …

Chloe knew she could either give up once and for all, and who knew what dreadful things would come of that, or she could hold on to her last tiny mustard seed of hope and fight back.

Chloe swung into action. She grabbed a broken piece of ladder from the piles of wood littering the board, and just before the huge snake slid right up to them and swallowed them in one big gulp, she *rammed* the wood into its mouth, preventing the jaws from snapping shut over their heads.

'Quick thinking, Chloe,' uttered a shaken Trevor, while Hoppy chirruped triumphantly.

'Now, get on to the snake's back with me, Trevor …' shouted Chloe.

'What? No … I can't, I'm too scared …'

'We have to get on to the beach before the game collapses. This is the only way!'

Other snakes started crawling up towards them, ready to snap. '**QUICK!**'

Chloe leapt on to the blackened back of the snake she had stunned and slid down it at speed towards the shallower sea below – but when she looked back she realised with horror that Trevor hadn't followed her in time. He was surrounded. There was no escape left for him …

17

THE GAME IS ON!

Chloe splashed into the dark water and started for the safety of the now greying beach as fast as she could. She looked back over her shoulder only to see the big snake she had just slid down **CRUNCH** through the piece of wood in its mouth. Splinters spat from between its teeth and it whipped round its massive head and caught Trevor's jacket.

Chloe turned back, grabbing the huge snake's tail as it flailed past her, and pulled it with her on to the beach, though the snake was so long it barely seemed to notice.

'Help!' shrieked Trevor. 'I knew I shouldn't have hoped. I will never see Evie again …'

But Chloe wasn't giving up. She could see Godfrey was still trying to move the storm clouds away; he wasn't giving up either. And then the answer hit her.

'Yes, yes,' said Hoppy in her ear. 'That's the key! I

will tell Godfrey straight away.'

'Quick, Hoppy, quick …' ordered Chloe, as Hoppy sped up to Godfrey as fast as she could, her little wings flapping as frantically as they had ever flapped.

You see, Chloe and Hoppy had thought of a **BRILLIANT** plan. Godfrey had to use the power of the Shadow Bandits' storm against them. If he could direct a lightning bolt to the seabed and destroy the vine root, Chloe was sure all the power of the snakes and vines would disappear …

BUT she had to get Trevor to safety first. He wouldn't survive the impact of the lightning bolt. He was still clinging to the last remaining corner of the board, with only his jacket between him and the mouth of a huge, violent snake.

'Barnie!' she yelled desperately. '**BARNIE!**'

Barnie came out from behind the taverna and stood stock-still, as if he couldn't believe his eyes. WHAT HAD HAPPENED? The truth is, after the fiasco with the football players he had been hiding in the taverna kitchen, mumbling to the waiter storks about how embarrassed he was, and designing a new drink to distract himself.

'Chloe! Oh my … Oh my …'

'Now, calm down, Barnie—'

'CALM DOWN?' shrieked the Sand Prince. 'CALM DOWN?! **LOOK!**'

Barnie started trying to gather an army of chess pieces and footballers, but in his panic he was getting more and more muddled.

'Form a line, no, a circle … Just do something …!' he shouted. Which wasn't very helpful to the already *chaotic* chess pieces, and the footballers who were huddled in a circle arguing about who should be the captain and hero of the moment, and not actually achieving anything.

The broken ladders were tumbling into the black sea below Trevor, the board was liable to fall at any moment. By now Chloe could only just see Trevor's white hair emerging from the coiled upper half of the big snake that had snatched him – she was sure it was squeezing the very breath from him even as she watched.

Chloe still had the snake's tail in her hands, but it was thrashing around, pulling away from her as it tightened around Trevor.

'Barnie!' she tried again, but he couldn't hear her above the jabber of the panicking pawns, babbling bishops, cackling castles and frolicking footballers. Desperately, Chloe stuck her fingers in her mouth and did the loudest **WHISTLE** she could. As one, the chess pieces and footballers froze and turned their attention in Chloe's direction.

'**GET IN A LINE, GRAB THIS TAIL WITH ME, AND PULL!**' she shouted with sergeant-major-like authority. To her relief, all the footballers and chess pieces immediately followed Barnie's lead as he charged across the beach towards Chloe.

Behind them thundered the Sand King's walrus entourage, followed by a deeply concerned-looking King Sandy and Queen Sandra.

As Barnie reached Chloe's side, he grabbed her about the waist, then the football players got in a line behind him, and the chess pieces behind them, and the walruses behind them like a record-breaking game of tug of war, everyone digging their heels and edges and flippers into the sand, trying to pull the snake away from Trevor.

'Dig in hard!' shouted Chloe to her team.

'Dig in hard!' shouted Chloe to her team.

'Dig in hard!' echoed Barnie, not completely sure what was going on, but determined to help his new friend. '**Dig in, dig in!**'

'Yes, we know we have to dig in, young man!' said the white bishop curtly after Barnie's seventh time of shouting it. 'What do you think we are all doing?'

'*Pull!*' shouted Chloe.

'*Pull!*' repeated Barnie, and the bishop gave him a stern look.

By now they were all pulling together. Pull, **heave**, pull, **heave**.

And gradually the snake started losing its battle. Chloe, Barnie, the footballers, chess pieces and walrus chain moved further and further back up the beach, and the weakened snake began to uncoil from Trevor as they hauled it down the board.

'**PULL!**' Chloe yelled louder than ever, and with one last, huge heave the snake unravelled completely, sending Trevor whizzing off the board like a spinning top. The snake fell into the sea and Chloe's long chain of creatures tumbled back on to the beach like dominoes, one on top of the other.

In the very same moment that Trevor was spinning

towards the water, eagle-Godfrey emerged from the storm clouds riding a **LIGHTNING BOLT** so bright Chloe had to shield her eyes.

'He's going for the root – it's the only way to stop it. Get out of the sea, Trevor,' she screamed desperately.

With a massive thunderclap the bolt flew from underneath Godfrey and sped arrow-like down through the sky and into the turbulent black sea. The waters seemed to recoil from the electric touch, parting to reveal the seabed below where the shadow vine had planted itself, and as the bolt stabbed into the roots it split them in half and its tendrils instantly began to disintegrate.

The already brightening sea crashed back together, swallowing everything beneath it. A massive jet of water surged upwards as the waters met, bashing into the broken games board above and washing the rotten snakes into the sea.

But had Trevor made it?

'Where's Trevor? Oh, Barnie … did he get out of the sea in time?' Chloe could hardly breathe. She was suddenly sure that her plan meant they'd lost Trevor for ever.

But through the clouds swooped eagle-Godfrey, with Trevor and Hoppy safely perched on his shoulders. Godfrey had just caught him in time. The golden eagle swept over the beach, returning to Godfrey's usual form as his feet hit the sand.

There was a relieved, exhausted SILENCE.

Chloe could have cried with relief – it was over! The sun was already drying everything out, and in most places colour was returning everything to normal.

She pulled Barnie up to his feet and they ran down to the shoreline towards where the black snake that they had wrestled for so long had washed up. It had indeed lost its power as soon as the vine had been destroyed, and lay motionless. Just to be sure, Barnie grabbed the sword at his belt, held it in the air dramatically, then dealt a final blow to the snake's head, pinning it to the sand. He put his foot on the head and swung round for a victory pose, then fell over as his foot slipped on the snake and his leg and shorts became covered in black oil. Once he had steadied himself and posed again, he realised no one was looking – everyone was too busy leaping up and down around Chloe.

'Yup, no, course … Chloe's the hero … I mean heroine … But guys, look, I stuck my sword in … hello? Guys … the snake … Nope. Anyone?'

Trevor was running towards Chloe.

'Thank you, Chloe, thank you, thank you, thank you. Though that wasn't quite the *game* I was expecting!'

'Me neither,' agreed Chloe as she gave him a massive hug.

Barnie approached Chloe shyly. 'You are … well, completely **AWESOME**!' He blushed. 'Three cheers for Chloe. Hip hip …'

'**Hurrah!**' everyone shouted.

'Hip, hip …'

'**Hurrah!**'

'Hip hip …'

'**HURRAH!**'

'Ummm, I, the king, should have done the formal thank you actually!'

Chloe spun round to see the Sand King and Queen standing there.

'Thank you, Miss Chloe,' Queen Sandra said regally.

'I was about to say that,' said King Sandy. 'Yes, thank you, Miss …'

'I've already said it now,' said the queen, shaking her head at him.

'Well, hip, hip, hurrah for Chloe …' said the king instead.

'We've done that bit too …' Queen Sandra winked at Chloe and gave her loving husband a consoling hold of the hand.

Chloe was *overwhelmed*. She wanted to tell everyone that she didn't deserve this attention, that it wasn't just her.

Barnie saved her embarrassment. 'Right, I think that's enough game playing for now, all things considered,' he said, for once with slight authority. The chess pieces and footballers began to boo but Barnie ignored them. 'Back to tables!' he called. And all the pieces disappeared.

Chloe ran over to Godfrey and Hoppy. 'Are all the game pieces back safely on the tables now?' she said anxiously. 'Is everything all right again?'

'Go and have a look,' suggested Godfrey. Chloe walked cautiously back up to the taverna with Barnie and Trevor. And there they all were. In fact, the chess pieces were waving at her as they went back to being their inanimate selves.

Chloe rushed to the Snakes and Ladders board. Even that was reassembling itself on the table, with the ladders intact and the snakes smiling and **COLOURFUL** once more.

'It's mended,' she said with huge relief.

'Yes, because you saved it,' said Godfrey. 'You saved Trevor too – using your quick wits, imagination and **courage** ...'

'... and hope. Your hope in the face of adversity, Chloe, it's **INSPIRED** me!' said Trevor excitedly. 'When that snake had me, when I thought I was gone, I dared to remember those two weeks on holiday. Falling in *love*. My Evie. Well, the chance of having that again is worth any pain. I decided if I survived, to risk it. Better to have risked it, then not to have tried at all. So, THANK YOU. And now I'm off – I have a date. Yippeeee!'

'Go, Trevor,' whispered Godfrey, patting Trevor on the back. As he did so, Trevor suddenly looked like an innocent *little boy*. Chloe blinked, thinking he'd morphed into something, but the moment passed just as quickly as it had come.

'Yes that's great news, Trevor.' Chloe gave him another big hug. 'You **SHOULD** go. I am sure she'll be there! Evie is a lucky woman to have you.' Chloe knew she would miss this kind old man hugely when he was gone, but she wanted to feel *happy* for him too.

'And YOU must have hope ... do it for me, please,' said Trevor firmly, squeezing Chloe's hand. 'I'm sure things will get better for you.'

Chloe nodded as Trevor turned and ran off into the trees beyond the dunes – he seemed to thin and disappear a little as he stepped into the shade of the first tree, and then he was *gone*.

Chloe collapsed on to the beach. 'It's all so confusing,' she said glumly. 'I am glad Trevor feels better, but even after all that has just happened, I don't see how I am meant to feel hopeful – I still don't have my **SMILE** and I am beginning to wonder if I ever will again.'

'You know my answer to that, my dear girl – trust us,' said Godfrey. 'The time will come. You're *special*.

So very special. Your **SMILE** brings happiness to all those around you. The Shadow Bandits know that and they will do anything to stop you. They're growing in strength. Animals in *Magic Land* have never turned evil before …'

'I don't feel remotely special.'

'You don't always have to *feel* special to *be* special,' whispered Hoppy in her ear.

'You must believe in yourself,' said Godfrey. 'You must have *hope* for it to happen. If nothing else, you just need to remember this – a **SMILE** without hope isn't a real smile.'

'A **SMILE** without hope isn't a real smile …' Chloe repeated it back so it would sink in. 'I just … I just feel that I can't go on if there are going to be more battles. Life is so tiring at home without my **SMILE**.'

Chloe suddenly realised Barnie was still standing there. 'You heard all that?'

Barnie nodded.

'You probably think I am really weird and pathetic …?'

'I think you are a hero and um … my … umm … new *friend* …?'

'Even though I don't have a SMILE?'

'Urrh, I noticed you didn't have a smile ages ago, and I still wanted to be your *friend* ...'

Chloe couldn't have been more surprised.

'I am so glad you came to *Sand Land*,' said Prince Barnacle.

'Me too.'

Godfrey nodded approvingly. 'But now we need to get you home, Chloe. You need your rest.'

'Will I see you again?' Chloe asked. She turned to Godfrey. 'Will I?'

'Most definitely.'

'Good ... I think.'

They all stared at Chloe.

'I don't mean to be rude, it's just if I am going to see Barnie again ... well ... it may mean more battles too ...'

She clambered back on to Godfrey's shoulders and as they took off she waved goodbye to Barnie, his royal family, and the walruses. Then Godfrey morphed into his majestic eagle self once more, turned on the wind and headed back towards Elmswater Crescent. As they flew Chloe tried not to notice the patches below of darkness and grey where the colour wasn't returning, even after everything she had done in *Sand Land* that day.

They all knew Chloe needed to reclaim *Magic Land* once and for all … And time clearly wasn't on their side.

18

FAKE PANCAKES

The sun rose slowly but assuredly as ever in the east at the back of Chloe's house, shining its light over her cul-de-sac. Chloe woke to a snip, snip, snipping sound she knew well. She looked out of the window and there was Mr Sweet with his shears, getting more and more ambitious, making a topiary chipmunk this time with his hedges! It looked like it was going to be a hot day and Mrs Sweet was watering already. 'Aaaah there you go, were you thirsty, my loves?' she said as she drizzled water over her scarlet geraniums.

Mr Sweet started his lawnmower. That was strange, thought Chloe. She was sure there was a rule in the cul-de-sac of no mowing before 7.30 a.m. She looked at her watch. It was already a quarter past eight. 'Oh my goodness, I've overslept!' said Chloe.

She leapt out of bed and started rushing about putting on her school uniform. Before she ran out of her bedroom door, however, she paused. She had a strange feeling, one she hadn't felt for a long while. She suddenly felt that maybe everything was going to be all right today. Maybe things were going to get better generally. Maybe one day she would even have her own duvet. Maybe even her **SMILE** would sort itself out, somehow, someday.

This feeling, combined with the courage she'd been experiencing recently, made her feel a bit like a superhero – **SUPER CHLOE**! It was such an unusual *sensation* for Chloe to think that everything could be all right, she was almost unnerved. Then the extraordinary adventures of last night came back to her in a flash. Maybe this was **HOPE** ...

She looked down quickly at her bedside table – on top of it was a postcard from the taverna with a note from Trevor saying, *It was an honour to meet you Chloe, love Trevor* and another ornament, this time a miniature sand-coloured *lion*. She gathered both items up and put them in the treasure box Gran Gran had given her, for safekeeping, along with the Hoppy cupcake top and the penguin statuette from the day before.

As she made her way downstairs to the kitchen, she could hear Gran Gran chatting cheerily away to her parents. Chloe thought quickly – she would finish her homework at breakfast so her grandmother wouldn't notice her continued lack of SMILE.

As Chloe pushed open the kitchen door it was immediately obvious that her parents were still putting on a pretence for Gran Gran. There were pancakes and bacon and orange juice and the breakfast table was laid neatly with a *lovely* tablecloth and matching plates. Chloe couldn't remember the last time her parents had made her breakfast, certainly not one this elaborate.

'Morning, dear,' said Gran Gran. 'Aaah, you look a bit more yourself today.'

'Hello my, ummmm, cherub,' said her dad as her mum gave her an awkward hug. 'Your mother has made *pancakes*.'

'Not that there is anything unusual about that, is there, Mr Long?' said her mum. 'I always do *pancakes* on a Thursday, don't I?'

'Of course, yes,' said Mr Long, trying to ignore his wife's furious stare.

Chloe sat down. 'Sorry if I don't talk much, Gran Gran, but I didn't finish my homework last night, and I am running late.'

Chloe buried her head in her books so her grandmother couldn't see her face as she quickly ate her pancakes. Even though it wasn't true that her mum cooked pancakes every Thursday, she wasn't going to miss out on eating them. They happened to be one of her very **FAVOURITE** things.

'Right,' said Gran Gran. 'I'm off, I've got a busy day so I won't be getting under your feet. I don't want my stay here to be in any way inconvenient.'

'Inconvenient, don't be silly, we love you staying!' protested Mr and Mrs Long loudly.

'Oh good. Because I always like my birthday visits to be as **ADVENTUROUS** as possible for my *sunshine* granddaughter. Tell you what, I'll stay on and let's think of a fun family outing for the weekend. What larks we shall have.'

Mr and Mrs Long's fake smiles dropped.

'Oh, and I'm hoping to introduce you to a friend of mine who is staying not far from here who could come along too. But for now, my dears, my hair has an appointment with a lovely wash and blowdry, and then I'm going to take myself to the shops. I've lost a bit of weight since I started dancing so I am going to treat myself to a new *dress*. I'm thinking canary yellow, with pink spots! Ta-ta for now. Have a good day at school, Chloe, my little ray of *sunshine*.'

After the bang of the front door, and a brief pause, Mr Long muttered to himself, '*Sunshine*, my little ray of *sunshine*, she never calls **ME** that any more ...'

'YOU a ray of sunshine? Don't make me laugh. More likely that I become Prime Minister.'

'YOU Prime Minister – don't make ME laugh, what would your policies be – everyone must have long red nails otherwise they go to prison?'

'Oh do stop, because listen,' Mrs Long droned on grumpily. 'She wants to stay longer and bring friends round now ... what next, three-course meals, banquets, tiaras?'

'Don't start shouting at me, it's not my fault!'

'Yes it is. It's **YOUR** mother.'

'Well, we all have mothers. I can't be blamed for that, can I? Neither you nor I would be here right now, if we didn't have mothers!'

'Don't get clever with me!'

'Don't you—' Mr Long didn't have the chance to finish his sentence, as the door opened again and Gran Gran was back.

'Sorry, I forgot my purse, what a silly-billy!' Gran Gran *laughed* at herself. Mr and Mrs Long did such over-the-top silly fake smiles to hide their argument that they both looked like they were in pain, or needed the toilet urgently. Not a good effect!

Chloe had already started putting her homework in her rucksack, so she and Gran Gran met briefly in the hall on their way out. Chloe concentrated madly on doing up her shoes, keeping her face firmly downwards.

'You **WILL** have a good day at school, won't you, dear? Remember what I say:

'WHATEVER YOU'RE FEELING, THERE'S SOMETHING FUN TO FIND IN EVERY DAY.'

'And ... if there is something wrong, you know you can talk to your Gran Gran. You can tell me anything ...'

'I'm just still not feeling very well,' said Chloe. 'Same old me, *cheery* as ever, promise!'

Chloe felt bad for lying, but she just couldn't tell Gran Gran the truth. It would be too upsetting, for both of them. Thank goodness she had Godfrey and Hoppy to talk to about it all, and Barnie too now.

Gran Gran checked her watch and, with a last glance back at Chloe, headed out of the door, her neat little feet scuttling hurriedly towards the gate and then on to the pavement. She only had size two shoes, but she walked with such purpose you could always hear her coming.

Chloe looked back down the hall into the kitchen to see her mother furiously tidying up. She was standing on the other side of the kitchen from the bin, throwing all the leftover pancakes at it, accidentally on purpose hitting Mr Long with some debris from time to time. Mr Long was trying to remain calm, his head in his newspaper, even when a piece of pancake landed on his forehead and slowly started to slip down his face, leaving a trail of syrup.

Chloe suddenly felt so very sad. The nice things

that her parents were doing now, with Gran Gran
staying, didn't used to be pretend.

More vague *memories* of a few years ago bubbled
up in Chloe's mind, when her mum would make
steaming porridge with honey and berries and take
her to school herself, and they would chat and sing
and skip along the way.

Were these memories that kept popping up really
true? It seemed so long ago. But yes, she was sure.
Her mother would kneel down and *kiss* her before
sending her in through the school gates.

And when her father first got his job as a bus-
driver, they would sometimes meet him at the start
of his shift, and she would sit on his lap and pretend
to drive the bus, beeping the horn and making silly
announcements. 'We will shortly be stopping at
Trumpington Town: anyone wanting to trump, please
get off now.' Very silly.

PICNICS! She suddenly remembered summer
picnics. They **DID** do that. They were *happy*.

She remembered last night when she lay next
to Godfrey feeling safe and calm. She had once
had a similar feeling lying between her parents on a

. ☼ 227 ☼ .

picnic blanket, counting the clouds. And when she cried or dropped something, they still *loved* her – it didn't make them cross. Where had she gone wrong? When did her SMILE stop being enough?

She looked at them again now in the kitchen, her father wiping his furious frowning face, her mother angrily scrubbing a frying-pan. She realised something awful. She couldn't rustle up any of the *love* she used to feel for them. She just felt numb. Did … did losing her SMILE mean losing the ability to *love* too? The thought was so horrible, it made her want to run upstairs and hide under her blanket. But then she remembered the evil shadow snakes they'd faced down last night against all the odds. She thought of Trevor, of how brave he had been dashing off full of hope to meet the *love* of his life, despite the risk she might never turn up. She thought of how much *Magic Land* needed her, and she rallied.

Chloe made herself turn back to the kitchen doorway and say brightly, 'Bye, Mum. Bye, Dad. Have a lovely day.' Mr and Mrs Long stared at her in confusion – they hadn't exactly noticed that Chloe hadn't been herself recently, but this sudden *kindness* came as a bit of a shock nonetheless. It had been days since anyone had said something so friendly to either of them.

Chloe could almost see this in their eyes and to her own surprise she found herself adding, 'And … and I really hope that one day we can go on a family PICNIC again. Bye.' She dashed out of the door.

'Well, er … What **IS** the girl talking about?' said Mrs Long.

'Exactly!' blustered Mr Long after a moment. 'A picnic indeed?!'

'I mean, what do we want with a picnic. In fact, this is our picnic rug and I am now using it as a tablecloth, so that would be just unhygienic. It needs a wash.'

With that, Mrs Long whipped it off the table from underneath her husband's elbows, sending him sprawling face-first into a sticky patch of honey on the rug.

'I'd only just wiped that syrup off my face!' shouted Mr Long.

Mrs Long tugged impatiently at the rug.

'Stop pulling, I'm stuck in the tablecloth!'

shouted Mr Long. He fell to the floor while Mrs Long was trying to drag him, as well as the rug, into the washing machine!

Chloe's dad pulled himself free, straightened his tie indignantly and stormed out of the kitchen. 'I have work to go to,' he yelled back over his shoulder. 'Buses to drive, traffic fumes to inhale, people to ignore!'

He left Mrs Long holding the tablecloth, looking at it as if remembering for herself the **PICNICS** that Chloe had made her think about. 'But ... I haven't got the energy for picnics, I'm EXHAUSTED.' She gave herself a brisk shake, threw the cloth into the washing machine and rushed to the living room to escape into her third magazine of the day. At least life was calm and rosy in her magazines.

Chloe was glad she was late for school in the end as it meant she could run all the way there with her head down, and if anyone said good morning she could just keep running and shout that she was late, without having to look a single person in the eye. That way she wouldn't feel guilty that she couldn't **SMILE**. It was her mission in life to bring people cheer and if she couldn't do that, she was beginning to feel, well, almost like she didn't really *exist*. Empty. Like she was somehow fading away.

Mr and Mrs Sweet tried to stop her for a chat as she left the house.

'Morning, Chloe,' said Mrs Sweet. 'I—'

'Running late …' shouted Chloe, waving behind her as she shot off towards school.

'Literally running late,' said Mr Sweet to Mrs Sweet as Chloe passed. 'Look how fast she is going.'

'I tell you, there's something wrong with young Chloe.'

'Don't you worry, sweetpea, she's just growing up, she has more important things on her mind than chatting to her elderly neighbours.'

'Elderly?' Mrs Sweet nudged her husband affectionately. 'Forty-three is **NOT** elderly, excuse me! But really, my sweet, I know there is something wrong.'

'Don't go upsetting yourself, sweetpea,' calmed Mr Sweet. Mrs Sweet went back to her plants and poured all the *love* into her garden that she had never been able to pour into a child of her own.

As the Sweets went back to their gardening, Chloe was sprinting over the zebra crossing, even before the lollipop lady had stopped the traffic.

'Careful, Chloe!' the lollipop lady shouted after her. Chloe dashed onwards, smacking right into the postman's trolley, sending it rolling down the street without her noticing.

'**Oi!**' shouted the postman furiously as he chased after his trundling trolley, whilst other people walking to work had to leap out of the way.

Eventually Chloe arrived at the school as assembly was ending. She quickly joined the pack of pupils leaving the hall and headed to her chemistry lesson.

Chloe was the last person into the classroom and noticed immediately that not only were Benjamin, Ruby and Hannah not paying her any attention, but the bench that she normally sat at with them already had four people on it. Another girl had taken her place – **GLORIOUS GLORIA**. The person everyone wanted on their table for chemistry as she was a science whizz kid.

Chloe walked past her once-friends to the back of the room to find a place. That hollow sad feeling hit her again. She felt a bit like a ghost, almost as see-through as one of the terrible Shadow Bandits. No wonder her old friends didn't want her around.

'Hope, hope, hope,' she chanted to herself resiliently. This feeling wasn't going to last. It couldn't. She **WAS** going to save *Magic Land* and get her SMILE back. Eventually.

Chloe went through the school day in a kind of haze, all on her own. In fact she managed it without looking up once or saying a single word to another person.

At last it was the final lesson before the end of school. She was nearly free. Then she realised with **HORROR** that Thursday meant the last lesson of the day was swimming. And Chloe had forgotten her swimming costume. Which meant wearing something from the dreaded **LOST PROPERTY CUPBOARD**.

She delved amongst the options for something to wear, and the best was an all-in-one stripy orange knitted swimsuit from the 1960s. Yes, that was the BEST option, you can but imagine the others. And it had been in the cupboard for so long it even smelt old. **NIGHTMARE!**

Chloe walked at the back of the class group all the way to the leisure centre, dreading what she would look like in the costume. Well, surely this was the worst her day could get?

But ... sadly not. It got worse, almost immediately.

They were only one block away from the pool when up ahead everyone became aware of a ruckus. A man was having an argument just around the corner. He was getting so het up that his gruff voice was becoming higher and higher pitched, until it sounded like a tiny parrot squawking.

Chloe's class was laughing at this man even before they could see him, but she had a dreadful feeling that the voice was only too familiar. Before she could do anything about it, however, the class turned the corner – and there was a bus, with its very tall bus-driver standing on the street, refusing to let a woman with a guitar case aboard.

All the passengers were leaning out of their

windows, booing him, but he continued shouting regardless, his voice getting higher still, his arms flailing so vigorously that people thought he might actually take off!

As Chloe drew closer she saw the thing she was dreading was indeed the case. The bus-driver was Mr Long.

Oh no. Could life get any more embarrassing?

19

HOPE IS REAL

'How can I guarantee that you won't start playing that ghastly thing **ON MY BUS**?' Chloe's dad was spluttering.

'We can't hear you, your voice has gone too high,' called out one of the passengers, and Chloe's class giggled. Mr Long had to slowly bring his voice back to a normal pitch.

'I said …' He cleared his throat. 'I don't want you playing that thing on my bus … plus, I should probably charge you two fares, since that monstrosity will take up a whole seat!'

'We might all enjoy a singsong,' called another passenger. 'She might be good!'

'No music on my bus! I just want to go about my day in PEACE and QUIET. There's a baby on board I don't want crying, and this woman next to it would sing very loudly, since she's as deaf as a post.'

'No, I don't want to go left to the coast,' shouted the lady, pretending she thought that was what Mr Long had said.

'Winding me up ... I said you are as *deaf* as a *post* ...'

'Did he just say I looked like a ghost?!' shouted the old lady. The passengers all howled with *laughter*.

'Will you all just PIPE DOWN?' shouted Mr Long.

Oh dear, this wasn't going well. The saddest thing was, Chloe could remember a time when her dad's bus route used to take him past the school gates – they would wave at each other, and Chloe would *laugh* as he instigated a sing-along for all his passengers.

'The wheels on the bus go round and round ... round and round ... round and round ...'

Even adults would join in merrily on this jolliest of bus rides. But oh how things had changed. Now it seemed Mr Long hated most people and all noise.

As Chloe ducked down at the back of the class crocodile, just wanting to melt into the ground, her classmates immediately started *laughing* and joining in with the jeering passengers. '**Spoilsport!**' called Princess.

The woman with the guitar started playing 'The Sun Has Got His Hat On' in the road right in front of the bus, so it couldn't drive on … and before their teacher knew it, all the schoolchildren had dropped their swimming bags and started dancing in and out of the crowd.

'I said, **PIPE DOWN**!' shouted Mr Long.

At that moment, life did indeed get even more embarrassing for Chloe.

'Hang on? Isn't that … Chloe's dad?' said Benjamin. Unfortunately for Chloe he said it just as there was a break between guitar songs and **EVERYONE** heard. Within seconds the whole class was going 'Can't be', 'Really?', 'That's Chloe Long's dad – how embarrassing!' and they were spinning about looking for her, *laughing* and pointing.

For a moment Chloe froze. Then …

'That's **NOT** my dad!' Chloe found herself shouting as she rushed past them all and into the leisure centre. What she didn't realise as she flung herself into a cubicle and locked the door behind her was that Mr Long had clearly heard her pretend he wasn't her father.

Well, her day couldn't get worse or more embarrassing than THAT, surely? thought Chloe.

It turns out ... it could. The walk of shame from the changing room to the poolside in the ancient orange swimsuit of doom, as it sagged and swayed around her bottom, was one thing.

She sensed everyone's heads around the pool slowly turning to look at this strange vision, and tried to stride stylishly, full of *confidence* in her outfit. Unfortunately her confident walk went into a kind of *bounce* and she found herself tripping over and falling into a stack of pool floats, which all went flying into the pool on top of the class doing their front crawl race. She thought not even Prince Barnie could cause such chaos.

And this was all before her dive attempt in front of the whole class ended up with the swimsuit of doom getting so saggy and weighed down with water that as she swam up to the surface, she realised the costume had not come with her, and was firmly at the bottom of the pool. She was stark naked! It was like the worst kind of nightmare!

Quick thinking as ever, she *dived* back into the stack of pool floats, only just tidied again, to hide herself before Mrs Bucks rushed over with her towel.

Grabbing the towel, she ran back to the changing room, but had time to see that the whole situation had been topped with another layer of embarrassment: Mrs Bucks was wearing the same costume.

She had borrowed one of Mrs Bucks's old costumes.

The class was in hysterics. What an ordeal – IMAGINE! **HORRENDOUS!** MORTIFYING!

Chloe was now rushing home, her hair and clothes sticking to her uncomfortably – she had fled the changing rooms at such speed she hadn't had time to dry herself properly. Any feelings of hope had slowly dwindled throughout what must have been her worst day at school ever ever.

'More like no hope, no hope, there's no **HOPE** …' said Chloe, not realising she was speaking her thoughts out loud.

'Yes dear, do I know you?' said a woman, as Chloe

passed her on the street.

'What?' said Chloe, turning back to face her. She found herself looking at a beautifully *curvy* lady in a bright orange outfit. The woman was *beaming* a wonderful SMILE at her. Almost as big as Godfrey's, Chloe thought. She had RADIANT black skin and hair piled high, tied with a colourful scarf.

'Did you want me?' she said.

'No, I don't think so,' said Chloe, confused.

'It's just, you shouted my name.'

'Did I?' said Chloe. 'What's your name?'

'Hope,' said Hope.

'**Hope!** Your name is Hope? What a lovely name.'

'Thank you, my dear, yes, I like it.'

'Well, I wasn't actually saying your name, I was just saying *hope* wondering if there really was such a thing.'

'Ooooh yes, there's **ALWAYS** hope!' Hope said loudly with a big *laugh*. And she started doing a little bop in the middle of the street and singing in a deep warm voice, 'There's always Hope! There's always Hope!' pointing to herself jokingly.

Three other ladies came over to join their friend,

laughing. 'Oh yes, there's always Hope,' they joined in and Chloe suddenly realised that one of Hope's friends was the lady with the guitar her father wouldn't let on his bus.

'She's always saying "there's always Hope". She's fifty-six, you would have thought she'd have got tired of the joke by now,' said the guitar woman. 'Come on now, ladies, we're going to be late.'

'Nice to meet you, young woman,' said Hope, holding out her hand.

'Nice to meet you too, Hope.' Chloe shook her hand. Then Hope and her three friends bundled into the local hall opposite, *warbling* as they went.

Chloe couldn't resist: she waited a moment, then crossed the road and peered inside. Hope and her three friends were up on a stage, joining a larger group of women. As Chloe watched they started SINGING – they had to be a choir of some sort. But not like one Chloe had ever seen before. It was **AMAZING**.

They were performing a song Chloe thought she recognised called 'Lean on Me', clapping and dancing in unison as they sang. Their voices were so strong that they didn't really need a band, but the lady with the guitar was strumming along, and three men tapped their feet as they played their **UKULELES**. Chloe thought of Trevor and how much he would have *loved* to play for these joy-filled women. She'd only met him last night but already she missed him.

She remembered him asking her to keep hope, and so having met Hope, she turned to head home, this time chanting, 'There IS hope, hope, hope,' with determination.

Things at home were surprisingly calm when she got back. Mrs Long had taken her magazines outside and was lying on an old sunlounger, getting what she thought was more and more beautifully bronzed, but actually was just more and more red as she burnt.

Chloe knew about sun cream and she was only eleven. Why her mother hadn't worked it out yet, she didn't know. She tiptoed out and left some sunscreen by her lounger – she hoped her mum would get the hint. Mr Long was still at work and Gran Gran had left a note to say that she wouldn't be back until late because her friend was taking to her a dinner dance so she would see them all in the morning.

Chloe went upstairs to her room. She felt safer than ever in there tonight as she was sure Godfrey and Hoppy would be coming soon. And she couldn't wait to see them again, even if it meant facing another mission.

Chloe settled down on the floor below her window, her back to the wall, putting the **horrific** school day behind her, and made a start on her homework. This time she would wait patiently. She *hummed* the song Hope's choir had been singing, and tried not to look at the clock.

As dusk arrived at last, she heard Mrs Sweet clattering about in her kitchen. She poked her head out of the window to see if it might be dark enough for Godfrey and Hoppy to arrive.

But just as she did so, guess what? Mr Sweet arrived in his bedroom in just his pants and socks, to get changed for dinner. He waved at her *cheerfully.*

What bad timing! She knew if she hadn't lost her SMILE she would be really *giggling* right now. She ducked back down again and left it a few minutes before she risked raising her head once more. Luckily both Mr and Mrs Sweet were now downstairs in their kitchen, tucking into tea this time. That was TWICE now she had seen Mr Sweet in his PANTS!

Chloe crossed her arms along the windowsill so her chin rested gently on her hand. And waited. Hopefully and patiently. Though she felt tired. Somehow, not speaking to people all day and feeling so empty was more tiring than you would think. She leant her head on her arms and closed her eyes. Within minutes she was fast asleep.

20

SNUFFLEDOM

Chloe woke with a start. It was completely dark and someone was tapping her on the shoulder. Her eyes adjusted to the darkness and she saw the now familiar brim of Godfrey's hat at the window and the shining face of Hoppy as she flitted about beside him. They both SMILED widely at Chloe as she stretched and rubbed her arms where she'd been lying on them.

'Good evening, dear Chloe,' said Godfrey through the open window. 'Sorry to wake you.'

'We need you to come with us, quickly!' Hoppy seemed even more excitable than usual. But Chloe noticed a look of worry in Godfrey's eyes.

'What's wrong?' she asked.

'Come quickly, my girl, no time for questions!' Chloe scrambled for her shoes, still dazed. Godfrey had said no time for questions, but she HAD to pose one she had been desperate to ask.

'Godfrey, did you deliberately make me bump into someone called Hope on the street today?'

'We couldn't possibly say,' winked Godfrey with a grin. 'We were very proud of you today, Chloe. We know how much you hoped and how patiently you waited. Now come on, we've NO time to lose …'

Chloe's stomach churned. Godfrey's new sense of urgency must mean something serious. 'Something bad has happened, hasn't it? I'm scared.'

'*Sand Land* needs us, *Magic Land* needs us. Well, it needs YOU. Now, deep breath and put that fear aside. You were brave yesterday. Tonight you might just have to be that bit braver. We'll go the quickest route.'

Moving quickly, Hoppy reached for Chloe's littlest finger on her right side and Godfrey enveloped her left hand in his own.

'Hold on,' said Hoppy, as Chloe perched on the windowsill, looking out over the dark gardens.

Before she had time to ask how they were travelling, Godfrey launched them into the air like a rocket, shooting straight upwards, all three of them in a circle holding hands. The cul-de-sac disappeared below Chloe faster than ever. This time she wasn't sitting on Godfrey's back or on his eagle wings, her feet were actually dangling in the air beneath her.

She was about to get spooked about the fact that somehow she seemed to be flying too, when it suddenly got lighter. They had shot straight upwards so fast that they had broken through the night clouds way up above and were now in the clearest of starry skies, with puffy clouds at their feet. As they slowed their ascent Godfrey let go of Chloe's hand.

'**Don't let go!**' screamed Chloe.

'Don't worry!' Godfrey pointed downwards. 'See?' Chloe looked down and realised her feet were resting lightly on a **CLOUD**, and it *wasn't* giving way beneath her. It wasn't even giving way beneath Godfrey, despite his immense size.

'No way!'

'Yes way!' said Hoppy, releasing Chloe's finger and hopping over to the next cloud along. 'Come on.'

Chloe took a tentative step – the cloud felt *springy* underfoot. 'Wow. I am actually walking on clouds.'

'Yes you are,' boomed Godfrey.

'We had to travel this way, it's even faster than the eagle,' said Hoppy.

'We need to get to *Sand Land* as quickly as possible. I'll show you just how fast ...' Godfrey bounced off so quickly, Chloe had lost sight of him within seconds.

Hoppy fluttered to Chloe's shoulder and quickly explained how to push off from cloud to cloud. 'Just one little cloud push and you will travel up to a mile or more at a time. Then it's just a case of landing, and pushing off again.' Hoppy made it sound so easy but Chloe was frightened. Jumping a mile through the air – would she be able to breathe, could she be sure the cloud would catch her when she came down, how high would she go?

'No time for any of those thoughts,' said Hoppy. 'You are just going to have to **DO IT**!'

It was so unlike Hoppy to sound this firm that Chloe knew it had to be important.

She took a deep breath, bent her legs and ... pushed off. W H O O O S S S S H H H !

The first jump was the scariest – the wind whistled in her ears, her stomach *flipped* and the clouds beneath seemed to hurtle towards her at a terrifying rate as she began to drop. But as her foot touched down, the cloud seemed to clasp it so gently, she felt as light as a feather. After that, it didn't take long for the sensation of flying through the air to hook Chloe in. And with each leap she got better at it, travelling further every time. Now it didn't feel like taking scary massive leaps. It felt like FREEDOM.

If only pavements at home were like this, Chloe thought. She would try to see them like that from now on. Friendly concrete supporting her little feet on their way. She doubted they would ever speak to her, though, like the clouds began to now. Yes, the clouds SPOKE! All lovely encouraging words like '*Happy travels*', '*Travel safe*', '*Nearly there*', '*Happy cloud bouncing*'. There was no way a pavement in the real world would ever say, '*Happy pavement walking*'!

Chloe and Hoppy arrived at what looked like the top of a big *whirlpool* in the clouds.

'Godfrey's made us a cloud slide so that we can get down to *Sand Land* at speed. Ready?'

'I think so,' said Chloe. But all her earlier fears came flooding back – what would she be faced with when she got down there? What was all this urgency?

'Remember your courage,' Godfrey's voice

echoed up the cloud slide.

'DO IT!' Hoppy was whispering, but with a determined energy. Chloe bounced on the spot to get herself going, then leapt towards the *spiralling* hole.

The cloud slide was exactly like a HELTER-SKELTER but made from soft cloud. Luckily Godfrey had made it wide so the turns weren't too tight. It had to be such a long cloud slide to get all the way down to the beach that they would have got way too dizzy otherwise. As it was, it was like going down a very long, very wide corkscrew with puffy edges.

'Wheeeeeeeeee!' Hoppy squealed in Chloe's ear as they glided downwards. And seconds later they flew out of the end of the slide and bumped bottom first on to the familiar sandy beach. The minute they landed the slide whisked back up into the sky and disappeared into the clouds with a friendly, '*Thanks for travelling by cloud!*'

Godfrey was ahead of them, talking to King Sandy and Queen Sandra. They all wore serious expressions on their faces and Godfrey kept looking around as if he was expecting something or someone to arrive. Chloe was sure the Shadow Bandits must be coming back any minute, perhaps with another shadow vine, perhaps with something even worse. Why else would Godfrey and Hoppy have rushed her here?

She noticed too that **Sand Land** didn't quite feel the same as before. The air was muggier and dirtier somehow. The green tufts in the sand dunes were now looking black and wilted. The sand had lost its sparkle and the sea was murkier – in some patches you couldn't even see the sand at the bottom of it. Chloe wondered if the rest of *Magic Land* had been similarly affected. The look on Godfrey's face told her it probably had.

Hoppy and Chloe curtseyed at King Sandy and Queen Sandra as they approached them. The royal couple was watching their crab cavaliers performing military drills on the sand outside their castle. The crabs were just like the ones Chloe was used to at home, except they were several times the size, as big as large dogs in fact. Prince Barnie was leading one of the groups of crab cavaliers: 'left, left, left, left' (the crabs made strong fighters and had great pincher movements, though they could of course only move sideways) but he sneaked a wave to Chloe, despite his equally serious expression. Chloe waved back – even in the circumstances she felt a small *happy* lurch inside her at seeing Barnie again.

'Welcome back,' said King Sandy.

'It's good to see you again,' added Queen Sandra.

'I have *told* you about doing that,' said King Sandy wearily to his wife. 'I am meant to do all the talking.' He turned back to Chloe. 'Thank you for your part in our battle yesterday—'

'Yes, thank you very much, you were very brave …' interrupted Queen Sandra.

'What have I just said? I am trying to maintain my status as king here … Oh, *clicking crabs*, I give up!' The king bowed hurriedly at Chloe and headed back towards his cavaliers. The walrus trumpeters gave him a quick **FANFARE** as he passed.

Chloe looked around and saw that Godfrey and Hoppy had gone on ahead to the taverna, in deep discussion. Suddenly Godfrey started to grow, up and **up,** until he was the greatest height you could imagine – he had to be the size of a skyscraper. Chloe realised this meant he could see for miles. Seconds later, he returned to his normal size to report to Hoppy. There was something about the way he kept glancing over at Chloe as well that made her stomach plunge ...

Chloe was about to catch up with them, to ask what they were keeping from her – she was ready to know what was going on now – when she felt a gentle tap on her shoulder. It was Prince Barnacle. He bowed, she curtseyed.

'Hello,' he said.

'Hello,' she said back, suddenly feeling a bit shy. 'Please excuse me, but I have to go to the taverna. I think there is something really wrong.' She headed off and Barnie followed, concerned for his new friend.

Chloe turned around but weirdly couldn't see him.

'I'm here.' He sprang up in front of her, giving her a fright. 'Sorry, so sorry, I tripped over that washed-up jellyfish ... sorry ...' he said, brushing off the sand from his face. If there was anything to trip on, Prince Barnacle would find it.

By the time Chloe and Barnie (having tripped up twice more on the way) reached the taverna, Godfrey was describing what he had seen. And it wasn't good.

'The Shadow Bandits are amassing a huge army on the mountain-top and they look stronger and more solid than ever. There's no colour left up there, nothing living at all. It's just … **BLANK**.'

Chloe gulped and dared to ask the worst. 'Could you … could you see the lakes and the river and King Percy and the dolphins? Are they all right …?' She trailed off as Godfrey shook his head sadly.

'Oh my girl, I'm sorry, but I couldn't see anything – it was all in shadow.'

'It's my fault, isn't it? I wasn't enough to save things at home, and now I have ruined my *Magic Land*.' Chloe flopped down hopelessly. It made her feel even sadder when she noticed she was sitting on the same chair that lovely Trevor had sat on only twenty-four hours earlier – another friend she had lost since losing her **SMILE**. 'I can't even feel *love* any more, I don't care enough for anyone, except you, of course. I mean, back home. I just feel … numb and … not here.'

Godfrey knelt down in front of Chloe's chair and for the first time since she had met him he looked genuinely worried. 'This is **NOT** your fault. But things are more severe here than I thought. We know you are our hero, Chloe, but we're not sure you are ready yet. Not when the shadows have turned out in such force already. Time is not on our side.'

Chloe looked from Godfrey's wide-eyed concern to Hoppy, who had come to sit comfortingly on her shoulder. She felt like such a failure. There was a silence, and it felt like none of them knew what to do.

But at that moment, Prince Barnie leant over and whispered something in Godfrey's giant ear.

'What did you say?' Chloe's giant friend whipped his head round in surprise, so fast Barnie had to duck out of the way of his hat, for once not falling over.

'Permission to take her to *Snuffledom*?' said Prince Barnie, this time for everyone to hear.

'Oh, of course! Good thinking, sir.' Godfrey leapt to his feet. 'Permission granted, Your Highness.' Godfrey bowed deeply, then leant down and patted the prince on the back. 'And well done, **well done**.'

Prince Barnie *flushed* delightedly until he was the colour of sunburn.

Godfrey nudged Chloe, which she took to be a hint that she should curtsey, so she did. Though she had no idea why and what the sudden change of mood was about. Prince Barnie bowed to her in return.

'It's the perfect idea,' Godfrey continued, bowing

again to the prince, who bowed back. Chloe curtseyed, just in case she was meant to.

'One of the best ideas ever, probably,' Hoppy chattered.

'Well, thank you,' said the prince.

'My pleasure, Your Majesty, sir,' said Hoppy, bowing midair. Prince Barnie bowed back. And then to Chloe, who curtseyed back **AGAIN**.

'Off you go!' urged Godfrey. 'No time to lose.'

'Excuse me!' said Chloe loudly. 'No one has asked **ME** if I want to go to this place. What is *Snuffledom*? And why am I going there now?'

'Oh, don't ruin the surprise, Prince Barnacle, sir, it will be better for her just to see it without trying to describe it first,' tinkled Hoppy.

'What happens if I don't want to go? I mean, no offence, Prince Barnie,' Chloe curtseyed again, 'but it sounds a bit … *flu-like.*'

'Ummm, well … you will be safe and have fun with me, if, umm, I may be so bold,' said Prince Barnie and he bowed again at her, so she had to curtsey back yet again. There was far too much bowing and curtseying going on here!

Chloe tugged Godfrey's long coat until he bent back down to her, and she whispered, 'Fun? Now? But shouldn't we be preparing for something ... what about the Shadow Bandits? I thought we had no time to lose?'

Godfrey looked Chloe in the eye. 'You can trust us. *Snuffledom* is where you need to go. You won't be long, and we'll be right here keeping an eye on things. It's the right thing to do.'

Chloe took a deep breath. 'Nothing to lose!'

'That's my girl.'

'Please ...' Prince Barnie stepped forward and took her hand, escorting her away from the beach, along a path beyond the sand dunes and into the once green, now lank and greying hills.

But before long they were climbing so high, they were in a place where the colour was unaffected. There were bright striped fields – literally striped, with red, yellow and green grasses and flowers. There were orchards, where the trees were laden with everything from grapes the size of melons, to melons the size of beach balls – and then, to Chloe's surprise, a giant beach ball tree, so you could pluck one before a trip to the beach. Ordinarily Chloe would have asked to stop and spend time amongst the trees, sampling their delights (especially when she passed a boiled sweet tree – **IMAGINE!**) but not today – she let Barnie lead her onwards towards *Snuffledom*, whatever it might be. It still sounded very odd to her.

Finally, just as Chloe was beginning to feel out of breath from all the hill climbing, they turned a corner so the sea was lost from sight and there in the craggy cliff face was a large tunnel entrance. Like what you might see for a road or train line that routes through a mountain.

'*Snuffledom* is through here,' said Barnie. 'Ready?'

Chloe nodded a little apprehensively, and they stepped into the cool shade of the tunnel. Their footsteps echoed around them as they marched into the darkness, but after only a short while it started to get lighter and seconds later they emerged into sunlight and something so brilliant that Chloe could never have believed it possible.

You see, *Snuffledom* was a land entirely inhabited by baby animals, specifically tiny, furry, cuddly, climby,

SNUFFLY puppies and cubs. Of every animal kind you can think of. There were MEADOWS of puppies of every breed. Tiny little waddling chihuahuas, as well as bounding Alsatian pups. And just imagine the rolling balls of fluff that were the husky puppies.

There were fields of bear cubs, bumbling about endearingly. Woodlands full of wily wolf pups and fox cubs. Large sandy areas for the tumbling tiger cubs. A pool of barking seal pups. And a snowy ice mound of naughty polar bear cubs.

Everything was soft. Everything was fluffy, and it was a place that would melt anyone's heart. The valley echoed with the sound of the animals yipping and yapping to one another *playfully*.

Prince Barnie smiled as he looked at Chloe's face. Her mouth was completely ajar! She couldn't SMILE, though Barnie thought that maybe her face was the closest he'd seen to SMILING since he first met her. But Chloe was sure there had been a mistake. She adored her new friend, but she was pretty sure he had got things a little wrong.

'Oh, Barnie,' she breathed eventually. 'It's PERFECT – but we can't stay here. Not with everything that's happening back in **Sand Land**. This can't be right. Shouldn't we be going somewhere for me to … I don't know, toughen up … or train, or something?'

'Nope.' Barnie shook his head firmly. 'As Godfrey said, this is exactly where we are meant to be – I promise.'

Chloe knew Godfrey would simply say, as ever, 'Trust me', so that was what she was going to do. 'Can we … can we play with them?'

'OH YES!' said Barnie. 'They are all tame and friendly.'

'In that case …' Chloe took off for the nearest field and within seconds she was tussling in the long grass of one of the meadows with puppies all around her. Then she dashed over to slide down the snowy piles with the polar bear cubs and land in a tangled heap with them at the bottom. She stroked the fluffy bear cubs – their fur like the softest fleece you could ever imagine touching, and their eyes so dark and deep they seemed full of kindness and wisdom.

Gradually she began to feel her emptiness ease. And when an adorable seal pup leapt out of its pool and slid up alongside her to lie in the warm sun, her heart did a sudden *hiccup*. She rubbed its tummy comfortingly before it leapt back into the pool, turning somersaults in the water, and felt nothing but *love* for it.

Barnie spent most of his time with the wolf pups and bear cubs, trying to look manly, but Chloe noticed that whenever he thought she wasn't looking he rushed to play with the tiny chihuahua puppies!

She lay there with the pups and cubs crawling all over her, snuggling against her side, licking her and nudging her with their little wet, cold noses, their whole bodies wriggling as their tails wagged maniacally, showing nothing but *love*.

'It's very nice not having to be all princely when I'm with you,' Barnie blurted out suddenly.

'Then come and play with this tiny sausage-dog puppy, I know you want to!' Chloe said. She understood, because spending time in *Snuffledom* with her new friend had made her realise how amazing it was for her not to have to hide her lack of SMILE, to be just herself, exactly how she was feeling at that moment.

She missed her school friends so very much, but perhaps she needn't be without them. She and Barnie were becoming the best of friends despite her lack of SMILE – if she gave Hannah, Benjamin and Ruby the chance, might they be just as understanding …?

As she stroked the tiny sausage pup, her *love* for her friends, her beloved Chaos Crew, flooded back in an overwhelming wave. She thought of her grumpy parents, and as she looked into the melting eyes of one of the Labrador puppies, her *love* whooshed back for them too. And for all her world back home, as she continued to play in the wonders of *Snuffledom*.

At the same moment, waiting at the tunnel entrance, Godfrey, with Hoppy perched on the brim of his hat, was bracing himself. Above them an army of near-solid Shadow Bandits had gathered on the mountain-top, ready to attack while Chloe's heart was mending …

They knew how important she was to *Magic Land* – and now they were going to strike. As the skies darkened and a storm rumbled, they prepared to swoop. And Godfrey and Hoppy prepared themselves to protect their Chloe – to the death, if necessary.

21

DARKNESS COMES

Godfrey was positioned in the *Snuffledom* tunnel entrance, bigger and brighter than he had ever been before. Some of the Shadow Bandits that raged above him now had large, dark, bat-like wings and they began to whirl downwards in an attack formation, spinning like tornadoes and making a horrible hissing sound as they fell.

One by one the bandits flung themselves at Godfrey – and because they were no longer insubstantial shadows but had taken on a thicker, almost muscular form, Godfrey found he couldn't blow or bat them away as before. He reached into one of his pockets and pulled out an impossibly long, glowing *sword* which he swung about, and where it connected with the shadows they squealed and shrivelled up midair.

But there were so many of them and they kept coming; slowly breaking through his defence. When they did, they didn't bite or fight – they simply swept their dark wings over Godfrey's arm, or hand, or body, and the colour seemed to seep from his skin and clothes. There was a terrible bitter smell, like something burning. At one point Hoppy took off from Godfrey's hat, ready to help, but the giant shouted, '**No!**', caught the edge of her dress and placed her safely into one of his pockets. What chance did someone as small as Hoppy have against these shadowy fiends, now they were so strong?

As his fist and sword swung, he knocked, punched, sliced and kicked the Shadow Bandits away. But as they grew in numbers and strength they began to attack in groups, smothering Godfrey in thick black smoke as he fought back. Godfrey seemed to disappear altogether into the darkness … until a giant **GOLDEN EAGLE** burst out and swept clear into the air. It was eagle-Godfrey, now ready to attack in earnest from the air. His great beak snapped shut on shadow after shadow, disintegrating them on the spot, and his strong wings disrupted their attacking patterns.

As eagle-Godfrey attacked from the air, Hoppy zipped back and forth between any Shadow Bandits that were closer to the ground. Godfrey might have wanted her to hide away, but there was no way she wasn't going to help him.

Besides, she didn't need to fight to come to his aid. She had other powers. All she had to do was *whisper* – in the ears of the seething shadow forms – and they would thin and DISAPPEAR on the spot. We all know how much it can hurt when people say horrible things to us. Well, an evil Shadow Bandit with darkness inside instead of a heart can shrivel on hearing the opposite – how strong Chloe was, how her *love* was growing back bigger than ever, how much good she was going to do, how beloved and special her *Magic Land* was, and how all her friends who lived there were on her side. It made the shadows sick.

But their fight got harder as more Shadow Bandits kept coming – from the air on wings and streaming down the mountain paths. The sky darkened until it seemed almost like night, and the flowers on the highest peaks drooped their petals now like snow or ash. The darker it got, the more POWERFUL the shadow beings seemed; and the more powerful they were, the more **darkness** they brought.

Godfrey knew Chloe was special, but the ferocity of this attack was more than even he had expected. He and Hoppy were becoming weak and exhausted. If there was such a thing as *limping* flying, that's what they were doing. They were not going to win this battle without help. Godfrey hadn't wanted to risk anyone else getting involved and possibly hurt, but now he didn't have a choice.

As if they'd heard him, suddenly there was a rhythmic 'click, click, click' sound and the Royal *Sand Land* Family's crab cavaliers appeared around the corner, ready to attack. Riding the two biggest and foremost crabs were the king and queen themselves, with King Sandy ROARING instructions until his reddening face looked like it might explode.

The crabs began to wield their dangerous-looking pincers through the air, snapping them shut on shadow arms and wings and weapons. The shadows exploded into puffs of black smoke whenever the crabs made contact, and the air thickened even further, making everyone cough and splutter.

'Crab troops – quick march, left, left, left, left, left, left,' Queen Sandra commanded calmly as she spotted a fresh wave of shadows approaching.

'Er, **I** do the commanding,' retorted the king, before realising she was spot-on and much better at this than he was, and given the circumstances it might be best if he just kept quiet and followed her lead. Why don't I always do that, he thought.

For a moment it looked like the additional troops might make the difference. Then Hoppy suddenly squeaked, 'Godfrey, **WATCH OUT**!' But he hadn't heard her or seen what she was warning him about. Flying at great speed towards eagle-Godfrey was an enormous new shadow form pelting towards him from behind. Before Hoppy could reach her great friend to tell him to turn around, the giant shadow drew a long, smoking black blade from its scabbard and thrust it straight into Godfrey's side.

For a second, everything froze, and then the eagle began to plummet from the sky towards the beach far, far below.

But even as he fell, Godfrey caught Hoppy's eye. Instantly the look of horror on her tiny face was transformed. 'Of *course*!' she tweeted, z o o m i n g after him through the air.

By the time Godfrey's body thumped to the – thankfully soft – sandy ground below he was back to his giant self. Blackened feathers fell to the floor around him, but he was once more in his trousers and many-pocketed long coat, though lying fragile and weak in a way Hoppy had never seen him before. She took a second to check he was still breathing before she darted into his smallest pocket, where she wriggled about for a moment before emerging bottom-first and holding the pocket open to the air.

Nothing happened at first, but then a small, brightly glowing dot appeared and zigzagged into the sky. It shone out strongly against the darkness all around. Seconds later another followed, then another and **another,** until there was a constant flow of flickering lights streaming into the sky above, like a string of fairy lights, only this one was alive. It was Godfrey's collection of fireflies and glow-worms, of course. The one he used to guide himself in to Chloe's window.

Everywhere they went they brought *light*, and the shadows pulled back, hissing as if they'd been scalded, or flapped about chaotically, as if they'd been blinded.

The Shadow Bandits began to retreat as one, flapping or marching back up into the hills with the biggest, sword-bearing shadow at the front.

They weren't beaten by any means, but the light had stopped them temporarily. And it couldn't have come sooner for poor, battered Godfrey and Hoppy and the crab troops.

As silence fell over *Sand Land* once more, Hoppy joined Godfrey on the beach, exhausted. The crab cavaliers started slowly back down the hills, trying to ignore the blackened patches of nothingness all around, where colour and life would normally be. King Sandy and Queen Sandra joined Hoppy and Godfrey on the beach, catching their breath.

The silence was deafening. They didn't know what to say to each other. They all knew this could be the beginning of the end.

22

THE BIG BATTLE

Chloe could happily stay in *Snuffledom* for ever, but she knew Godfrey and Hoppy would want to know how much better she was feeling. And they had been so worried when they'd arrived in *Magic Land* earlier – she owed it to them to get back and see what she could do to help. Maybe she could be as strong as they needed her to be, after all.

'Thank you so much for bringing me here, Prince Barnie.' She curtseyed, suddenly feeling shy again as she understood how kind he had been.

Barnie bowed. 'My pleasure. I am so glad you liked it.'

Chloe curtseyed again. It seemed only polite – and he *was* a prince after all. But Barnie shook his head. 'I think maybe we can stop all the bowing and curtseying now! We are friends. Oh and umm … You may be having a difficult time but you are still really *lovely* to be with. You are so brave and fun and interesting and creative and … well … you know …' He trailed off, embarrassed.

Chloe felt her cheeks flush. She nodded her thanks, before spinning round and heading for the tunnel entrance. 'Last one down the hill has to get the drinks!' she called over her shoulder before starting to run. She ran all the way back through the hills towards the dunes, eager to tell Godfrey and Hoppy all about *Snuffledom*, slipping down the slopes at such speed she ended up tumbling and *somersaulting* down most of them.

Barnie galloped behind her, trying to keep up. 'Chloe PANT PANT, hang on PANT PANT, it's not that I'm out of breath or anything, I'm actually very fit, all that soldier drilling, you know PANT PANT, but—'

'Godfrey, Hoppy,' she yelled JUBILANTLY as she hit the beach at last and began to run towards them. 'I feel it. I feel *love* again. *Snuffledom* was AMAZING and I think … I think I'm ready for anything and …'

Chloe's voice trailed off as she took in the state of Godfrey and Hoppy. Godfrey's usually bright, beaming face was ashen and serious, his hat was askew, and the patches on his pockets were no longer all the colours of the rainbow, they were torn and grey. Worse than that, despite his great size he seemed shrunken somehow.

In his hand he cradled Hoppy's tiny form – she was sitting up but her face was as white as her dress. Chloe looked about and saw what she had missed in her haste to get back to the beach – the patches of grey and nothingness all around, the exhausted crab troops being tended to by the king and queen themselves. Barnie rushed towards them to help.

'Wha-what happened?' Chloe wailed. 'Was it the Shadow Bandits again? It must have been. And it's all my fault for not being ready to help, isn't it?'

Godfrey pulled Chloe to his side and gave her a tight hug.

'Chloe – you're not to blame. And I am so glad *Snuffledom* has helped you to feel stronger – that was Barnie's intention and why I wanted you to go. But you're right that we have been fighting to protect *Magic Land* once and for all, and without you at our side we have not been powerful enough. You need to be ready now. We've no time left – you're going to need all your courage, talent and strength for what's coming. You can do it, Chloe, WE know you can. But do **YOU**?'

A sudden shudder went through *Sand Land*, like an earthquake. The very sand beneath their feet trembled. Everyone was rooted to the spot. What was happening?

A loud stamping began and suddenly it was clear what had caused the shudder. At the top of the dunes above the long stretch of beach, as far as the eye could see, was a line of the dreaded Shadow Bandits. Even more of them than before. They were marching with such anger and force that sand kicked into the air all around them, creating sandstorms that mingled with their shadowiness and turned to choking smoke. It spun down the beach towards them, making Chloe's nose crinkle and her throat scratch.

'Can't we just blow them away again?' asked Chloe desperately.

'They've become too strong,' said Godfrey grimly.

'What are we going to do?' Chloe panicked. The noise of the sandstorm was already almost deafening so she had to **SHOUT** to be heard.

'Quick, before we are blinded by the sand and smoke …' Godfrey morphed into his majestic eagle form once more. But for the first time Chloe could see the strain in his face as he did so, almost as if it was painful. And he didn't stop there – once he'd reached his eagle form he began to grow, and grow and grow, until he was so big he seemed to take up the whole beach.

Chloe nearly cried when she saw how damaged his beautiful wings were – some of his most colourful feathers were grey and singed, or missing altogether, and his tail feathers drooped weakly. But the gleam in his eyes was as warm and determined as ever. As Chloe watched, he stretched one wing out close to the ground and everyone fell to their bellies and slid underneath it. It was quieter under there, with protection from the sandstorm, and won them some time to think.

Chloe lay there on her stomach, listening to the *eerie* screech of the storm outside. All around her she could feel the others staring at her and the weight of their expectations. Despite what she had said after her visit to *Snuffledom*, she was suddenly terrified.

What could SHE, an ordinary girl without a SMILE, do against such a force of evil? How could she **SAVE** them all?

She could feel herself starting to panic when she felt something nudge her hand gently. She looked down to see Hoppy crawling limply on to her palm. The little bird-girl seemed smaller than ever. Her wings were crumpled and her hair looked floppy and limp for the first time, but she looked up at Chloe and began to *sing* – she had the prettiest, tiniest, tinkliest singing voice Chloe had ever heard.

'What are you doing? What is there to *sing* about right now?!' Chloe asked.

'The shadows hate it when we *sing*. Their power lessens in the face of anything happy or joyful. You should *sing* too, Chloe. Remember Hope's choir.'

'No – I can't, I'm ... I'm too scared ...' But all around her the others were beginning to join in with Hoppy as she took up her song once more. The crabs clicked their claws in time, and the king and queen and Barnie sang along, though in their case, not necessarily in tune. Chloe realised it was the same song that Hope's choir had been *singing*. Hesitatingly at first, and then with more strength, Chloe joined in. 'Lean on me … when you're not strong.' And surprisingly she did begin to feel calmer.

As if sensing this, Godfrey stuck his eagle head under his own wing. 'They're nearly upon us, Chloe – are you ready?' he squawked. 'Remember how SPECIAL you are – it's up to you now … but we will be with you every step of the way.'

And with that, eagle-Godfrey swooped off to try and knock down as many of the enemy as possible.

Chloe and her friends scrambled to their feet, still singing, and faced the dark army – the beach and skies were so thick with them it was like a solid wall of shadows. There was no colour left anywhere, the air was as thick as soup and hard to breathe, and the rasping noise of the Shadow Bandits' movement made Chloe want to clap her hands over her ears and disappear.

But she couldn't.

These mighty furious warriors with dark hearts were here for Chloe and her *Magic Land.* She had to step up.

As Chloe's determination grew, as her voice grew

stronger, the anger of the darkness increased.

There was a shifting sensation amongst the bandits, and the largest shadow form pushed its way to the front. This was the same bandit that had stuck Godfrey with its blackened sword – a sword it still brandished almost laughingly, although the creatures didn't seem to have mouths as far as Chloe could see. The shadows' leader, as Chloe took this thing to be, raised its empty hand and pointed ominously at her, before taking a spinning leap and beginning to whirl across the sand between them. The other bandits followed as one.

'Tell us what to do, Chloe!' yelled Barnie.

'But I … what … er …' was all Chloe could manage.

'I know what you're still thinking,' chirruped Hoppy. 'But you're not just about your **SMILE**, Chloe Long, you are caring too, and creative and brave and fun. And above all, you have an **IMAGINATION** beyond compare – just look around you at *Magic Land* for the proof.'

'But how does that help?' Chloe moaned. 'I still don't know what to do.'

'You **DO** know what to do. You must **DRAW** your weapons …'

'What weapons?' said Chloe, desperately scanning about her.

'Draw your weapons,' whispered Hoppy again weakly.

'Draw them …' said Chloe to herself thoughtfully. 'Draw my weapons, as in …?' She suddenly realised what she needed to do. But she needed more time to do it.

'Barnie – I need a distraction – **QUICK**!'

'Right. Got it. Leave it with us. On it. Er …' Barnie sprinted off in the direction of the Sand Castle. King Sandy gave Chloe a hasty bow before leaping on to the back of his biggest crab and, Queen Sandra beside him, they urged their crab troops into a line and advanced on the shadow army.

Chloe tipped Hoppy carefully into her pocket, then ran down to the wetter sand at the shoreline, fell to her knees and frantically started *drawing* in the sand. Prince Barnacle emerged from the Sand Castle with the castle walruses in a long line behind him. They were blowing jubilantly on their trumpets and flip-flapping into battle behind their prince, even if he did look terrified. All of this was distracting the shadows and winning Chloe the time she needed.

She started with horses, but not just any old horses: horses for battle, with knights on their backs carrying **GIANT** swords. She drew as many as she could in as much detail as she could manage, so they were big and strong and menacing. It was as if all the drawing of horses she used to do when she was younger had been preparation for this very moment. She stood up, snapped her eyes shut and ... **IMAGINED**.

Just like before, the sand rippled and rumbled, and when Chloe opened her eyes there were rows and rows of sand-coloured, snorting, pawing battle horses, dancing on the beach, striking their hooves impatiently. They were **MAGNIFICENT** – Chloe couldn't believe they were really there, standing in front of her. Their sandy flanks gleamed warmly and their dark eyes stared at Chloe, as did the helmeted troops on their backs. Chloe nodded and the troops kicked the horses' sides, galloping off into battle. Seconds later, Chloe heard the clash of sword on sword behind her. But she didn't even have time to look round. Her knees were soaked, her back ached, but she kept drawing. She knew the others couldn't hold the shadows off for ever without her help. And she couldn't ignore the fact that all around her more and more shells were turning grey; lifeless, colourless fish were beginning to wash up on to the beach. She hadn't done enough yet.

On and on Chloe drew. Slowly but surely a vast sand-horse army was created, lined up along the beach beside her. When at last she thought she could draw no more she turned around and screamed, 'GO **WIN** THIS BATTLE, GO, GO, **GO**!' From her pocket she thought she heard a small, Hoppy-sized cheer.

As the newest sand horses mobilised, heading towards the shadow army, it was clear they outnumbered the bandits two to one. Chloe gasped with relief. There was no way that the shadows on the ground would win against Chloe's mighty horses, with their speed, power and knightly weaponry.

At that moment, Barnie galloped up on the back of one of Chloe's sand horses. 'Keep going, Chloe, KEEP GOING!' he yelled.

Chloe looked up. She now needed to turn her attentions to the battle taking place in the air. Godfrey

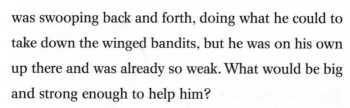

was swooping back and forth, doing what he could to take down the winged bandits, but he was on his own up there and was already so weak. What would be big and strong enough to help him?

Chloe looked down into Hoppy's eyes and Hoppy just had the energy to whisper what Chloe was just about to think. 'A **DRAGON** ...'

'YES. A dragon. Barnie ... help me,' said Chloe. 'I need to draw the biggest dragon EVER.'

'It's the one thing I *can* draw,' said Barnie, dismounting his horse. 'I will run far down the beach and start at the tail, you start the head here, and we'll meet in the middle.'

Chloe clapped her hands. 'You're *brilliant*, Barnie! Yes!'

The prince beamed so widely a nearby Shadow Bandit spontaneously combusted. Chloe and Barnie kept singing to keep their strength up and the bandits away from them as they drew. Eagle-Godfrey needed back-up, and QUICK.

Chloe began to *draw*. Barnie did the same from where he had run to. It didn't take Chloe long to carve out the dragon's long neck, spiked back and angry face. Barnie met her part-way along the beach, having given their fire-breathing weapon a fat tail – perfect for swiping with – and four strong legs and clawed feet. Together they added two **MAGNIFICENT** wings.

'Close your eyes, Barnie – imagine it *real*!' Chloe closed her eyes and imagined a real-life dragon, stomping up and down the *Sand Land* beach, snorting fire into the air. When she opened her eyes that was exactly what she saw. She didn't even have to say anything – the dragon bent its head briefly in her direction, then leapt into the sky with a near-deafening **ROAR**.

The battle above began in earnest. As the sand dragon swept overhead, eagle-Godfrey found his second wind and together they began to beat back the winged Shadow Bandits. There were shrieks as their dark forms were swiped at by sharp talons, a massive beak and bright, hot flames. There were loud **THWACKS** of heavy wings as Godfrey and the sand dragon threw themselves into the shadows, over and over again, screaming in pain as their colour and *light* were sucked from them, but they were driving onwards nonetheless, determined to win this battle.

Chloe could hardly bear to watch, but she couldn't look away either. She knew she had drawn the biggest army she could, and that nothing could beat the size of the dragon she and Barnie had created. She dared to count: the greatness of the dragon was working and the number of shadows was diminishing, above *and* below. Rather than fighting back, the weakened bandits began to shrink away from the flames, hissing and shrivelling up like autumn leaves until they disappeared altogether, or POPPING like balloons as Godfrey's sharp beak skewered them. The shadows on the ground were being trampled into the sand by Chloe's army of horses. But Chloe was struggling to see the biggest of the Shadow Bandits, the one who had stabbed Godfrey, and she knew they needed to defeat it to win this battle once and for all.

Just at that thought, out of the smudged clouds that very Shadow Bandit appeared. It was even bigger now and its wings seemed to take up the whole horizon, while its sword of smoke had doubled in size and seemed to suck light into itself as it swung side to side. Before Chloe could even scream, the bandit leader – which Chloe assumed it must be – threw itself on to Godfrey's back and pulled the eagle's wings into his sides. With one flick of its long fingers, a thick rope of blackness unravelled from its hand and wrapped itself tightly around the great bird. Tied up like this, the already weakened Godfrey began to plummet from the sky, heading straight for the waters below.

Seconds later he splashed down.

He did not re-emerge.

Without pausing for breath, the sand dragon *dived* in after him.

Everyone turned to face Chloe. Barnie broke the silence. 'Chloe, what do we do?'

23

THE FINAL DRAW

Chloe knew Barnie had just spoken but she was **TRANSFIXED**, unable to respond. With Godfrey gone, the shadow general had turned its empty gaze on her, and it was headed her way. Fast. And as it approached, it was puffing out new shadows – small at first but growing to full-size within seconds. So this was where they were all coming from … At this rate, they would be back to full strength within minutes.

Whatever happened now, Chloe knew the battle to save *Magic Land* was about to be won or lost for good – by her. She had to destroy the bandit leader, or they would never win. She didn't have time to be frightened. She dropped to her knees one last time and started drawing.

She drew her sand lion again, only this time his shoulders were even broader and stronger and his smile was not a friendly one – instead his teeth were

She swung up on to his back, checked that Hoppy was safely in her pocket, leant forward and whispered in her sand lion's ear, 'CHARGE!'

long and pointed, his claws were sharp as *knives*, and his eyes smouldered darkly, even in the sand. The beach shook slightly each time he **THUMPED** a heavy paw to the ground.

In other circumstances, Chloe might have felt a little afraid of him, but not today. She swung up on to his back, checked that Hoppy was safely in her pocket, leant forward and whispered in her sand lion's ear, '**CHARGE!**'

He took off like a rocket – Chloe could feel the power in his haunches as he thundered across the beach, head to head with the bandit leader.

In turn, the giant shadow creature half-ran, half-flew across the sand towards them. It was like a medieval joust. Except in a joust both sides would usually have a weapon, whereas all Chloe had was the *shell* she'd been drawing with, clutched tightly in her hand.

Her mind was racing – what was going to happen next, would her lion fight for her, what if she came into contact with the shadow itself, would she sizzle and burn like Godfrey and the others, what could **SHE**, just a schoolgirl, do to stop all this? But she forced herself to silence these unhelpful doubts. Her new friends and *Magic Land* were relying on her – even if she died trying, she would face this shadowy horror down.

'**Courage**,' she chanted to herself. '**Courage**. **HOPE**. *Love*.' In her pocket she heard Hoppy join in squeakily. '**Courage**. **HOPE**. *Love*.' She leant forward and whispered in her beautiful lion's ear: '**Courage**. **HOPE**. *Love*.'

Over and over she said it. Louder and louder. And just as they drew almost level with the blackened form, the smell of sulphur thick in the air around her, she looked up, fixed her gaze fearlessly into the black hole eyes of the shadow leader, and shouted it again, then sang it. Sang as loudly as she could, Hoppy joining in. '**Courage**. **HOPE**. *Love*.'

To Chloe's amazement the huge, evil creature cringed. Her sand lion reared up and roared a mighty lion roar, then snapped his jaws shut around the shadow's head. There was a soft pop, the rest of its dark body disappeared into *nothingness* and the very few remaining shadows thinned and disappeared as one.

THE BATTLE WAS OVER! For good this time.

'Click, click, click,' cheered the crab troops as the king and queen dismounted quickly and ran down the beach to pull a bedraggled but alive eagle-Godfrey out of the waves and back on to the beach.

Chloe let out a breath that she didn't even realise she'd been holding.

Her sand horses reared **VICTORIOUSLY**, their knights clinging to their backs, before galloping off to line the top of the sand dunes where the bandit army had stood what seemed like days earlier, though it hadn't even been hours. Their sandy backs glinted in the *sun* just starting to peek through the dark clouds, and it seemed to Chloe that they all looked at her for a moment and nodded.

As they galloped triumphantly back down the dunes towards her, they dissipated into the sand, until nothing was left.

Sand showered Chloe from above as the **DRAGON** did the same and, beside her, her lion gave her cheek one almighty, sand-raspy lick before he too disappeared in a puff. Their work was done.

Chloe began to look around. Though the others

seemed to be celebrating and there was no doubt the battle was won, *Sand Land* looked terrible and Chloe assumed the rest of *Magic Land* was the same.

On the beach, the usually golden sand looked dirty and grey; all the plants and trees for as far as she could see were burnt-looking, where the angry footsteps of the Shadow Bandits had passed. Even the sea looked muddy and the few fish she could just make out were the colour of ash. The monkey ropes in the trees had been torn down, the taverna had just one wall standing, and while the Sand Castle was still there, it was certainly war-torn too. Two turrets were broken, their top sections scattered on the ground below. The moat waters looked oily and the pretty shells and bits of glass that usually adorned the walls were either shattered or dull and colourless.

The effects of the battle were clear to see.

Godfrey, in his ordinary giant form once more, limped across the beach to Chloe and scooped her proudly up in his arms, and Hoppy emerged from her pocket. Godfrey broke the silence with a gentle, 'Well done, Chloe!'

The royal walrus trumpeters blasted out three long, loud notes.

CLICK CLACK CLICK CLACK.

King Sandy, Queen Sandra and Prince Barnie approached with their crab cavaliers behind them. Some of the crabs were now missing a claw or had cracks in their giant shells, but they seemed cheery nonetheless.

The king stopped in front of them and Godfrey bowed formally, lowering Chloe to the sand so she could curtsey.

Then King Sandy and Godfrey started speaking at the time. Godfrey was apologising for the damage to *Sand Land*; King Sandy was thanking them for protecting their land and all of *Magic Land*. Then King Sandy was saying, 'No, please, no need to apologise,' as Godfrey was saying, 'No need to thank us, it was our duty, besides it was Chloe who won the war.' Then King Sandy started saying sorry and 'After you, after you' over and over again as Godfrey was saying, 'Forgive me, Your Majesty, how rude of me to interrupt.'

And neither of them seemed to be able to stop,

both apologising and thanking and explaining and excusing themselves over and over. It went on and on!

'Oh, do **SHUT UP**!' Queen Sandy suddenly exclaimed, much to everyone's surprise. But they were all rather relieved too, since the conversation was getting more than a little *ridiculous*. Especially considering the circumstances – I mean, they had nearly died in the biggest battle over *Sand Land*, and here they were being over-polite with a lot of nonsense jabbering!

'In that case, may I take this opportunity …' Prince Barnie appeared from behind the king and queen with a new determination in his step, '… to extend that thanks again in particular to Miss Chloe, as without her sand-animal army, the shadows would not have been defeated and *Magic Land* would be gone for ever!'

'Hear, hear!' boomed Godfrey, and one by one everyone around them gave Chloe a solemn salute.

The walruses began playing a much jauntier tune than usual on their trumpets, and the crabs began a peculiar-looking *dance* that basically meant them running along the beach, left to right and back again, over and over. Even the king and queen joined in. Hoppy flitted into the air above them all, finally *giggling* again.

Godfrey bent down to Chloe. 'Would you like to go and see the rest of *Magic Land* – tell them the danger is over?' But his face fell when he saw Chloe's.

'But look around you – *Magic Land* is ruined.' Chloe swallowed a sob. 'Ruined. And all because I took too long to get it right.' She looked up at Godfrey. 'You were wrong. I was never enough. I don't think I want to be important or special in this world,' she added quietly. 'It's too much. Please take me *home*.'

'But Chloe—' Godfrey started, then he stopped at the look in Chloe's eyes. 'You're right. For now, it's time to get you home.'

Godfrey beckoned to Hoppy and, with a wave of his hand, a flume of cloud appeared a few metres from them on the beach, ready to suck them back up to the sky at speed. Chloe felt so tired she barely had the strength to say goodbye to anyone, but she managed a weak *wave* at a concerned-looking Barnie. Then she stepped into the cloud and felt herself being sucked upwards and away.

Up in the clouds, Godfrey bounced ahead of her with Hoppy on his shoulder. They seemed to be whispering to each other but Chloe couldn't bring herself to care what about. The gentle giant's movements were slower than they had been on the way out, probably because of his injuries, but his strides were still several times what Chloe's were and within seconds he was well in front. And suddenly Chloe was struck by something. It hit her like a physical *punch* and she found herself on her knees on the clouds, unable to move.

'I can't go home!' she shouted after Godfrey.

'What?' He turned around and started bounding back to her.

'I still haven't **SMILED**. After everything, after all our **ADVENTURES**, after *Snuffledom*, after beating the shadows, I **STILL** haven't got my **SMILE** back. And everything is still ruined. I have to go back, I have to go back and get my **SMILE**.'

'Chloe—' Hoppy began gently.

'No more clever answers, please. Where is it? Why hasn't it come back? TELL ME WHY?'

Chloe was so upset she could barely breathe – tears were *streaming* down her face – but she began to crawl back across the clouds, determined to return to *Magic Land* and find her SMILE.

'We have to get you home now,' said Godfrey authoritatively. 'Trust us.'

'You keep saying that, but how can I trust you when it keeps not happening? I want to go back!'

'We're nearly home,' said Godfrey. 'If you want to talk, let's find somewhere more cosy.' He took Chloe's hand, Hoppy took the other, and suddenly she found herself falling slowly down through the misty clouds, emerging into the dark sky below. They were over the woodlands near Chloe's town.

Godfrey spied an empty nest in one of the trees.

He slowly shrank smaller and smaller, and Chloe found herself becoming smaller and smaller with him. She hadn't morphed with him before – it felt *strange*, like she imagined it might feel to be pressed between the pages of a book, only painless. By the time Godfrey was the size of a pigeon and Chloe the size of a chick, they were sitting in the nest with Hoppy, tinier than ever, leaning kindly on Chloe's ear.

Chloe sat there with her legs up to her chest and her hands tight around them, in a tense ball. 'You always say you know how I feel, but if you really knew how I felt, you would have let me get my SMILE back by now.'

'Dear girl, listen to me. We're piecing you back together again, don't you see?' said Godfrey gently. 'What would a SMILE be without *love*, without HOPE, without **bravery**? There is no genuine SMILE if it's not filled with all of those.'

'But you keep saying I have all of those now. You said I was special and I would save *Magic Land* and I would find my SMILE and NONE OF IT'S TRUE!'

'I don't like it when people shout at me,' said Hoppy sadly in Chloe's ear.

'I don't want to shout at any of you,' said Chloe, very much **SHOUTING**!

'She's shouting! She's shouting!' said Hoppy, clamping her hands over her ears and humming loudly.

Godfrey tried to take Chloe's hand again but she pulled away from him, too furious and upset. In fact, her mind felt like it was going to **EXPLODE** with all the bad things she was feeling right now.

Godfrey didn't try to talk to her again after that, and even Hoppy fell quiet, though after a few minutes she tried a tentative soothing stroke of Chloe's hair. When Chloe didn't stop her, she continued stroking. Despite everything, Chloe felt her eyes getting heavier and heavier and before she knew it, and unsurprisingly after all she had been through, she was fast asleep.

24

TRICKY TIMES

Chloe woke very early the next morning, well before her alarm. She immediately remembered everything from the night before, including being shrunk down and falling asleep in a nest, but she didn't remember being dropped home. She thrashed about in her bed for a bit, trying to get back to sleep, but her mind was too *full*. In the end, she just got up.

She felt a surge of confusion when she saw that once again Godfrey and Hoppy had left something on her bedside table. Three little SNOW GLOBES, and in each one was a miniature pup or cub from *Snuffledom*. There was a polar bear cub, a golden retriever pup and a tiger cub. Sparkling bits of fake snow fell when she shook them, and she could almost hear the baby animals' playful yapping. There was also a sand-coloured horse ornament to match her lion.

They were such thoughtful, *loving* gifts and she

felt so grateful for them, but she was angry too. Why had they let her believe it could all be different? Her head was still spinning – it was like she was feeling every kind of human emotion at once. She snatched up the snow globes, placed them in her **TREASURE BOX**, then slammed it firmly shut.

As she slammed the lid, she made a decision. It was time to face the fact that cheery Chloe was gone for good, her **SMILE** never coming back. She'd done everything Godfrey and Hoppy had told her to, after all, and there was still no sign of it. Clearly, she had failed somehow and didn't deserve to be that girl any more. They had probably realised the same – she'd probably never hear from them again, now she'd let *Magic Land* down. So it was time … time to get on with life without a **SMILE**.

As she had woken early, the house was silent. She crept out of her room and peered into her parents' bedroom. For some reason her dad was sleeping on the floor beside the bed. He must have fallen out in the middle of the night. And her mum was asleep on her back in a starfish position taking up the whole bed, snoring to her heart's content.

Chloe looked at her parents and suddenly had a vivid memory of the times they had all lain in that bed to open Christmas presents together. She remembered the times she would sleep in between them if she was ill. The memories were coming back again and this time in full TECHNICOLOUR detail and, with memories of *Snuffledom*, a wave of love surged through her for them. They **HAD** all *loved* each other once. She **DID** *love* them. She didn't know what had gone wrong over the last year or so exactly, or her part in it (Mr Long was always saying that children got more demanding as they grew up), but surely with her new-found battle strength and *love*, smile or no SMILE, she could repair it all. Yes – another decision!

She crept downstairs and out into the garden, where the grass was still wet with the morning dew. She peered through the shed's small window to see Gran Gran fast asleep on her little made-up bed, all cosy and with a broad SMILE on her face, obviously having wonderful, jolly dreams.

Chloe felt a pang of jealousy at the sight of Gran Gran's SMILE, but quickly swallowed it back. She had decided to make her family breakfast. Show them how much she really did **love** them, even if she couldn't **SMILE** at them. Actions speak louder than words, she had heard Gran Gran say before, and this would be her way of trying to repair some of the sadness in the family. Perhaps then, one day, her parents wouldn't have to just **PRETEND** they were happy.

She went back into the house and prepared the pot of tea Dad said he needed in the mornings before he could 'face another day of bus boredom!' and made the cup of coffee her mum would have beside her as she started on her first magazine of the day. She cooked scrambled eggs, Dad's **FAVOURITE,** and she lined up Mum's magazines and nail kit so they were within easy reach of the kitchen table. Just as she laid the last piece of cutlery, her parents appeared.

'Chloe, there you are,' said Mr Long gruffly. 'Actually your mother and I, we rather need to talk to you and—' Mrs Long, who was staring at the kitchen in astonishment, nudged him urgently and he looked up from straightening his tie. 'Oh,' he said. 'Er … What's all this?'

'I just wanted to do something nice for you both, help out around the house a bit,' Chloe said quickly.

She looked at her parents and, although her mother was still in her grubby old dressing-gown and her father's brow was still furrowed, she could see beyond that again, to the GOOD and *warm* people she knew were still there underneath.

'Oh, well that's … nice,' said Mr Long.

'Lovely,' agreed Mrs Long quietly.

'Wh-what was it you wanted to tell me?' asked Chloe as she put down some eggs in front of her dad. She had a strange sense of dread, but she couldn't quite put her finger on where it was coming from.

'Oh right, yes, you see …' He looked anxiously at Chloe's mum. Chloe put down a coffee in front of her.

'Yes, right …' said Mrs Long. 'I, er, don't think this is the time after all, is it, Mr Long …?'

'No, right, we'll speak to you about it later.'

Chloe breathed a sigh of relief. 'Good idea – I mean, this is such a nice moment we should probably all just enjoy it. Together. Yes …?' She trailed off when her parents didn't answer and sat down with them to eat her cereal. She was hoping that in time, if she got things right, she might be allowed a toaster back in the kitchen for her favourite hot buttered toast.

But for now Crispy Crackles would do. 'Shall I wake Gran Gran up?'

'No, best leave her,' said Mr Long. 'She didn't get home until very late last night. She was out with her new friend.' Then he mumbled to himself, 'And I could do without her chirping in my ear first thing.'

They ate their breakfasts in silence but Chloe noticed that Dad hadn't buried his head in the newspaper and Mum was ignoring her magazines. So that was a good sign, wasn't it? While she was eating Chloe began planning her next move – to get her best friends back! Maybe she couldn't make them *laugh* any more, but she could show them how much she cared. Barnie had taught her that.

Oh dear – Chloe's stomach lurched as she thought of how she had left him last night – she probably wouldn't see him again either, and it nearly made her cry. Get a grip, Chloe! she told herself firmly. She had her life to get on with now.

Before leaving for school, she went upstairs to her bedroom to get the snow globes from her **TREASURE BOX** – they would be perfect for her Chaos Crew …

When Chloe came back downstairs with her school

rucksack, her parents were in the hall, still looking a bit baffled, so she summoned up all her courage and said, 'I *love* you,' before running out of the door. 'See you later!' She was too scared to stick around and see if they said it back, in case they didn't, but she was pleased she had managed to say it herself. After all, she knew now it was true. And surely it would help them feel better. Surely. And surely there would be less arguing. Surely … maybe …

Outside, Mrs Sweet was giving Mr Sweet his packed lunch for work. 'Morning, Chloe,' waved Mrs Sweet.

'Morning, Mr and Mrs Sweet,' said Chloe enthusiastically. 'Your garden is looking more **BEAUTIFUL** than ever this summer. Have a lovely day.' And she turned to head off to school.

Mr and Mrs Sweet looked at each other. 'Oh, what a relief,' said Mrs Sweet, welling up. Mr Sweet *kissed* her warmly and got in his car to head off to work. His car was full of the fifty *garden gnomes* that he'd brought home for Mrs Sweet, but that she had told him in no uncertain terms **NOT** to remove from the car. She had no intention of ruining her garden with such ridiculous things! 'Oh my sweetpea, you are silly!' she said to herself as he drove off with one of the fishing gnomes on his lap.

Chloe didn't exactly enjoy having to keep her head down the whole way to school – she was still desperate to **SMILE** at people on the street (and she kept walking into lampposts) – but she told herself firmly that things could certainly be worse.

She found Hannah, Ruby and Benjamin chatting in the corridor. She wished she could **SMILE** at them and break the barrier that way, but instead she had to be brave, go straight up and talk to them.

'Hi!' she said.

The three of them looked blankly at her.

'I wanted to ask you something ...'

'Umm, you can't suddenly decide you want to speak to us again after dumping us ...' said Hannah indignantly.

'Yes, actually, I think that's right, and would certainly be in the friendship rulebook if there was such a thing,' said Benjamin.

'**SOB!**' said Ruby. And the three of them turned on their heels and marched into assembly.

This was going to be harder than Chloe had thought.

During assembly, Chloe sat a few rows behind her old gang, avoiding the cool girls' bench so they would know she wasn't really friends with them, and hatched a plan. She got out Benjamin's **SUMMER NOTEBOOK** and started writing a note. She tried to do it subtly, but unfortunately Mr Broderick – who was feeling particularly tired and grumpy again this morning – was checking closely for school uniform infringements or people falling asleep or ... he saw Chloe, head down, scribbling.

'Chloe Long!' he suddenly thundered. The whole assembly hushed and all eyes turned to Chloe. 'Put that notebook away and concentrate please. You know the assembly rules!' His nostrils flared. 'That's two minutes' silence for everyone and no snack shop at break.' The whole school moaned. '**SILENCE!**' boomed Mr B, as he set the clock for two minutes.

But Chloe was not going to give up. During breaktime she sat on a bench by the playground and was so busy writing her note to her friends that she didn't notice everyone was furious with her about not getting any snacks. If they were thirsty they only had milk as an option today, thanks to Chloe. **YUCK!**

As the end-of-break bell rang, Chloe had only just finished writing (it had taken her twenty-seven drafts to get it exactly right). There were Ruby, Hannah and Benjamin, together as always, *laughing*. But when she tried to bring herself to approach them, she found she was too nervous. They had to read this note. This was the answer, she was sure. She waited for them to go to class and slipped the final draft into Hannah's locker. They would get it at lunchtime and she hoped they'd then come to meet her at their oak tree. She'd written this:

Dear Ruby, Hannah and Benjamin, my bestest friends ever,

This might sound really odd, but here's the thing, and please keep reading till the end. You see, last week I lost my smile – I'm not sure where or exactly how, but I was too sad and worried to tell you, so I hid it from you and hoped it would come back. I have tried lots of things but it hasn't returned. I decided to protect you all from whatever was happening to me, but I see now I ended up shutting you all out and made you feel *bad* too. Also, the reason I got grumpy on my birthday was because my mum and dad *forgot* (don't think too badly of them). All they seem to do at the moment is argue and that might be because of *me too*, I guess.

I am so *SO* sorry for upsetting you – I didn't mean to. I *really* miss you and I hope you will *forgive me*. And still like me, even *without* a smile. If you do, please meet me under our oak tree at lunchtime today. I have *presents* for you all too.

Love you, your friend, Chloe xxx

Magic Land was her special secret and she knew she would never tell anyone about that, but it didn't mean that she couldn't share some of her gifts with her friends, like her cub-filled SNOW GLOBES.

She had no idea whether the note would work but at least they would read it, and at least she had done all she could by being honest with them.

At lunch break Chloe rushed off to the lovely shaded patch of grass underneath their oak tree. She checked that the snow globes were still in her rucksack and felt excited about giving them to her friends. In fact, she was SO excited to be reunited with them she couldn't sit still, and found herself *jogging* up and down on the spot. Ten minutes later she was still waiting, but she had stopped jogging. She waited another five minutes. Still no sign of them. They had had time by now to get out of class, read the note and head to the tree. Was it possible they'd read her note and … they weren't coming anyway?

Just then she heard a loud tapping sound. **TAP TAP TAP!** She turned around to face the trunk of the tree and saw two woodpeckers pecking loudly at it. As she looked at them more closely, she realised that one of them wasn't a woodpecker at all, but a tiny girl with crazy blonde hair and woodpecker-like wings; the woodpecker next to her had a small black hat on its head. Chloe gasped. It was Godfrey and Hoppy. In daytime. In her school field.

'Hello, Chloe,' Hoppy said softly.

Chloe gulped. She'd made up her mind, she didn't need them any more. She was just getting on with her life now, smile or no smile, doing it how she wanted. She had to be strong. 'Just … go away! I am waiting for my friends and I don't want them thinking I am even *weirder* than they do already, which they will if they see me talking to two woodpeckers!'

'Please come with us on a final **ADVENTURE** tonight,' said Hoppy. 'Please. Trust us one last time.'

'I can't risk coming with you. I can't take any more disappointment. I can't face any more battles, or failures, or hearing you say yet again that it isn't the right time. I just can't go through that again. I don't think my **SMILE** is even out there for me to find.'

Even in the form of a woodpecker, Godfrey looked more disappointed than Chloe had ever seen him before, and it nearly made her cry that she was the one causing it. 'I am grateful to you, really,' Chloe went on more graciously. 'I have learnt so much, but … I'll be fine as I am …'

'But we **P E C K** want you **P E C K** to be *more* than just fine,' said Godfrey.

'You have to go now before anyone sees me chatting to birds. PLEASE. Just GO …'

Godfrey and Hoppy took off from the trunk and circled her head closely for a moment before flying into the higher branches of the tree until Chloe couldn't see them any more.

But she could hear them. 'We'll always be here, whenever you need us, just call out …' said Hoppy and then there was silence once more. An unending s i l e n c e – eventually Chloe had to admit to herself, her friends were definitely not coming. Her plan hadn't worked, and she'd been so very sure it would.

It was hard to concentrate in class for the rest of the afternoon – Chloe found she couldn't even look in the direction of her once-friends, she was so mortified. But she told herself even THIS was FINE – maybe honesty wasn't the best way to go after all, maybe Barnie had got that wrong, and at least now she could focus all her smile-less energies on being brave and hopeful at home.

At the end of the day Chloe pelted out of the classroom and across the playground almost before the bell had finished ringing. She was in such a rush to get home that she bumped *smack* into Mr Broderick heading to his car. His papers went *flying*.

'Now look what you have done!' said the headmaster grumpily. 'What is wrong with you these days, Chloe?'

'Sorry, Mr Broderick.' Chloe paused. 'And sorry about assembly earlier. It was really important, I promise, otherwise I wouldn't have got distracted. You know I **LOVE** your assemblies!'

'Love them? Really? Well, I am not sure any student **LOVES** assembly, do they, however fun one might try to make them, but well, I do try …' said Mr Broderick, looking cheered. 'Now then, get along with you, and leave these with me.' He waved a hand at his scattered papers, which Chloe was still trying to pick up.

'Sorry again, Mr Broderick.'

And then she was off, rushing again to get home.

But whatever her plans, little did Chloe know that they were about to be **TRAMPLED** all over as soon as she got there …

25

THE BIG BAD NEWS

Chloe opened her front door and called, 'Hello, I'm home,' with as much *cheer* as she could. It was what she used to do, in the days there was an answering call of welcome and she would rush into the sitting room and give her mum a hug. Yes, she was remembering it all now. When she would feel cosy and *loved* in her mum's arms. Today she wasn't exactly expecting a response, but she also wasn't expecting to enter the sitting room and be confronted with a sombre-looking Mum and Dad sitting together on the sofa as if waiting for her to get back.

'Chloe, sit down,' said Mrs Long. Chloe sat down slowly in the chair opposite their sofa.

'Now, as you know, we wanted to talk to you this morning,' said her dad. He glanced rather sadly at her mum. 'But we decided to wait until you got back from school.'

'Is Gran Gran all right?' was Chloe's first thought. What if her trip to meet a mysterious friend had been a cover-up? 'Is she ill?'

'No, your grandmother is fine,' said Mr Long. 'Now let me speak—' But as he was about to continue, the door flew open.

'Coo-ee!' said Gran Gran's voice, trilling like a little songbird.

'Oh for goodness sake!' Mr Long muttered angrily. Chloe jumped out of her chair and gave her Gran Gran the biggest hug ever, inhaling her lovely *lemony-lavender* scent. The thought she had had of losing her was so awful she didn't want to let go.

'Well, this is lovely!' Gran Gran patted Chloe's back. 'But you'll have to let me go at some point, dear! And listen here, I ... well, I have some **BIG** news to share.'

'Really?' said Chloe, stepping back. 'You as well?' She looked from her parents to Gran Gran and back again. Whatever was going on?

'I do, I do.' Gran Gran seemed twitchy, and her voice had gone even more shrill. 'Gosh, I don't know why but I feel rather nervous telling you this, even though it's such **THRILLING** news. For me. I just hope it is for you too.'

'What is it? What is it?' Chloe was nearly bursting, she wanted to know so badly.

'I'll just say it … I am getting **MARRIED**!' said Gran Gran with a little excited leap.

'You what?' Mr Long exclaimed. 'What do you mean? Who are you getting married to?'

'Well, that's not exactly the *jolly* reaction I was hoping for!' chirped Gran Gran.

'Oh, Gran Gran, I am so happy for you,' said Chloe. 'You deserve to be happy.' But as she hugged her grandmother again she was swallowing down fresh panic. How could she get away with a lost **SMILE** after being given news like this? She might have to tell her family too – and what if they reacted as badly as her friends had?

'Well?' said Gran Gran pointedly to her son. 'I know it must be strange thinking of your mum getting married again, and not to your father, but I lost him so long ago that this feels very different. Like a different time. I feel young again …'

'Umm, urrh, we don't want too many details!'

said Mr Long, shuddering.

'At **YOUR** AGE!' Chloe's mum couldn't hold it in any longer. 'Isn't it a bit ... unnecessary ...?'

'Unnecessary?' Gran Gran looked shocked. 'What's got into you two? Of course it's not unnecessary. I don't care how old anyone is, everyone deserves *love* and *love* is certainly **NOT** unnecessary.'

'I think it's **WONDERFUL**, Gran Gran,' said Chloe. 'You won't be on your own any more.'

'Thank you, dear. I'll be bringing him to meet you all soon. And you ...' she pointed sharply at Chloe's mum and dad, '... you'd better be a bit more polite to him than you have just been to me!'

'In fact, I am so excited,' Chloe went on, thinking quickly, 'I am going upstairs right now to start drawing you the perfect wedding dress, because you know how much I *love* to draw ... rightio, see you shortly,' and she dashed from the room before anyone noticed her strange face.

'Ooh, what a wonderful idea,' called Gran Gran after her. 'Tell you what, I'll pop back out to pick up my dress material samples for us to look at together. See you in a wee while.' Seconds later Chloe heard the

front door bang and Gran Gran was gone, busy and adventurous as ever, her feet almost *clip-clopping* like a trotting pony down the cul-de-sac.

Chloe collapsed on to her bed, feeling, well, really strange. She was happy for Gran Gran, definitely, but it was *tinged* with worry. She suddenly realised she would have to SHARE her beloved grandmother now. What if that meant she wasn't around as much as before …? What if she couldn't be with her on her birthdays or go on adventures with her …? They still hadn't gone in a hot air balloon, like they had planned – and Gran Gran wanted to skydive before she was seventy! And what if Chloe didn't like her new step-grandfather?

Chloe closed her eyes and tried to imagine *Magic Land*. It was how she would usually end a difficult day or calm her whirring mind, and it was calling to her. She saw in her IMAGINATION the two lakes, dolphins waving their flippers at her and penguins skating happily.

But of course IMAGINING it was nothing like actually being there, actually feeling and seeing and *smelling* it, being part of it all and sharing it with Godfrey and Hoppy. And Barnie and Trevor too. Even in her mind the colours seemed duller, and while she tried to fight it, some of the wreckage she had witnessed the other night kept creeping in. If she didn't concentrate really hard the trees would start to shrivel, and she might see a Shadow Bandit swallow a penguin or tarnish a galloping pony-bunny with that dark evil oil she once saw in the sea below the Snakes and Ladders.

As she lay there with her eyes shut and her brows furrowed in desperation, she didn't see the two small birds perching on her windowsill, one in a black hat, watching and waiting for her. Desperate for her to call out to them. Instead, she fell into a light sleep.

Minutes later she awoke from her worried doze on hearing a loud screech from next door. She leant out of her window. It happened again. It was coming from the Sweets' house. Then she saw Mrs Sweet running out of her front door, in fact practically *galloping*, still screeching. Chloe couldn't work out whether she was happy or had just seen a snake in her sitting room and was freaking out!

Mr Sweet was just at that moment pulling up by their garage. 'Sweetpea, sweetheart, my darling!' Mrs Sweet yelled and she ran towards him and threw her arms around him as he got out of the car. Phew, thought Chloe. It was clearly a *happy* thing that was happening. Then Mr Sweet started screeching and galloping around too. They both looked like mad jumping jacks! The neighbours started coming out of their houses to see what the fuss was all about.

Mrs Sweet shouted down the cul-de-sac, 'We're having a baby! I can't believe it!'

Everyone whooped and cheered and went to hug them both. 'We're having a baby!' Mr and Mrs Sweet kept saying over and over.

Chloe lay back on her bed. First Gran Gran's news, now this – life was going to be really tough without a SMILE to share at such *happy* moments, but it was nice to be reminded of how good life could be with all this excellent news, even though she didn't have any excellent news of her own.

Life really was fine. And that was, well, fine. Wasn't it? It was certainly better than being hurt or disappointed all the time, Chloe thought.

And look, this morning over breakfast her parents seemed different already, didn't they? They seemed to be arguing far less. Everything seemed much stiller and quieter. They weren't exactly laughing and *joking* around yet, but Chloe told herself that the effort she was putting in was obviously making a difference.

As if by **MAGIC**, there was a soft knock on her door. Her mum and her dad came in together and sat down on Chloe's bed. They hadn't been in her room for so long. She felt *excited*. Perhaps they were planning a belated birthday tea or were coming to say they were proud of her, or even *loved* her. Whatever it was, it had to be positive, surely, her parents coming to see her together. Chloe sat up.

'Chloe,' said Mr Long rather seriously. 'You remember we wanted to speak to you?'

'Oh yes,' said Chloe, feeling upbeat.

'Well …' Chloe's dad trailed off and looked imploringly at his wife.

'The thing is, Chloe, your dad and I, we're thinking of getting a divorce.' Her mum swallowed loudly. 'Or a trial separation at least.'

Chloe stared at them. '*What?*'

'I am sorry, Chloe,' added Mr Long, looking as long-faced as ever, not knowing what else to say.

Chloe started to cry. 'But why? I have been good, haven't I, making breakfast and clearing up, and you

know I *love* you, and just because—'

'But Chloe—' interrupted her mum.

'Where will I live?' Chloe continued regardless. 'I want to be a *happy* family again. The Longs against the World again. All together. I don't want this!'

'You're going to be fine,' her dad tried. 'It's only me and your mother who are separating.'

Suddenly Chloe's mum stood up and ran from the room, her for once unmanicured hand to her face. Mr Long looked at his daughter. 'Sorry, Chloe,' he said again, 'it's for the best.' He patted her knee awkwardly but when she didn't respond he left too. Chloe was completely **SHELLSHOCKED**. And alone. Her life had just fallen apart. What was she going to do now – she had no plans left to make things better – she had failed in every way.

The sound of the front door opening and closing downstairs barely registered with Chloe. But she did hear the low murmuring of voices that followed, then the unmistakable sound of Gran Gran's feet coming up the stairs. Chloe threw herself into her grandmother's arms, crying uncontrollably. 'I … I thought you'd gone out,' Chloe managed between sobs.

'Thankfully your mother had the sense to come after me and I'd only got as far as the bus stop – I'm so sorry, Chloe, they just told me. Come here, my *sunshine*.' She hugged Chloe tighter, pressing the girl's wet face into her fluffy jumper in such a way that Chloe felt more **loved** than ever before. 'I've been so wrapped up in my own happy news I've not been paying proper attention to what's been happening here. It seems like things haven't been right with your mum and dad for a while,' Gran Gran went on, almost talking to herself now. 'I should have realised. And there's something else I've not given proper attention to, Chloe, and that's your *beautiful* SMILE. I've had to admit to myself that I've not seen that once since I got back, have I? Oh, my little ray of *sunshine*, you must have been hurting so much … I wish you had told me.'

The warmth of her grandmother's hug was nearly as calming as Godfrey's, and gradually she found the big hurting lump of sadness and guilt inside her was throbbing a little less painfully and she could whisper, 'I didn't want to worry or disappoint you. You always say to look on the bright side of life and be light and jolly for others around you, and I was letting you down every day by not living like that.'

Gran Gran *gasped* and pushed Chloe away from her by her shoulders so she could look her in the eye. 'Don't you know that you could **NEVER** disappoint me, my PERFECT girl? A SMILE is important in life, but so is being honest about how you are feeling, so those who *love* you can help you when your SMILE is flagging. There will be difficult days and times in every person's life. And that's all right. All you have to do is share, and ask for what you need. I'd *love* you even if you never SMILED again, but I don't believe for a minute that your SMILE is gone for good. I believe it will come back when you are ready for it.'

Chloe stared at Gran Gran. She sounded a bit like Godfrey. She pushed Chloe's hair back from her face. 'I'm going to go downstairs and get you a glass of water, and then we're going to talk some more.'

The minute her grandmother had left, Chloe jumped up. Godfrey was right. Being just fine was NOT fine, and it didn't have to be. She just hoped she wasn't too late. She leant out of the window and whispered, tears streaming down her face, 'Are you there?'

26

SHOW TIME

Chloe turned back sadly. They had probably left her for good after what she said to them at the oak tree. Then, in an instant, Godfrey and Hoppy leapt into her bedroom from their positions in the tree outside her window, unintentionally giving Chloe a massive but brilliant **FRIGHT**.

Godfrey shifted from bird to large man in seconds – he was still big enough to have to bend down so as not to smash into her overhead light with his hat, but when he sat himself down carefully on her desk chair he fitted. Hoppy perched on the table next to him. It was odd seeing them in daylight in her bedroom.

Chloe flung herself at them, crying. 'I'm sorry, I'm sorry, I'm sorry,' she said over and over again.

'Shush, shush,' he said. 'Shush, my girl.' His deep calming voice instantly worked its *magic* on her and she found her tears had already dried.

'You never need to apologise to us,' said Hoppy, stroking her hair. 'Never. We *love* you so much, whatever happens, and we are always waiting for you if you need us. We never left you.'

'Even if everything is my fault, I'm just not ME without my **SMILE**.' Chloe took a breath. 'So you know what I want to ask you?' she said a little nervously.

'You can ask,' said Godfrey, beaming broadly.

'She wants to go get her **SMILE** back!' shrieked Hoppy. 'Sorry, I know you wanted to say it … I'm just very excited.' She bounced from Chloe's desk, to her shoulder, and on to Chloe's bed, where she boinged manically back and forth.

'I want to get my **SMILE** back,' Chloe agreed. 'But we need to leave now. Gran Gran will be back any minute.'

'Oh, don't you worry. We can be there and back before she's even turned the tap on,' Godfrey assured her. 'But it's daytime, so we'll need to travel differently. Are you ready for this, Chloe? I'm going to have to turn **YOU** into a **BIRD**!'

'Me?' Chloe squealed. 'Yes PLEASE!'

'Now, take a deep breath. This might feel a little

funny …' Godfrey put his big hand on her head, she closed her eyes and … nothing …

Godfrey took his hand away and Chloe opened her eyes and, 'ARGH!' Why did her desk and window suddenly look so **MASSIVE**? And why did her legs feel funny, almost as if they weren't there? Chloe opened her mouth to ask Godfrey what had gone wrong and all that came out was '**TWEET, CHIRP, SQUAWK**'. Chloe snapped her mouth, or rather *beak*, shut. She spun round to look in her mirror and came face to face with a small, colourful PARROT with a shocked expression on its face. It was whirring its wings madly and hovering in the air in front of the mirror. It was … her.

As she stared, Hoppy appeared on one side of her, her own bird's wings shimmering back and forth; and on the other side was a large woodpecker, with a black hat on. The woodpecker – Godfrey of course – winked and darted out of the window. Hoppy nudged Chloe with a soft wing and took off too. Chloe had to follow, so she began to flap.

Chloe had flown before: in a plane, on Godfrey's back, on an eagle, even holding Godfrey's hand, but

this was something else altogether. As she soared into the sky above Elmswater Crescent she felt the immense *power* in her broad wings, she felt the way her feathers caught the wind and held it, so she could swoop and *soar* in whatever direction she chose. She had never felt freer. She had never felt lighter. She almost forgot where they were going or why – she felt like she could stay as a bird, exploring the skies, for evermore. But deep down she knew that wasn't possible, and as *Magic Land* and Chloe's favourite lakes came into view at last, she got ready to face her **FINAL** task.

As they came in to land, Chloe felt something shift inside her, and as her feet touched the ground she was already Chloe the girl once more.

She looked around and her heart fell. As she had suspected, *Magic Land* had been damaged and, well, killed, all over by the Shadow Bandits – the plants and trees, even the sausage bushes and toffee apple trees along the lake shorelines, were shrivelled and colourless; the ice lake was all but melted, and her summer lake was dried up altogether at one end, the waterfall reduced to a tiny trickle.

Chloe couldn't even look at her penguin friends. She had let them down so badly by not stopping the shadows and these were the dreaded consequences. She couldn't bear to see the same look in their eyes as she had seen in Ruby, Hannah and Benjamin's so recently. It was hard to imagine how this could be the place she would find her **SMILE**, but she was determined to remember her lessons this time – **courage**, **HOPE** and **love**. They would get her through.

Godfrey didn't let her linger. He was back in his giant form and he strode off wordlessly into the woods beyond the lakes, somewhere Chloe had never ventured before. She followed quickly, Hoppy zipping along at her side. It was hard to keep up. Godfrey was able to simply step over the fallen trees and matted undergrowth, whereas Chloe had to find her way over, under and through it all. But eventually she found him in a large clearing near the middle of the woods.

A little **AMPHITHEATRE** nestled into the clearing. It was only about five rows high and quite small widthwise. Like it could fit in a sitting room. There was one main seat in front of the stage with a big cushion on it and Hoppy ushered Chloe towards it.

She had the best view in the house. In fact, she had the *only* view in the house – as she sat and waited, none of the other seats filled; they were an audience of just three, and since Godfrey and Hoppy had seated themselves right at the back in the top row, Chloe felt very much like the only person in the audience. What on earth was going to happen next?

What Chloe didn't expect and definitely wouldn't have guessed was for a troupe of woodland animals to march on stage and take a bow in front of her. They were actually going to watch … a *performance* of some sort? It was the same troupe that made up the woodland band Chloe had heard play when Godfrey first brought her to *Magic Land*. The badger in a bow tie began the proceedings by announcing in a low, very theatrical voice:

'Welcome to your very OWN performance from the woodland theatre troupe. Tonight your play is called "The Lost Child". *Please to enjoy, we thank you.'*

The animals left the stage and suddenly it went dark. A flute began to play a gentle tune. Chloe looked up and saw it was a blackbird (playing a specially designed *flute* you can use

with a beak) in the top of the tree next to the stage. Then all around the stage soft glowing lights appeared – glow-worms and fireflies again, pulsating gently in time with the song. A tiny squirrel skittered up to Chloe's feet and presented her with a still-warm box of **POPCORN**. Some of the kernels were still popping – pinging out of the container and into Chloe's mouth without her having to lift a finger. It nearly made her *giggle*, if only she could …

Two foxes carrying a tiny hedgehog curled up in a ball entered stage left and sat down in the chairs set out on the stage for them. The *performance* began.

It was the story of a young family, starting from the birth of the little hedgehog onwards. Initially it was fun to see the hedgehog as a baby, being rocked by the two foxes playing her parents (trying not to get prickled the whole time); and then as she started to learn to walk, they were there to catch her if she fell (also a little prickly) and play games and go on fun outings with her; but as the little hedgehog continued to grow up – played by successively larger hedgehog actors – the fox parents seemed more and more tired. They started arguing and barking at

each other angrily. The fox mother grumbled about her job as a chicken hunter because the chickens were so noisy and the farmers she had to avoid were so smelly and mean; the fox father became more and more obsessed with accessorising the den, not wanting to spend time with his noisy family. It became increasingly upsetting to watch. Chloe desperately wanted to turn away, but Hoppy appeared in her lap at exactly the right moment.

'It's all right, Chloe,' she whispered, 'things will change, remember?' Chloe took a big calming breath. She had complete trust in Godfrey and Hoppy now. And as she watched she saw how lonely the hedgehog was becoming as her fox parents became engrossed in their own woes and stopped paying their child any attention. How the little hedgehog hid that hurt inside rather than sharing it with anyone, determined to keep SMILING. Tears started rolling down Chloe's cheeks as she was mesmerised by the sad story playing out in front of her. She desperately wanted to scoop the little hedgehog up – prickly or otherwise – and protect her, tell her that she was a lovely hedgehog and everything was going to come good.

But then something new happened – the little hedgehog waddled from the stage, leaving the two foxes alone together. Chloe sat up quickly. What did that mean, was the show over? No, there was more … Now the scenes showed how the two foxes were cross and arguing with each other even when the little hedgehog wasn't around.

'If only you weren't so fed up all the time, maybe I wouldn't have to bury myself in woodland catalogues!' snapped the father fox.

'You have no idea how hard I work,' barked the mother fox, 'and all for nothing, it's not like anyone appreciates it.'

Chloe couldn't help it, she found herself out of her chair, shouting for the little hedgehog to come back. 'Come and see – it's not your fault you've lost your **SMILE,** it's not your fault your parents are arguing, you need to tell them how you really feel!'

'Yes, Chloe, yes!' squeaked a little voice at her feet – it was Hoppy, still on the floor where she had fallen when Chloe stood up so suddenly. What did Hoppy mean …

OH! OOOOHHH!

And the penny dropped for Chloe: the hedgehog's story was HER story. None of her family problems were her fault either. All the time she had blamed herself, but she was just an innocent girl who had been forgotten by her parents as they became more and more distracted by their own problems. The relief coursed through Chloe – she hadn't lost her SMILE at all, it had been taken from her. Losing her SMILE hadn't been a punishment for not being good enough, it had been a symptom all along of just how bad things had got.

This time the tears came in an uncontrollable flood, she couldn't stop. Chloe collapsed into her seat and cried and cried and cried, the tears dripping from her chin.

The woodland theatre troupe bowed as the blackbird played her flute finale – their *performance* had served its purpose. Silently, they walked off into the wings of the forest, unfazed by Chloe's sobs, and Godfrey appeared at her side to hug her. 'Well done,' whispered Hoppy in her ear.

'But … but I am crying, not s-s-smiling,' Chloe managed to say through the sobs.

'Let it happen,' said Godfrey warmly,

reaching into a patchwork pocket for one of his enormous handkerchiefs, and giving it to Chloe to wipe her tears. Hoppy gently stroked her back. 'Don't worry, it's just tears of relief. Let it all go. Let it all out. At last you can see that none of this is your fault.'

It took some time but eventually Chloe felt the sobs begin to subside, and she wiped her wet face with the corner of the gigantic hankie. She felt floppy and weak after so much crying so Godfrey popped her into one of his great pockets and strode back towards Chloe's FAVOURITE lakes, with Hoppy close behind. Chloe felt her strength begin to return. And she felt a lightness in her whole body. A weight she hadn't even realised she had been carrying was lifting off her. Almost like a thick, black shadow leaving her. And as Godfrey opened the gate to leave the amphitheatre, she felt a tingling at the corners of her mouth, a stretchiness in her lips, and before she knew it a BROAD GRIN had spread over her face. She was SMILING. She was actually SMILING. In fact, she couldn't stop.

'My SMILE, it's come back!' she yelled. 'My SMILE is back!!! I'M SMILING!'

'WHEEEE!' squealed Hoppy as she did a joyful

loop the loop in the air above Chloe's head. Godfrey scooped the rejuvenated Chloe from his pocket and held her at eye level.

'You see, my girl, a SMILE without courage, patience, hope and love is not a real smile at all – that's why this was always worth the battle.'

Chloe nodded gratefully. Was that why so many of the grown-ups she saw on her way to school didn't look happy? They had lost all those things that make up a proper smile. As Godfrey had once said, it takes real strength to smile when life is difficult. He placed her back on the ground so she could run about. She started skipping and dancing along the path back to the lakes.

'And look,' Hoppy whispered. Chloe looked where Hoppy was pointing and saw that blossoming up behind her was a trail of BRIGHT COLOURS, blooming flowers and celebrating animals. Wherever her hand or foot had touched *Magic Land*, even just in passing, the lost colour and life was beginning to return. Chloe began to run, trailing her hands through the grass and trees all around her.

When she reached the summer lake she leant over

the water and marvelled at the reflection of her SMILING face, then she dipped a single finger in the water and sat back to watch its turquoise colour return, the water level rising all the time. She found herself *giggling* loudly when the ecstatic dolphins leapt from the water in happy arcs and splashed back down, wetting her all over.

Chloe ran back and forth touching everything, returning it all to its former glory, her penguin pals waddling along behind her happily. There were the bright yellow spring daffodils, the multi-coloured Easter eggs being placed by the bright white bouncing bunny-ponies. There were the Christmas lights in the fir trees, with heaps of presents below them. And the winter hat and scarf trees – fabulously coloured knitwear hanging from the branches, ready to be plucked if you felt like snuggling up in soft wool. There were the autumnal piles of orange leaves and the red squirrels juggling the brown conkers. *Magic Land* was all there.

There was a loud grinding noise and the rock wall behind the waterfall began to shift outwards to let a herd of walruses through, bobbing along in the waters, carrying not their trumpets this time but the three members of the Royal *Sand Land* Family. Chloe, Godfrey and Hoppy rushed to meet them at the shoreline.

'I, the great king of *Sand Land,* just wanted to come by and say … actually, sorry, you do the formalities, my love.'

'We thank you. Your tears rained on us and restored our beaches to their rightful glory, and—' said the queen.

'Chloe, you're SMILING!' shrieked Prince Barnie.

'Now **he's** interrupting **me**!' said the queen, the king laughing now she knew what it felt like.

Without thinking, Barnie threw his arms round Chloe in delight. Then he suddenly realised what he was doing. 'I mean, er,' he pulled back swiftly, 'how *lovely* to see you.' He bowed formally. 'We've come to deliver a message of thanks which, er, I think my mum, I mean the queen, was just telling you, so … er, yes, I'll shut up now.'

Chloe *giggled*, and before the queen could get cross she fell into a deep curtsey and addressed her and the king.

'No, thank **YOU**,' Chloe looked back up, 'thank you everyone, for believing in me until I could believe in myself. I can't wait for tomorrow now, whatever happens. I just can't wait. I am going to SMILE at everyone and see the cheery side of all I can, but remember not to bottle it all up if I feel sad. And maybe SMILING at my friends will help to win them over too. But you are my bestest friend ever, Barnie, because I can share *Magic Land* with you.' She hugged him again, properly this time. 'Oh, and most of all I am going to SMILE at myself. Well done me! Thank you, thank you, thank you!'

The walruses bowed, forgetting they were in the water carrying the Royal *Sand Land* Family, who all fell head first into the summer lake, much to the hysterical laughter of Godfrey, Hoppy AND Chloe. Oh, how good it felt to laugh again, as she dive-bombed into the lake with her newfound beaming smile.

After swimming together, they shared a celebratory sausage and toffee apple feast as the heartfelt thanks and goodbyes continued. It was the most **WONDERFUL** *Magic Land* party Chloe could ever have dreamt of. Finally it was time for her to clamber on to eagle-Godfrey's back, more tired than she had ever been before, but still with her wide **SMILE** plastered across her sparkling face, as everyone in *Magic Land* waved her off.

'I *love* you, Godfrey, I *love* you, Hoppy,' said Chloe as she nestled into Godfrey's warm feathers. 'Thank you for helping me find my lost **SMILE**.'

'And we *love* you more,' said Godfrey.

Chloe hesitated as a sudden thought hit her. 'But now I have my **SMILE** back … will I ever see you or any of the others again?'

'Always remember, we're here whenever you need us,' said Godfrey firmly. 'But we think you are going to be more than fine, even on the days when a **SMILE** might be hard to come by.'

'Besides,' added Hoppy, 'you can always come to *Magic Land* in your **IMAGINATION**, and see us all.'

'It won't be the same though, will it?' said Chloe, as her bedroom window came into view.

'It's as it should be.' Eagle-Godfrey perched in the tree just outside her bedroom window. 'Quickly now, I'm taking a risk being out in daylight at this size.'

'I will miss you so much!' Chloe scrambled off

his back and on to her windowsill. 'I will never, ever forget you. EVER.'

'You'd better not!' quipped Hoppy.

'We *love* you, Chloe,' said Godfrey.

And with that, they were **GONE** … Chloe looked up into the sky and saw two bird shapes disappearing over the woods. She turned around and somehow there was a final gift on her bedside table – two more tiny porcelain *ornaments*. One was a miniature kingfisher, perfect in every detail. It was poised exactly as if it was about to take flight, its bright blue wings spread wide, and it looked as if it was winking at Chloe. The other, slightly bigger, statuette was of a magnificent golden eagle, and when Chloe lifted it up to look at it more closely she could have sworn she felt warm feathers ripple under her fingertips. She fell back on to her bed, the ornaments still in her hands.

At that moment, Gran Gran knocked on her door with a glass of water as if Chloe had never been away.

27

SMILES AND SURPRISES

Chloe could have shared her fresh new *smile* with her grandmother there and then. She could have rushed downstairs and tried it out on everyone, but she felt surprisingly tired and subdued, and wanted to savour the moment and all that she had been through on her adventures on her own first.

Plus, this was the first time in a long while that she was in her bedroom without the awful worry that she was in the way of her parents. She wanted to relish the *freedom* of just being there knowing nothing had been her fault. She needed to take in her parents' news. That remained a sadness in her life. But as Gran Gran had said, at least it meant they were facing up to their problems. Hopefully things could change, and for the better.

She grabbed the SUMMER NOTEBOOK Benjamin had given her, and her drawing pencils, and started drawing the sand animals from *Sand Land*, and then Prince Barnie and *Snuffledom*, Godfrey and Hoppy, and all the memories from her adventures. In the back of her mind she wondered whether she would ever see them all again; in the front of her mind, she was simply excited to be going to sleep so she could wake up the next day with her brand new SMILE and show it to the world.

She woke up still in her school uniform having fallen asleep with her drawing pencils in her hand. Oh well, she thought, I am now ready to go straight to school, I don't even need to get dressed! She rushed to the mirror. YES! Her smile was still there. It was a half-day at school before the summer holidays, but she was going to make the most of it.

She dug out her joke notebook and read out the first joke she came to.

HOW DID THE FARMER FIX HIS JEANS?
WITH A CABBAGE PATCH.

'**HA!**' snorted Chloe. She felt her **SMILE** grow a little.

Another one.

WHY DO HUMMINGBIRDS HUM?

BECAUSE THEY CAN'T REMEMBER THE WORDS.

Hoppy would *love* that one. Can't remember the words ... **HILARIOUS!**

Just one more, then she really needed to get to school.

WHAT'S BROWN, LONG AND STICKY? A STICK.

Chloe collapsed into her chair, *giggling* hysterically. It probably wasn't even that funny a joke but it felt SO GOOD just to LAUGH!

She looked out of the window as she gathered her books from her desk.

There was Mrs Sweet sitting on a chair in the shade watching Mr Sweet finishing his hedge chipmunk. Perhaps she was going to take it easy now she was pregnant and enjoy bossing Mr Sweet around.

'Morning!' shouted Chloe, *beaming* at them both.

'Morning, Chloe!' they shouted back.

'Oh my dear, you look **WONDERFUL,** look at that **SMILE**,' said Mrs Sweet. 'We have missed that this past week.'

'You are going to make an amazing mum, Mrs Sweet,' Chloe said, before dashing downstairs and into the kitchen.

She couldn't wait to do her walk to school.

'I think I am just going to grab a breakfast bar and head straight to school,' said Chloe to her parents, selecting one from the cupboard and heading back out. 'See you later, *love* you. Oh.' She'd almost forgotten in her rush … She stepped back into the room and looked at her mum and dad, both in their own silent worlds, having their separate breakfasts. She cleared her throat loudly so they both looked up, then she stared them both in the eyes, one by one, and **SMILED** broadly at them. A long, loud, *loving* SMILE.

And what do you know, her dad ... **SMILED** back. He suddenly found he couldn't help it when he saw his daughter looking so *happy*, so happy for the first time in a long time. He **SMILED** and that made Chloe SMILE even more. With that she left for school.

As Chloe left, Mrs Long was looking at her husband oddly.

'I haven't seen you SMILE in SO long,' she said pensively. And she **SMILED** at him in turn as she said it, a little tentatively it was true, but a smile nonetheless.

Chloe set off walking. She **SMILED** at the postman.

She **SMILED** at the traffic warden.

She **SMILED** at the stressed mother.

She **SMILED** at the exhausted jogging father.

She **SMILED** at the lollipop lady.

Each time she **SMILED** at someone, they couldn't help but **SMILE** back, and they felt a little lighter and the world looked a little *brighter*, even to Chloe. In fact, it wasn't a lot less colourful than *Magic Land* after all. A smile is free and so easy to give and yet it is such a gift, Chloe thought. Gran Gran was right.

When she got to school, she saw Mr Broderick crawling out of his car, with his usual grey face and litre of coffee. He looked up as he shut his car door and saw Chloe coming towards him, **SMILING** at him. A big thankful grin for being headmaster of her *lovely* school. And Mr Broderick began to **SMILE** too. Chloe walked into school and Mr B turned back to get something from his car. Might that be his *guitar*?

As she walked down the corridor Chloe even **SMILED** at Princess and her friends. All she got in return was a collection of scowls, but Chloe didn't mind.

That morning's assembly was more bonkers than ever as Mr B played one of his most embarrassing tunes yet. This time it was about **HOLIDAYS** and even included him attempting a naff Hawaiian dance at one point. Having not had his songs for a while, the pupils hadn't realised how much they'd truly missed them. They were dancing in the aisles. Turns out, it was much better to have a jolly headmaster than a grumpy one. Even the grumpiest of teachers were on their feet dancing. The whole school finally appreciated Mr Broderick's songs, and didn't care a jot how embarrassing he might be – which was lucky, as Mr B was now getting out a Hawaiian garland.

Chloe played a game of School-amentary to herself. *'And there's Mr B dancing, looking like a flamingo with a sore bottom!'*

What Chloe didn't know, as she went about her school morning SMILING at EVERYONE, was what was unfolding at home.

Not long after Chloe set off for school and her dad left for work, Mrs Long went into Chloe's bedroom. At first, she tidied up some of Chloe's clothes and straightened her drawing pencils, then she started to make her bed. She hadn't done this in a long time but today she had felt compelled. Chloe was such a good, *kind* daughter and she had a horrible feeling she hadn't been treating her that well for far too long.

She sat down thoughtfully on Chloe's bed, and noticed how thin and uncomfortable her bedding was. Had she really been sleeping with just this scratchy blanket? As she had that thought, a little yellow and white BUTTERFLY flew in through the open window and fluttered straight past her. And as it went past she had a lightning-bolt idea: a *duvet*. She would get Chloe a duvet. The butterfly fluttered back out of the window where it hovered momentarily, then ... winked at Mrs Long. Mrs Long shook her head impatiently. Winked?! She didn't have time for nonsensical thoughts like that, she needed to get downstairs and order a new duvet.

Meanwhile the school was nearing the end of sports day, the final bit of school before they broke up. Next up – the seniors vs teachers three-legged race!

Chloe raced over to the oak tree before the final races, to say goodbye to it for the summer holidays. She gave the trunk a hug. She didn't feel silly doing this – she really felt like the tree was an old friend.

Suddenly she heard a strange rushing, screaming noise and she was knocked to the ground by a six-legged, six-armed bundle of ... Hannah, Ruby and Benjamin. 'Chloe, we *love* you,' they were *laughing* and crying (Ruby, naturally).

What was happening? Chloe hadn't even had a chance to SMILE at them yet, but they were coming back to her anyway? She had kept trying to find the right time to SMILE at them, but they were all in different classes and races.

'Oh, we've missed you!' said Ruby, tearfully squeezing Chloe so hard she might pop.

'What do you mean? But ...' Chloe gabbled. 'My note. You didn't come ... I thought ...'

'We only just got it.' Hannah now piled in on the hug as Ruby didn't seem to be letting go. 'You put it in the wrong locker, silly, the one next door to mine. Gloria found it and passed it over this morning.'

'As if we wouldn't forgive you *anything*, especially when you've been feeling so bad,' Benjamin added. 'Why didn't you just tell us? We could have helped. But hang on, you're smiling ...'

Chloe nodded smilingly. 'It's back, my smile is back.' They all whooped and cheered and bounced, still in a group hug.

'Wait,' said Benjamin. 'Can we just be very clear here please. We want to be your friends with or without a smile.'

'Of course, fancy you not knowing that!' sniffed Ruby emotionally.

'You've got us whatever mood you're in, silly,' agreed Hannah.

'Thanks, **CHAOS CREW**! You're my best friends for ever,' said Chloe.

'And group lesson, everybody,' added Hannah

bossily. 'Next time one of us feels sad or upset we say so STRAIGHT AWAY. Deal?'

'DEAL!'

'It's all **TOO MUCH**!' said Ruby dramatically. 'I am SO HAPPY I could cry.'

'You **ARE** crying,' laughed Benjamin, Hannah and Chloe.

'Come on, let's go and watch the three-legged race,' suggested Benjamin.

'Bye, *oak tree*,' said Chloe.

'Bye, *oak tree*!' they all joined in and ran across the playing fields hand in hand, nearly knocking over Gran Gran on the way.

'Hello! I'm a bit early to pick you up, dear,' she said to Chloe, with a cheery hello to her friends.

'No, that's fine, Gran Gran. **LOOK!**' And Chloe beamed her new smile.

'Oh, oh, oh – look at that SMILE, oh my little ray of *sunshine*, there she is. I am so glad you are feeling better … oh, that makes this so much easier … You see … I have a little surprise for you.' Gran Gran took Chloe by her hand and led her back down towards the car park and school gates.

'Are we going on an **ADVENTURE**?' asked Chloe excitedly.

'Actually, I've brought someone to meet you,' said Gran Gran a little nervously. 'He is just waiting by his car, come and say hello …'

Chloe followed Gran Gran. Someone stepped out of the car, waving at her. And, well, this was the most unexpected thing that had ever happened to Chloe. And that's saying something, given what she had been through. Because the man waving was … Trevor. Trevor from *Sand Land.* Chloe's Trevor. THAT Trevor!

Chloe froze, open-mouthed.

Gran Gran tugged at her arm. 'Chloe, this is—'

'Trevor,' said Chloe, at exactly the same time as Gran Gran.

'Yes, Trevor,' said Gran Gran, looking perplexed.

From behind her back Trevor gave Chloe a knowing wink. 'Well, what a lucky guess, young lady. And how *lovely* to meet you at last. I've heard a lot about you!'

There was so much going through Chloe's mind she couldn't even respond. But Trevor pulled her into a warm hug, and Chloe found her SMILE all over again.

Which made Trevor's SMILE even wider.

'Evie,' Chloe whispered incredulously in the old man's ear. 'Evie was Evelyn, **MY** GRAN GRAN, all along?'

'Yes,' said Trevor quietly. 'How *perfect* is that?'

Then he took Gran Gran's hand. 'Shall we all head home?' she said jovially. Chloe ran back to say goodbye to her friends and suggest they meet tomorrow at the park to start their SUMMER adventures.

They were all in hysterics as she approached – Chloe looked at the race track and saw why. Princess had been paired with Mrs Bucks and was being dragged along on the ground by the teacher, who hadn't realised Princess had fallen over at the start of the race. They could not help laughing as Princess was pulled through the mud screeching, 'My hair, my perfect hair!'

Chloe gave her friends a parting School-amentary quip: *'And here we have the chair-bottomed, turtle-like teacher dragging what looks like a muddy old scarf along with her as she runs, slower than any being has ever run before, even a tortoise would overtake,'* said Chloe, her gang getting even more hysterical.

Over the course of the car journey home with Gran Gran and Trevor, Chloe had to do some pretty clever quizzing of her grandmother to work out what had happened since she last saw Trevor, without giving either of them away.

In the end it didn't take much coaxing to get Gran Gran to explain how they'd met and fallen in *love* on holiday, but she had got her holiday dates wrong and realised that she had to get back twenty-four hours earlier than planned for Chloe's birthday. 'Remember how I nearly didn't make your birthday bash at all last year and only got there in the late afternoon?' Chloe did – she remembered how relieved she'd been, too, given how things already were with her parents. Gran Gran explained that she went to find Trevor to say that she was catching a flight that morning and wouldn't be at the dinner, but he had gone out on a boat trip on one of the mountain lakes.

'Why didn't you just tell me that in your note?' said Trevor. 'I would have understood you wanting to get home for Chloe's birthday.'

'Because ... well ... it may sound silly ... but I suddenly began to doubt your feelings for me. I suddenly worried I had got carried away, been a foolish old lady – we had only known each other so fleetingly. But I knew if you felt the same way as me, then you'd wait, you'd come back. And if you didn't, you'd be free. I have to admit, I didn't think you'd be there when the day finally came.'

'Neither did Trevor!' exclaimed Chloe. 'I mean, I bet you didn't, did you, Trevor, not that I would know …'

Trevor smiled at her in the rear-view mirror. 'You're right, Chloe, I had exactly the same concerns.' Then he reached out one hand as he drove and took Gran Gran's. 'Aren't we *silly fools*.'

'And then he asked you to marry him?' prompted Chloe.

'And I said, "Yes. Yes please."'

'**HOORAY!**' cheered Chloe.

Trevor glanced at her in his mirror again. 'And as soon as Evie told me about her wonderful granddaughter, and how special she was, I felt as if I knew her myself, almost as if I had actually met her. I just know we are going to get on like a house on fire!'

Chloe beamed. 'Me too!' Gran Gran had chosen her birthday even over someone as perfect for her as

Trevor. She wasn't losing a grandmother, she wasn't even sharing her, but she **WAS** gaining the best grandfather ever.

When she got home, Chloe's parents were both outside in the garden, doing a bit of weeding and tidying up. The Sweets had peeked over the fence and seen this and were delighted the plants were finally getting some attention. And the Longs were actually chatting. Normally. Not shouting. At all. And Chloe noticed that her mum had thrown out a large pile of her magazines, while her dad had found a box of some sort in the shed and was dusting it down.

Chloe ran upstairs to put her schoolbag away before heading outside to join them. She leapt on to her bed to get a joke from the book under her pillow, but forget the book – her bed was ... **SOFT**. Really soft. And smooth. She looked down at her knees – there was a *duvet* on her bed. She had a duvet! And there was a note on her bedside table:

Happy 11th Birthday, Chloe. Love, Mum

She rushed back downstairs and into the garden.

'Thank you, Mum.' She gave Mrs Long a tentative hug. Her mum hugged her back a little awkwardly, but she clung on just the same.

'No, thank **YOU,** Chloe. Whatever happens, we'll do better from here on in, I promise.'

As she turned back around she heard her dad say, 'Trevor, I don't know if you know how to play Snakes and Ladders,' he waved a box from the shed, 'but I was a bit of a whizz in my time – fancy a game?'

Chloe caught Trevor's eye – and to everyone's surprise they both burst out *laughing.*

Everything seemed all right for a moment. Chloe knew now that life wasn't always going to be perfect but she knew she could cope – whatever it might bring. And if she ever needed help then she knew who to call upon – in *both* worlds.

She had a feeling it was going to be a good summer ahead with her friends and family, and a *wedding* to plan. But deep down, she was sure she was going to see Godfrey and Hoppy again one day …

Well, life would be boring without **ADVENTURES,** wouldn't it?

EPILOGUE

'*The wheels on the bus go round and* round*, round and* round*, round and* round *... The wheels on the bus go round and* round*, all day long.*' Singing was to be heard on Mr Long's bus as they trundled out of town on a trip. Chloe's dad looked *cheerfully* out of the front window – getting out of town meant a break from busy traffic and angry commuters and he felt transformed. Why hadn't they made a trip like this for so long?

Trevor started strumming his **UKULELE,** picking out a different tune. Hope nudged her friend and she joined in on her *guitar,* followed moments later by Mr Broderick on his. Hope's rich warm voice started warbling out the words, '*We're all going on a summer holiday ...*'

The Sweets were sitting up at the back near Gran Gran, exchanging gardening tips. And Chloe's mum was sitting at the front of the bus, reading the map and passing Mr Long snacks as he drove.

Chloe looked around at all her favourite people in one place,
on a belated birthday trip just for HER. It was perfect.

The bus *whizzed* along country lanes in search of the perfect beach and picnic spot.

Hannah, Ruby and Benjamin sat up front, huddled alongside Chloe, as she entertained them all with her impression of Princess trying to suppress a burp. As they collapsed into *laughter*, Chloe looked around at all her FAVOURITE people in one place, on a belated birthday trip just for **HER**. It was perfect.

She looked out of the window and saw an eagle flying overhead. Could it be …? She peered closer. Flying beside the eagle there appeared to be a much smaller bird, more the size of a hummingbird, so small it was only a dot. Then something else caught her eye – something waving frantically on the back of the eagle. A small figure, in a crown and … were they, yes, *flip-flops*. Chloe SMILED and gave a quick wave out the window, before the trio swooped off over the distant horizon. She turned back and SMILED at everyone on the bus – then she joined in the *singing*, noticing her dad was even beginning to hum along too.

'We're all going on a summer holiday …' they all sang as they trundled merrily along through the rolling hills on a perfect summer's day …

ACKNOWLEDGEMENTS

I feel very lucky that there are always a number of people I could thank for helping in various ways to support my work and life. I dedicate this book to my nephew and niece Alfie and Jemima and I would like to thank them and their parents, my wonderful sister and brother-in-law Alice and Christopher, for being such rocks in my life. They are the people who provide me with laughter, a sense of adventure, and a reminder that every day is to be rejoiced over and lived to the max. That is partly why this book came about and indeed what it is about.

But I want to acknowledge just two other people as regards this book, to highlight their importance. Hannah Black – my colleague and friend who has been there tirelessly through times of smiles and lost smiles, and Ruth Alltimes – a new Hodder colleague without whom this book wouldn't have turned from my shambolic ramblings of an idea, to something worthy of publication. Together with my literary agent Gordon Wise and amazing illustrator Kate Hindley, they treated my vision for my first children's book with love and respect and worked incredibly hard to get it on those shelves. Forever grateful.